SURGE

R. L. HADLEY

SURGE

Copyright © 2010 R. L. Hadley
Published by Sandpile Press

ISBN# 978-0-615-39194-6

Printed in the USA

Chapter 1

The old 1970's model farm truck with wooden rails built and mounted on the sides, looked as if it could quit at any minute. The truck rocked back and forth across the dirt road in Northern Mexico, creeping slowly in the darkness heading for the border. It carried a load of twenty people who had purchased their freedom in Mexico and were traveling in hopes of reaching America.

They were quiet as they sat with their own thoughts. Some of the people were families, some were couples, and some were coyotes that had made the trip many times traveling into and out of Mexico smuggling people for a hefty price.

Those that were seeking a new life for their families knew that if they got caught trying to cross the border, that the worst thing that would happen is that they would be returned to Mexico. And they would continue to try until finally they would succeed.

Pedro Sanchez was a regular at going back and forth across the border. He knew the route like the back of his hand. His first trip across the border was in 1956, as a child with his family. He had grown up in America as a forged citizen. His father made his living smuggling items into and out of America. Of course he didn't see it as a crime, but a way of life. Most Mexicans believed that Texas was still part of their country anyway. To them, a piece of paper would never change that fact. There were groups of Mexicans that had been planning for years, the downfall of America. They were all tied together and operated as one, positioned in different parts of the United States.

Pedro was one of those people. He was a leader of one of the groups positioned in Arkansas. There were three other men on the truck that were riding along with Pedro, his protectors. They acted as if they didn't know each other. Their papers had been forged so as to not link the men if they were caught trying to cross the border. Since the group had some of the U. S. border guards in their pocket, it was usually no problem for them to cross the border, as the guards looked the other way.

Pedro had seen the explosion of growth of the group in recent years with the addition of some of the Islamic extremists. The only obstacle standing in their way was Columbia, which was only a matter of time. The routine smuggling route started with Iran. They supplied the weapons to Venezuela in pieces. From there, they would travel through Colombia, make their way into Mexico and right up into the United States where the pieces of the puzzle would be distributed and reassembled at the final destination.

Like a football being passed from one player to the other until finally a touchdown, Pedro thought to himself. He did like that American game.

The truck slowed down and then screeched to a halt. The passengers on the truck had received instructions before the trip. "When the truck stops, run," the driver said.

Pedro was ready. He and the three men jumped from the truck and ran. They knew the trails and lay of the land. When they got closer to the border, Pedro and the men looked to see if their man was in place. He was and their crossing was uneventful as they squeezed through the barb wire and ran quietly back across the border.

Freedom, thought Pedro.

The word Freedom meant something different to the Mexican people. "Free, dumb." If a Mexican made it into America, everything was free; food, electricity, clothes, housing, education for their children, transportation, and medical care. And Americans were dumb enough to allow it, with their politicians on Capital Hill passing new legislation every day, Pedro thought. And Pedro had been watching the events unfolding in America. He smiled to himself at his brilliant idea as he walked along the dirt road.

When 9-11 happened, Americans awoke from their slumber. They were outraged at the attack on their untouchable country, Pedro thought. The people of America waved their little flags and came together and protested. Pedro sneered thinking about how ridiculous it was. Words, what good were they? The terrorists didn't care about the words of the Americans. Neither did he.

It didn't take long for the American people to return to their old patterns. Once again they were oblivious to things going on around them, not caring about anyone but themselves. Pedro knew that once they returned to their old habits and it was business as usual, it would be easy to put his plan in motion.

But he had to get in to see the men in charge. He knew that he had to bring his brilliant plan to the leaders. It was just pure luck that he learned that his uncle was a friend of a friend of one of the leaders. It hadn't been easy, but he convinced his uncle to help him arrange a meeting with Salvatore Ramirez.

Pedro thought back to the day that he met with Ramirez. He was impressed with the back door approach that Pedro talked about. It was going to take some planning, restructuring their group, and a lot of money. The Group had the money, Pedro had the plan, and over the past few years the group had recruited new members to grow their organization to pull his plan off.

Merging their Mexican group with a Muslim group was something that hadn't been done before. The Muslim group liked the plan even if they despised the Mexican people. The average American person could not even tell a Muslim from a Mexican if they passed one on the street.

Pedro had seen as the red dots continued to grow in numbers and take over American businesses. Hotels and gas stations. People had to sleep. And people had to have gas. Members of the merged group began to purchase gas stations and hotels. Americans had gotten conditioned to the diverse mixture of people, so it would be easy to do

6

right under their noses. These businesses were not purchased to make money, but as tools, to topple the big giant.

Mexican members of the merged group sought out jobs on farms and went to work, business as usual. There they would obtain some of the materials that the group would use to bring the United States to its knees. A stump blaster, Ammonium Nitrate, a simple fertilizer mixed with kerosene which they purchased at the local hardware store, and a fuse. Boom.

Salvatore shook his head. "We would need a lot of it to be effective. It might raise suspicion." Pedro explained the rest of the plan.

"If we already own the gas stations, a little bomb in a big tank of gas will create a very big explosion, with enough chaos to divert attention to the big plan. At the same time, set off a small bomb in the hotels and we create more chaos. These businesses will be purchased in major cities. The ammonium nitrate will be taken a little at a time from the farms across America and then delivered to our strategic locations in the cities. We would then synchronize the exact date and time for our members to detonate their packages all across America. As we have seen in the past, America does not react well to an attack on their soil. Their police and emergency system would collapse. Then the biggest blow of all would bring them down. An Electromagnetic Pulse," he finished excitedly.

Salvatore sat watching Pedro as he played the scenario in his head. It was possible. It would be very difficult to obtain the EMP technology. But if it could be done, Salvatore was all for it. And so it began.

Salvatore returned home to Mexico and began to make inquiries. He approached the Muslim groups that had joined them and they began to help in the search for the materials needed for the EMP.

And then, when a Muslim was elected to the highest office, Pedro knew it was time. The American people had just thanked the Muslims for bombing their country, without saying a word. This new president was definitely changing America. Some people thought that he was a member of the Trilateral Commission, an organization led by some of the wealthiest people in the world, seeking a New World Order. For that to happen, the old way of doing things would have to be extinguished. This new president was doing a bang up job. Trillions of dollars printed to "bail out" some of the largest

7

Corporations in the world. Food prices were rising, millions of people were out of work and homeless. Tent cities dotted landscapes now as people were forced out of their homes.

Pedro began to laugh, breaking the silence that he and his men had endured for the past six hours. Pedro just couldn't believe that the American people didn't see it. His laughter grew as he thought about it. He began to skip and dance around, as he and his men walked along the path leading to their pick up destination. The three other men glanced over at their leader and kept walking. Soon they began to laugh with him, not knowing what the joke was. Pedro's laughter grew until he was crying, thinking of the other men being so clueless. Just like the American people, the joke was on them.

And soon when all was said and done, he would reclaim his country and return it to his people.

Chapter 2

The six year old boy crouched in the dark woods, holding his breath and listening to the approaching sound of footsteps moving closer to him. He struggled to be silent as the sweat trickled down his cheek and dripped onto a leaf, sounding like a rock splashing into a lake. The July heat was nearly unbearable. He waved a mosquito away from his ear just as the puppy came into view with his tail wagging, happy to see the boy.

"Hey, that's not fair!" Simon said to his sister. "You cheated!"

"It's not my fault that we have waaay too many dogs." Cassie said as she walked up behind the puppy. The puppy began sniffing the ground, and was soon following a curious trail behind her. The fifteen year old girl was not happy to be babysitting her little brother on a Friday night. She was even less happy about playing hide and seek in the creepy woods.

"Time to head back and get ready for bed," she said.

"I'm not sleepy," Simon protested.

"Yeah right, I'll beat you to the house," Cassie said as she turned to run.

"Hey! Wait! Where is Max?" Simon asked his sister. In a split second, the pup had disappeared. Cassie gasped, stopped in her tracks and turned around to look for the German shepherd puppy. He was nowhere to be seen.

Mom will be furious if she finds out that she lost one of her clients dogs, she thought.

"Oh great!" Mom is gonna kill us if we don't find that dog!

"You lost him!"

"Shut up!" she said, reaching into her front pants pocket to retrieve her cell phone, but it wasn't there.

"Great," she said.

"It was your bright idea to bring him. Next time, why don't you bring one of our dogs?" Simon said to his sister, being the obnoxious little brother.

"Help me look for the mutt." She snarled at him through clenched teeth.

"Max, come. Here pup," Cassie called the pup, making her way deeper into the woods.

"C'mon puppy," Simon called behind Cassie.

After an hour of walking and calling to the puppy, they were getting tired.

"I need a break," Cassie said to her brother as she sat down on the ground. He fell to the ground next to her and leaned over on her. "I'm sleepy," he told her.

"So am I." Her voice softened as she reached over to hug him to her. She didn't want him know that they were lost.

The mosquitoes seemed to follow them everywhere. Cassie swatted at the biting insects, trying to keep them off of Simon.

"Okay, let's head back to the house. Maybe Max went home," she said, rising from the ground.

She started out at a slow jog pulling Simon with her as she went and pushing the limbs out to the way in front of them. Simon struggled to keep up with his sister.

"Stop, Cassie! You're going the wrong way!" Simon snatched his hand from hers and walked over to a tree and sat down.

"I'm thirsty," he said sleepily.

Cassie was out of breath when she stopped running. She looked around her, unsure of which direction to take. Nothing looked familiar to her. Her heart began to race with fear. She slowed her breathing and tried to calm herself.

Why couldn't we live in New York City or Boston? Why on a farm in the deep woods of Arkansas? One day, I will leave this place and I will never come back, she thought to herself, as she joined Simon on the ground.

"Okay, we will rest for a few minutes," she said to her little brother. Even though they argued a lot, they were still close. Sometimes when their mother was gone on a business trip Simon would sneak into her room in the middle of the night and crawl into bed with her. She would awaken the next morning to him pressed up against her back.

She pulled him onto her lap, hugged him to her and leaned back against the tree. She sat listening to the sounds of the woods until finally sleep overcame her.

Cassie awoke with a start. She heard something in the woods. She gently woke Simon from his deep sleep. "Shhh, be quiet," she whispered before bringing her finger up to her lips and motioning for him to be quiet and to listen.

There were voices in the distance. They sounded foreign and she couldn't make out everything that they were saying. "….see you.. ……September…….have everything….Nitrate……Pedro…" Cassie wondered who they were and why they were in the middle of the woods talking like they just ran into each other at the store or something. Cassie and Simon waited quietly, still as statues, afraid to show themselves. She could feel his heart beating rapidly. She rubbed his arm and smiled at him, trying to reassure him that everything would be okay. A few minutes later they heard two cars start and then drive away.

There was a road.

"Come on." Cassie pushed Simon to his feet and grabbed his hand. The boy was like a zombie as he put one foot in front of the other, following his sister.

"I can't Cassie," the boy whined. "I'm too tired."

"Okay," she said as she crouched down in front of him and turned her back to him. "Climb on."

She carried him on her back for half a mile. It was just past midnight. She was tired, every bone in her body hurt and she had blisters on her heels.

When they started their game of hide and seek, they had walked down to the small pond on the south side of their farm. When they arrived at the road, they had traveled two miles south of their farm and were in the National forest that joined their land. Now, with the moon shining, Cassie could see the entrance to their driveway in the distance.

How was she going to explain this? She had lost a clients dog. Their mother was not going to be happy about it. Not to mention, taking Simon out in the woods in the middle of the night. The boy thought he was Daniel Boone already.

She was in big trouble.

Cassie heard a vehicle approaching from behind them just over the hill. Frightened that the men may have returned, she turned and headed off the road and into the woods.

"Simon, get down," she told her brother as she let him slide off her back onto the ground.

"I'm scared Cassie! Are they gonna shoot us?" he asked fearfully with big eyes.

"No. Be quiet," she commanded, before pulling him into a crouching position behind a tree to wait for what looked to be a truck to pass.

The truck slowed down and slowly moved along the road until it reached the area where Cassie and Simon had hurried into the woods. The truck stopped and someone stepped out. The man had a flashlight and was shining it into the woods. He had seen them, thought Cassie.

"Cassie? Simon?" Ethan called out to his children. Cassie sighed with relief and dread at the same time.

"Daddy!" Simon sprang up and ran to his father. Ethan lifted him up into his arms and held him close.

Cassie hobbled out of the woods just in time to see the puppy in the truck looking out of the window.

"I'm sorry Dad," she said.

He reached out and hugged her to him.

"Let's get home," he said. Ethan carried Simon to the truck and placed him in the passenger seat next to Cassie and shut the door.

Simon leaned over on his sister, touched her arm and turned his face up to her. "Who is Pedro?" Simon mumbled sleepily and drifted off to sleep.

Chapter 3

Rachel slowly pulled the van to a stop and turned the engine off. She stretched her arms out to her side and arched her back. "I'm getting too old for this," she said to Zeus, her German shepherd dog seated in the passenger seat.

At age forty-two she looked ten years younger. Her 5'7" slim build with golden brown hair and green eyes made men turn and look twice when she walked by. She had never thought much about her beauty, she was too busy living and raising her four children.

She reached down for her purse and opened the door to the van, leaving the keys in the ignition. "Watch it, Zeus" she told the dog. Her long legs carried her into the service station. The cashier behind the counter looked foreign. Maybe from India she thought to herself. "I'm filling up on pump four," she told him.

"Have a gooooood day," he said in his foreign drawl, after she handed him a hundred dollar bill. She returned to her van and pumped the gas. When she finished pumping the gas and returned from getting her change, she got into the van and moved it over to the side of the gas station.

Zeus was ready to get out of the van. After four hours on the road, everyone was ready to stretch their legs. Rachel went to the back of the van and opened the doors to the six German shepherd dogs that were in their crates. All of the dogs started barking with their tails wagging. They knew the routine. Time to pee, get fresh water and return to their crates for the remainder of the trip home. She opened the first two crates that held Sasha and Sarah. The two dogs jumped out of the van and stood standing anxiously, waiting for her command. "Go potty" she said to the two dogs who then bounded towards the grassy area.

As she stood waiting for the other dogs to finish, she was aware of people nearby watching the beautiful dogs. Often times she was approached by strangers with questions and children wanting to pet the dogs.

When they were finished doing their business, each dog ran to the van and returned to their crate, just in time for Rachel to hear Zeus growling. She shut the doors and walked around to the driver side of the van to see a man approaching.

"Hello, I'm Mitch Carlson," he said, extending his hand towards her. "I met you a few months back at Governor Russell's party, in Dallas." Zeus began to bark frantically, worried about Rachel. She let him continue to bark as she shook the man's hand.

"Yes, I remember," she said, remembering that his date was a drop dead gorgeous supermodel who she couldn't quite name.

"Can I buy you a cup of coffee? I might have a business proposal for you," he shouted over the barking dog, and motioned towards the small diner next to the service station.

"Zeus, wait," she commanded the dog to be quiet, and he did.

"Sure. Let me finish up and I'll be right over," she said.

"Okay. I'll order our coffee," he said and turned to go to the diner.

Rachel couldn't help but notice the way that he walked with a long confident stride. He was over six feet tall, with dark brown hair and blue eyes that seemed to look right into your soul.

She finished giving Zeus water and then reached up to the air conditioner that was in the ceiling of the van, and turned it on until she returned.

Mitch watched her as she crossed the parking lot. Her hair was pulled up in a pony tail and she had on her sunglasses. She looked like she was dressed for the gym, in shorts and tennis shoes. He remembered seeing her at the party with her husband Ethan Reed. Too bad she's married, he thought to himself.

She slid into the booth across from him and asked, "So, what can I do for you Mr. Carlson?"

"Please, call me Mitch. I am looking for a dog trainer that might have some dogs for sale. Do you have any?" he asked, picking up the coffee pot and reaching over to pour her a cup.

"What type of trainer are you looking for?" she asked.

"Someone, who can train a dog for ranch work. We are looking for a few dogs, trained in herding, with basic obedience and some protection work," Mitch said.

"I see. Well, we have a kennel with around forty dogs that are in training for obedience, protection, herding, tracking or assistance work. I have some dogs that will be available soon," she said. "You are welcome to come out and take a look at what we have to offer or I can send you a video."

"That sounds great. I'd like to take a look at your kennel." he said, taking a sip of his coffee.

"You are a long way from the border. What brings you up this way? Rachel asked. She remembered that he lived near the Mexico border.

"I came up to buy some Angus heifers."

"How many head of cattle do you run?"

"We have around two thousand head."

Rachel leaned back in the booth and laughed. "That is a lot of cows," she said, shaking her head, trying to imagine what his life must be like. "You may need more than just a few dogs," she said smiling.

My god, what a smile, he thought.

"You are probably right," he smiled back at her, amused that she thought that two thousand was a lot of cows.

"So, how do you know Governor Russell?" she asked him.

"My brother William knows him. He couldn't make it to the party and asked me to go to represent our family," he explained.

"And you?" he asked.

"He is my Godfather," she said proudly. "He and Lisa took me under their wings when I was a teenager."

"It is amazing that he became Governor and that little known fact was kept quiet," he said. He had voted for the man and liked that he stood for stronger immigration and little gun control.

"He is a very private man that puts his family first," she said smiling.

Mitch could see that she loved the Governor very much.

"Were you his campaign manager? You sold me. And for the record, I voted for the man," Mitch laughed.

They continued to talk and before they knew it, almost two hours had passed. Rachel glanced at her watch.

"I have got to hit the road," she said standing.

"I'll walk you out," he said, dropping some cash on the table.

They walked to her van slowly and Mitch realized that he had enjoyed talking to her and was not looking forward to parting ways.

"Let me get you a business card," she said, opening the driver side door and reaching into her purse. Mitch stepped back a step, unsure of the dog in the van. She handed Mitch the business card while Zeus kept his eyes on the stranger.

"We live two hours from here" she told him. "Give me a call tomorrow and I will be glad to arrange a meeting." She extended her hand to him. Mitch grasped her warm hand in his and felt the strength behind her grip. She released his hand and smiled as she stepped up and into the van. He glanced down at the card and read her name. "Will do, Ms. Reed," he said.

He turned to walk back to his car as Rachel shut the door to the van. She turned the key in the ignition and put it into gear. She was anxious to get home as she returned to the road and her thoughts.

As she drove, she thought about Mitch Carlson. She knew that he was a widower, and he had lost his wife and child some years back. There had been many rumors that he was about to marry over the years, but it had never happened. What she didn't get was why he hadn't remarried. He was a good looking man and she couldn't believe that someone hadn't snatched him up.

Rachel's thoughts were interrupted by her buzzing cell phone. She reached for it and flipped it open. "Hey Ethan," she said to her ex-husband. "Hey baby. Where are you?" he asked.

"Just outside of town," she said. "I should be home in about twenty minutes," she told him.

"How was the show?"

"We did great. Sasha won winners bitch, Sarah won her class, and the puppies placed in their classes. I can't complain."

"That sounds good. Well, we had a scare last night," Ethan began. He told her about Cassie and Simon and their big adventure.

"Luckily, Max came home by himself." Ethan told her how he had loaded the pup into the truck and set out to find the children and how scared the two of them looked when he finally found them.

"Thank God that everything worked out!" Rachel said knowing that they could have easily disappeared into the National forest.

"Yeah, we need to have a talk with the two of them. Hurry home, we missed you," he said.

Rachel flipped her phone shut and tossed it up onto the dashboard.

She was eighteen years old, when she met Ethan. After graduating from the Ellison Institute, she was home for the summer before going on to College. One Friday night, she had gone into a nightclub where her mother was at with her friend Cindy, and sat down with them at the bar. Rachel looked older for her age, so she ordered a drink. Ethan, the bartender, asked to see her I.D. She was underage but he didn't know that. He just wanted to find out her name. She handed him her license, and with one eyebrow raised, she leaned her head to the side flashed him a smile and asked, "How about that drink now?" She knew that he would serve her the drink, even though she was underage. He put the khamakazi onto the counter and smiled back at the beautiful girl.

She turned up the shot, swallowed and gritted her teeth. "Keep them coming," she said slapping the counter with the glass and turning the bar stool around to follow the older women to a table. As soon as she sat down, a man twice her age walked over and asked her to dance. As soon as they finished and she sat down again, someone else would ask her. Ethan watched from the bar until she finally sat down to rest. He decided that now was his chance, as he looked at his watch and told Ron the other bartender to take over.

"Don't do it man," Ron warned him. Ethan laughed and finished mixing the watered down drink and walked over to Rachel. He sat it down in front of Rachel. "Can I have this dance?" he asked. "Sure" she said carefully standing up. They danced the next three songs and when his break was over, he told her that he had to get back to work, as he walked her back to her table. She sat down and Rachel leaned over to Cindy and said "That is the man I'm going to marry." Cindy began to laugh and shook her head, thinking it was time to get the girl home.

Ethan and Rachel started dating the summer before her first year of college. He was five years older, and they were crazy about each other. He was working his way through college, studying to become an engineer and was in his last year. He was smart, good looking and funny. On their first date Rachel asked him if he liked dogs and he said he did. She laughed and told him that she "just couldn't date a guy that didn't like dogs."

By the end of the summer, Rachel knew that she was in love with Ethan. They had spent a lot of time together and when she was about to leave for college, she decided that it was time that he learned about her family.

Chapter 4

Britta Hardin, with her long grey hair neatly braided and twisted up on her head, sat on the church pew with Rachel's head leaned over on her shoulder. She had come to love this girl as her own, even though she was just her Nanny. Britta had miscarried two children in the early 1930's before the doctor told her she could never have children of her own. After her husband died, Britta returned home to her family land in southern Alabama to live out her days.

In 1968, a new subdivision had been built across the street from Britta. One of the families, the Gleason's, consisted of Kenneth and Mary with their four children Jeanie 12, Kenny 8, Samuel 4, and Rachel 2. She had watched the four children playing outside for a few weeks before she went over to introduce herself to the family. Not long after, Mrs. Gleason asked Britta to move in with them to be their Nanny.

She agreed with one stipulation. She was to have Sunday and Wednesday off for church. On those days Jeanie would watch the two boys while Britta would bring the baby with her to church. So, she moved into the house with the Gleason's and kept her house vacant across the street with all of her belongings.

Britta got up every morning and walked across the street to feed and water her three German shepherd dogs. Most days Rachel would go with her. If for some reason Rachel slept in, she would be seen coming across the street in her night gown looking for her surrogate mother. The girl loved the old woman more than anything, and she loved the dogs second most. At age three, Rachel would go into the kennel, pour the old water out of the buckets and bring the water buckets to and from the kennels. At age four she would feed and brush the dogs. It made Britta happy to see her so involved with them. She imagined that the girl would carry on her love for the breed. As Rachel grew, so did her knowledge of the German Shepherd dog. Britta would often tell her how the breed had evolved and were brought over to America, about the courage and loyalty that the dogs possessed, and that the dogs would die for her if need be.

"You should always treat them with respect and kindness, but have a firm hand in training them," she would say. Rachel would sit and listen attentively to the old woman and like a sponge soaked up every word.

At age twelve, Rachel would bring Pal, the last of the dogs, out of the kennel and put her through her obedience commands. When they finished, Rachel would lead Pal back to her kennel and sit with the old dog. One morning, Rachel arrived at the kennel to see a blanket thrown over the lifeless form. Pal had died the night before. Rachel walked over to Britta and with tears streaming down her face reached out and hugged the old woman. She didn't want to let go. Their hearts were broken. For weeks after, both Britta and Rachel seemed lost without Pal, as they went about their daily lives.

Rachel came home from school one afternoon and her Mother told her to go across the street to find Britta. Rachel slowly walked towards the kennels. She had not been back over since their loss of Pal. She heard a dog barking. Rachel hastened her steps to the kennel. She walked around the corner of the house to see a six month old, German shepherd puppy. She was saddened but yet glad to see the new pup. Rachel looked over at Britta, who was smiling at her. "She is all yours," she said to Rachel.

Rachel walked towards the fence. She began to cry as she opened the gate. She went in and went down on one knee. The pup ran up to her wagging her tail wanting to play. Rachel reached out and hugged the pup who then started licking the tears away. The girl cried until she had no tears left.

Every day upon returning home from school, Rachel would race across the street to see her new dog, Queen. Rachel had become a great trainer at the age of fourteen. The dog was already trained in hand signals and voice commands. Anything that Rachel asked of Queen she would happily do.

Britta and Rachel were on the way home from church one night when Rachel asked if she could take Queen to an obedience trial.

"Well, sure," the old woman said.

"Do you think that she is ready?"

"Well, you are the trainer, what do you think?"

"I know that she is."

Since Queen was registered, they contacted the Association for the next obedience trial in their area. On a Saturday in June, Rachel and Queen entered the obedience ring. When they left the ring Queen had earned a perfect score. It didn't take long for Queen to finish and earn her Companion Dog title. Then, she went on to earn her Companion Dog Excellent title.

Britta attended every trial. She was the only cheering section that Rachel had since her parents worked shift work at the local mills.

When her parents were not working, they were drinking or fighting. Britta shielded Rachel as much as she could from her parent's behavior. When they were not in church on Sunday and Wednesday, she would quietly take her across the street away from the abuse. Britta would make an excuse to go check on Queen, and Rachel didn't seem to catch on. The two older children Jeanie and Kenny had already moved out of the house. Jeanie had married at nineteen and two years later Kenny moved out, the day after his high school graduation and he seldom visited them.

Samuel had never liked Britta because he knew that she loved Rachel like her own. He was extremely jealous of Rachel because she received all of the attention. He was always gone whenever possible and seemed oblivious to the abuse. Rachel tried to reach out to her brother. She would offer him candy that Britta had hidden for her. Sometimes she would offer to do a chore for him, which he would jump at, although it never changed his dislike for her. He suspected that she was up to something and he had decided long ago that he wasn't going to fall for it.

No matter how much Britta tried to hide the abuse, Rachel was well aware of it. She remembered the first time that she had seen her father beating her mother. She was two years old and it was before Britta moved in. Rachel toddled up the steps of the den and into the kitchen. She looked down the hallway to see her father on top of her mother, beating her. Years later, when she asked about the incident, Jeanie had told her that he was beating their Mother because she didn't bring him the newspaper. Many times over the years, her father would come home from working the evening shift, drunk, and drag all of the children out of bed and whip them for misbehavior during the day. Her Mother never tried to step in to defend her children. She would sit by crying and beg him to stop hitting them.

On one occasion, when she could stand it no more, Britta stepped between the children and their father and defiantly dared him to hit her. Even in his drunken stupor he knew that it would be a mistake and turned and left the room.

Britta and Rachel had created their own little world. They shared the love of the dogs and each other.

One afternoon Britta asked Rachel to come with her across the street to her house. There was something she wanted to show her. Rachel followed her into the house, down the hall and into the back bedroom. Britta shuffled to the far wall and swung open the two doors of the old wooden schiffarobe. At age eighty-one, Britta was beginning to show her frailty as Rachel was becoming a beautiful young woman at age fifteen.

"Pull the string," she said with her gnarled hand pointing at the floor of the large wooden closet. Rachel reached into the closet and pulled the floorboard up by a string that was folded to the side. Rachel looked down into the blackness of the hole in the floor. She could see the top of a wooden ladder. Rachel told her to go into the basement and look around. "Do not bring anything up, just look," she told Rachel, handing her a flashlight. Britta sat down in a nearby chair to wait while Rachel explored the hidden room.

Rachel reluctantly stepped onto the ladder leading down into the hole and turned on the flashlight. Her legs were shaking. She made her way down into the basement. She counted eight steps as she made her way down. At first, it looked like the steps led to nowhere. When she got to the bottom of the concrete shelter, there was an opening to the left. She turned and pointed the light into the underground room. The room was twenty feet wide and twenty four feet long. The walls were lined with shelves from floor to ceiling with crates of cans of food, water, lamps, kerosene, linens, clothes and shoes. There were cases of guns and ammunition. M1's from World War II, .22 rifles and numerous caliber pistols.

At the end of the hidden room, there was a single bed and next to it a small bedside table. When Rachel was finished looking around, she climbed back up the steps. She emerged from the hole in the ground with an ashen face and big eyes. She and Britta closed the trap door to the hidden room and shut the doors to the large closet.

The old woman returned to the chair in the room and asked Rachel to come sit down next to her "There is a reason why I showed you my hidden room. When the time comes for me to join our Lord and I am no longer here to protect you, all of my property and belongings will be yours. Should there ever come a day when you need a safe place, you will have it. There is only one other person that knows about the basement He will come to you after I am gone. Tell no one," she said firmly.

Rachel looked at Britta, seeing a whole new side to the woman that she loved beyond words and nodded.

A few months after Britta shared the hidden room with her, Rachel stepped off the school bus to see Queen lying in the field waiting for her. The dog jumped up and ran to her mistress, with her tail wagging. "Good Girl," Rachel praised the dog. "Queen, heel," she commanded the dog, who quickly twisted around to her left side. Rachel and Queen walked through the field and behind six houses in the subdivision before finally reaching their house. "Okay," Rachel said to the dog, giving her freedom.

Rachel carried her book bag into the house and dropped it onto the couch. She called out for Britta but there was no answer. She bounded the three steps that led into the kitchen and turned to go down the hallway to her bedroom. She opened the door and saw Britta lying on the bed. Why is she sleeping so late? Rachel thought. "Britta, are you okay?" she asked reaching out to touch her shoulder and upon feeling her cold, hard body she recoiled in horror. She stood staring at the body that lay on the bed, her mind unable to comprehend. "Britta? Nooo! Britta, wake up!" she screamed. She threw her body over

27

Britta's, willing her to live. She sobbed uncontrollably for over an hour. Their lives together flashed before her as she remembered the love that only a mother and daughter would know. Exhausted, she slid to Britta's side of the bed, searching for life in the woman who had loved her so.

"I love you Britta," she said to the lifeless form that lay on the bed, before standing. And with her body shaking, she walked out the door of her bedroom. She walked, with Queen following her, across the street to Britta's house and went inside. She opened the doors that led to the secret room and felt her way down the eight ladder rungs in the dark and over to the little bed. She lay crying until finally sleep rescued her from the hole that now consumed her heart.

She awoke to Queen's cold nose under her arm. How did she get down those steps? She began to cry, knowing that the nightmare was real. She felt Queen's soft fur and wondered if the bitch sensed that Britta was gone.

Rachel reached over to the table and felt for the flashlight. She turned it on and made her way to the ladder. She climbed up the ladder and pulled the doors to the shelter shut. She then backed down the ladder and pulled the floor of the little closet down and closed. She returned to the room and sat down in the middle of the floor. The fear that had engulfed her was beginning to lift. She looked around the room to see a box with an envelope taped to it. It had her name written on it. She made her way over and tore the envelope from the box and pressed it to her chest before returning to the bed. She began to cry again as she thought of Britta. She drifted in and out of sleep clutching the envelope that held the last of Britta's thoughts. She awoke and was finally ready to open the letter.

My Dearest Rachel,

By now, I have left you and gone to be with our Lord. I know that you are heartbroken. I am so sorry that I could not stay with you longer. You are the light of my life and even in death our love will never die. You are the daughter that I could never have on my own. God brought you to me for a reason. I have watched you grow from a baby to a beautiful young woman. I have tried to instill in you the difference between right and wrong, with Gods help.

You are becoming a woman now. I know that you will go on to do great things in your life. Remember, that no matter where you go or what you do, always try to do Gods will and have a giving, loving heart.

I have left all of my worldly possessions to you. There is a small stipend that will enable you to live comfortably. There is also money set aside for you to go to college if you so choose. I once told you that after my death, someone will contact you. His name is Brian Russell. This man is trustworthy and I will rest easy knowing that you have him should you need help. He is a grandson of a long time friend. His grandfather served in the war with Jim and he is the executor of my estate. Should you ever need help, he is the man to call.

You will, over time, learn more about me and the life that I led before I became an old woman. I trust that you will not be ashamed.

This prayer is for you.

My joy, my heart, my love, I pray that our God will guide your every step in life. That our God will bless you, keep you and lift you up when life's trials are too difficult to bear and that you will be strengthened at every turn.

Good night my little champion.

Britta

A sob escaped her. Every night at bedtime, since she could remember, after she and Britta finished their prayers, Britta would tell her "Good night my little champion." Her tears began to flow again.

She folded the letter with care. With shaking hands, she placed it back in the envelope and clutched it to her chest.

She wondered if she would ever stop crying.

Chapter 5

The morning heat from the Texas sun shone into the windows of the twenty five floor building. Brian Russell felt it on his back as he pressed the button on his phone to answer the call that his secretary Olivia had put through. It was a Mr. Gleason. Brian hoped that this wasn't *the* Mr. Gleason. Britta had left Brian's name and phone number with Mr. and Mrs. Gleason in case something ever happened to her.

But it was. Mr. Gleason was calling to let him know that Britta had passed away, as per her instructions. He also said that his daughter Rachel was missing and that there was a search out for her. Brian gave Mr. Gleason his condolonces and hung up the phone. He pressed another button to summon Olivia.

"Yes, Mr. Russell?" she inquired as she walked into his office.

"Olivia, cancel all of my appointments for today and get me a flight out to Mobile, Alabama as soon as possible."

"Yes sir," she said hurrying from the room.

He was saddened by the news of Aunt Britta's death. He had known her his whole life and although they were not related by blood, he was very fond of her. Jim and Britta had stayed in contact with he and his family even after his grandfather died. Every birthday he received a card with a savings bond from them. Britta attended all major functions in his life even after Jim died. She had asked him to be her Executor of her estate after he joined his Grandfathers law firm ten years ago. Brian would often fly in to Mobile and help Britta with anything she might need. He had helped her move from the farm in Arkansas to her family home in Alabama. He was the one who had carried the boxes and crates down into the basement, one by one.

Brian knew the history of his Grandfather Paul and Jim. They had served in World War II together in Germany. Britta joined the Red Cross to be near her husband during the war. That is where she fell in love with the German shepherd dogs.

Brian grabbed his briefcase and started putting papers in it. He was not looking forward to this trip. He arrived at the Mobile Regional Airport and rented a car.

As he drove the route to Britta's house, he wondered if Rachel would be there. He suspected that she would have gone into the basement, to surround herself with the memory of Britta. It was dark when he pulled the car into the driveway and turned it off. He reached into his briefcase and retrieved the keys to Britta's house and a flashlight, and slowly entered. He knew the layout of the house, even in the dark.

Queen began to growl at the sound coming from above their heads. She nosed Rachel awake and laid her head down next to her. Rachel looked over towards the doorway of the room and saw a beam of light shine into the opening.

"Rachel, are you in there?" Brian called out to her. "It's Brian."

She remained silent, hoping that he would go away. She didn't want to be found and she wasn't ready to rejoin the world. Brian slowly made his way down the steps. Queen began to growl her warning to stay away. Rachel knew she couldn't hide any longer. "I'm here," she said to the stranger. Brian stepped into the doorway with the flashlight and reached up to turn the light on in the ceiling.

Rachel squeezed her eyes shut tight from the brightness until her eyes adjusted. She told Queen that it was okay and the bitch relaxed. Brian reached his hand out for the dog to smell him and she then stretched her paw out to shake hands. Brian smiled. Britta had told him about Rachel and Queen. He was happy to know that Britta had found a child to love. It had been Brian who had arranged for Queen to be shipped to Britta after Pal died.

"There are a lot of people worried about you," he told Rachel. He turned to look at the box that he had brought down just a few weeks earlier and saw that Rachel had found the letter.

"No one cares about me." Rachel said clutching the letter, as she tried to stop the tears, shaking her head.

"I care about you."

"You don't even know me."

Brian sat down on the floor of the basement and leaned up against a box as he told her about his relationship with Britta. How Britta had sent pictures of her through the years. That he had watched her grow through pictures and the letters that Britta sent to him. He had seen her from a distance, many times, while he was visiting Britta.

"I also know that Britta loved you more than life itself. That is good enough for me," he said to the young girl.

"We need to let your family know that you are safe and then we have some business to discuss. You already know that Britta left you everything. What you don't know is the extent of her estate. She did very well for herself after Jim died. We worked together to invest her money. She has a farm in Arkansas, the house and property here in Alabama, and a house in Germany. There is enough money for you to live on and if you are careful, you will never want for anything. Britta placed the estate in trust and I will oversee it just as I have for the past ten years. When you turn twenty one, it will be turned over to you."

Rachel shook her head back and forth. She didn't want any of these things. She wanted Britta and her life back. She wanted to continue on as before.

Brian reached out to take Rachel's hand in his. Tears came to his eyes. "I loved her too. I know that you are hurting right now. Each day will get a little easier."

She pulled her hand away. "I can't go back home. There is nothing there for me. I don't know those people that are supposed to be my family," she sobbed. "I don't even like them, much less love them. God forgive me for feeling like this! I want Britta and my life back!" she continued to sob, as Brian listened to the girl.

He looked at her, knowing that Britta had unintentionally alienated Rachel from her family. He couldn't blame her though. Britta loved Rachel so much that she didn't want her to get hurt.

"Rachel, you have options now. What about boarding School? There is a really good school near us that you could attend. Since school is almost out for the year, why don't you just think about it during the summer and we will talk about it a little later?"

She sat quietly thinking about what he had just said, and nodded her head fighting the sobs back.

"I am going back upstairs, so let me know when you are ready to go home," he said.

She nodded her head again and slowly rose to her feet trying to summon the courage to face the world without Britta.

"I'm ready," she said as she swiped at the tears that refused to stop flowing.

"Good girl," Brian said rising to his feet.

Rachel climbed the stairs and gave the command "Queen, come." The bitch jumped up to the fourth step and climbed the rest of the way out. Brian followed them out, shut the doors, locked them and slid the keys into his pocket.

The funeral was two days later. It was a small ceremony with just the Gleason family, Brian, his wife Lisa and a few of the church members in attendance. The room was filled with flowers from people all over the world. Britta had touched many lives with her contributions to charities.

Following the burial in the church cemetery, under an oak tree overlooking the pond, Brian, Lisa and the Gleason family returned to the church sanctuary for the reading of the will.

When everyone was seated, Brian began to read:
"I, Britta Hardin, being of sound mind and body, do hereby make my last will and testament.

I bequeath to:

Jeanie Gleason Gibson, Kenneth Gleason Jr. and Samuel Gleason, $10,000.00 each, to be used for their college education.
Kenneth and Mary Gleason all expenses paid for thirty days to the Alcohol treatment center of your choice.

Rachel Gleason, a scholarship to the Ellison Institute Boarding School, the remainder of my estate, and all of my love.

I appoint Brian Russell to be the trustee of my estate until Rachel Gleason reaches age twenty-one, at which time, my estate will be signed over to her.
Signed,
Britta Hardin"

Brian watched as Kenneth and Mary looked at each other with disgust.

"How dare that woman presume to think that we would need a treatment center," Mary said to the room full of people. She rose from her chair and walked out of the room. Rachel remained seated as she watched her family one by one, follow her mother out the door. When the door shut, Rachel wept into her hands. She just didn't understand it. She could not believe those ungrateful people. They didn't deserve anything, but yet Britta had included them in her will. When she had regained her composure, she looked at Brian and asked, "When do I leave?"

Chapter 6

The following month in June, on her sixteenth birthday, Rachel and the Gleason family celebrated with cake and ice cream. It was a somber occasion. She still missed Britta and was having a hard time adjusting to her death. She could hardly eat or sleep. She spent most of her spare time with Queen, across the street at Britta's house, now hers.

When it was time to open presents, Rachel glanced over into the corner of the room, to see a large item with a blanket over it. Rachel walked over to the item and pulled the blanket off of a beautiful cedar hope chest. On the front was an image of a German shepherd dog that had been burned into the wood. There was a card attached to it that read:

To my Champion, Love Britta

Rachel glanced over at her Mother with blood shot eyes and a cigarette hanging out of her mouth.

"It was delivered just before she died and we hid it across the street in the kennel house. Well, I guess I should say *YOUR* kennel house now."

Her mother, father and Jeanie had started drinking at noon, and by two o'clock in the afternoon they were just about to become nasty. Samuel had left right after eating cake and ice cream and Kenneth Jr. was at work. Rachel was alone with a house full of drunks.

Brian and Lisa arrived just after Rachel opened her presents. He carried a large box into the living room and sat it down. "We better get used to seeing you, huh?" Mary said in a slurred voice. Brian just smiled at her. Britta had told him about their drinking and how things could escalate quickly. He wanted to get Rachel out of there as soon as possible.

Rachel was glad to see Brian and Lisa. She had become fond of them after Britta died. She pulled the wrapping paper off of a box of a set of Gucci luggage.

"What do you need *that* for?" Mary asked drunkenly.
Kenneth, who had been sleeping some of his liquor off, awoke to the shrill tone of his wife's voice, and groggily looked around the room at the people, wondering where they had come from.

"Actually, that is why we are here. I came to discuss Rachel's education with you. Since Britta left the scholarship for Rachel to attend Ellison, I came to ask your permission for her to go." Brian said.

Mary looked at her husband, agitated. He was still trying to remember why they were all there.

"I don't want my baby going off to some school that I have never even seen before," Mary said. She was buying time and Brian suspected that she was going to milk it for all it was worth.

"I have taken the liberty of making reservations for you and Mr. Gleason to fly out to tour the school with Rachel. It is a fine school. If you agree to let Rachel go, Lisa and I live close enough to help her if she needs anything. We will be glad to visit and check in on her. If you would like, we could fly you up to see her on occasion. And of course, she will be coming home on holidays and vacations," Brian said. He could see the wheels turning in Mary's head. She looked like she had hit the jackpot.

"It sounds like you've thought of everything," Mary said. "I am sure that we can agree on something. Don't you honey?" she said, smiling sweetly at her husband.

Fifty thousand dollars and two weeks after her birthday, Rachel and her parents flew out to tour Ellison Institute. After two days of drinking and a very large hotel room service tab, the Gleason's agreed to allow Rachel to attend the school. It was an easy sale.

Brian and Lisa agreed to bring Queen up to their place while Rachel was attending Ellison. She would then be able to see the dog when they came to visit her on campus. They had a fenced in yard and had two German shepherd dogs of their own.

Brian asked Rachel what she wanted to do with the contents of the house that she had inherited from Britta.

"I want to keep it for a little while. I'm not ready to say goodbye to Britta yet," she said, tears welling up in her eyes.

With the cache in the house, they decided to block the entrance to the basement by moving all of the furniture into the one room, and blocking access to the contents in the hidden room. Brian advised her to change the wooden door with a metal door with two locks on it. Rachel also agreed to have a masonry fence built around the house with a locked gate.

"I really don't need any of that stuff in the basement," Rachel told Brian.

"You may, one day. You need to remember that Britta lived through the great depression, World War II and the Vietnam War. She watched the decline of this great country. She wanted to make sure that if you ever needed anything, you would have it. And if and when you decide, we will teach you how to handle the weapons," Brian said. She wondered who he meant by "we", but didn't ask.

With the house secure, Brian, Rachel and her mother left for the airport the following day. They had purchased a shipping crate for Queen. They would all be on the same flight, since Rachel was worried about her dog.

After Mary had signed all of the paperwork for her daughter to attend Ellison and Rachel was moved into her room, Brian escorted Mary to the airport. The woman protested that she was too tired to make the trip back, but Brian was adamant that she return to Alabama. He was glad to see her go, as he watched her board the plane.

Rachel was looking forward to starting her first day of school at Ellison. She had always excelled in her courses and she was hoping that this new school wouldn't be too difficult to master. She soon learned that she didn't have anything to worry about.

Her new roommate was named Tina. She was tall and athletic like Rachel, with strawberry blonde hair and blue eyes. They became friends right away, which was a first for Rachel as she had always been a loner.

By the time she had adjusted to her new routine, it was time for the Thanksgiving holiday. She chose to go to the Russell home instead of flying back to Alabama. She just didn't want to be forced to sit through a fiasco with a bunch of people that didn't even know her. Her parents wouldn't even notice. They would be three sheets to the wind by noon anyway, she thought.

Lisa arrived to pick Rachel up at school, and when she got to the parking lot, she saw Queen in the car waiting for her. The bitch was barking happily with her tail wagging. Rachel struggled with her bags as she ran towards the car.

She was glad to see her dog and Queen was glad to see her girl.

As they were loading her bags in the car, Lisa reached out gave her a big bear hug. "I am so glad that you are coming," she said.

Rachel smiled. "Thanks. It has been a long time since I felt like I belong somewhere," she said.

"You are always welcome with us."

Rachel believed that she meant it.

The day after Thanksgiving, Brian and Lisa asked her if she was ready to visit the farm that she had inherited from Britta.

"Yes! Can we take the dogs?"

"Of course, what would a trip to the farm be without the dogs?" Lisa teased her.

It was a beautiful day for a drive. The farm was about a hundred miles south west of Little Rock and consisted of two hundred acres, a large Victorian farmhouse, a small cottage, a big red barn, two stocked ponds and an indoor/outdoor kennel.

When they arrived at the driveway, Brian got out and unlocked the gate. At first it looked like they were driving into the woods. Brian followed the winding driveway and stopped at a second gate. He unlocked it and they continued on. They topped the hill and Brian again stopped the truck, this time for Rachel to see the glorious site in the distance. Where the woods ended, Heaven on earth began. Rachel felt like she had come home. The site before her would be etched in her mind forever. The large two story farmhouse sat perched on the hill in the distance behind a pond. The driveway curved to the right around the pond with massive cedar trees on the right of the drive and poplar trees lining the left of the drive. The yard was landscaped beautifully with boulder size rocks and flowers.

Brian got out of the truck again and walked a short ways up the drive, reached down and pulled a rope of three inch diameter barbwire out of the driveway. It was painted brown to blend in with the winter colors. Rachel would have never known that it was there.

They continued around the drive to the house and parked the truck. Brian, Lisa, and Rachel stepped out of the truck, as Rachel, awestruck, looked around her. She couldn't believe that this was hers. It was so secluded that she understood why Britta had moved back to Alabama.

She was due back at school in three days, so their trip to the farm would be a brief two day stay. After they had unpacked the truck, Rachel and the three dogs set out to explore the grounds. The two story red barn could house a lot of animals. It had a concrete floor with twenty stalls, a tack room, a feed room and a wash room. The stairs led to the hay loft above. At the back of the barn was a roofed over loafing shed.

Rachel looked out of the back of the barn to see a small pond in the distance. She wondered if it was part of the property as she turned away from the barn and headed to the kennel house. It was a small ten run kennel. It was made of concrete block and had a separate feed and grooming room.

Just past the kennel was the small cottage with cute little window boxes. The door was painted red and the exterior of the little house was white. There was a small white picket fence that surrounded it. It held a bedroom, a bathroom and a small kitchen area. It reminded her of the story of Little Red Riding Hood.

She returned to the main house for lunch. Afterwards, she walked through the big house, looking around. It was partially furnished since Britta had moved some of her things back to Alabama. There were five bedrooms, a study, the kitchen, living area, laundry room, a parlor in the entranceway, and a basement. The attic in the house was one huge room. Britta and Jim had planned on filling the

41

house with children, but when they couldn't, they decided to keep the house that they loved so much, and instead filled it with their beloved German shepherd dogs.

Rachel spent the rest of the second day with Brian, Lisa and the dogs. They fished in the pond and threw sticks for the dogs to chase and retrieve from the pond. By then, sadly, it was time to pack up for the trip back to reality.

Tina was glad to see her return since she had stayed on campus for the holiday.

Sometimes Rachel, Tina and some of the other girls would sneak out of their building and go to a bar. Rachel didn't want to look stupid so she just went along with them. She knew how to wing it, since she had grown up with drunks.

When she was bored, she would go out with her new friends. It was innocent fun.

When the Thanksgiving holiday arrived in their second year at Ellison, Tina came with them to the farm. Rachel, Tina, Brian and Lisa decorated the farm for Christmas and when they returned for the holiday the following month a light snow had fallen and dusted the landscape. Rachel had never seen snow before and she loved it.

The two years passed by quickly and when it was time to leave Ellison, Rachel and Tina promised each other to keep in touch, as they tearfully hugged each other goodbye.

Chapter 7

After Rachel attended her first year of college, she turned nineteen the following summer. She and Ethan continued to date. She decided that she didn't want to go to college and dropped out. She had talked to Brian, who was now like a father to her. She told him that she wanted to follow her dream of becoming a dog trainer. She asked him if he would arrange for her to go to Germany to become an apprentice at Heidelberg Kennels, where Britta had trained. It was one of the best. She was going to stay in the house that Britta had owned and live the life that Britta had lived, even if for a short while.

At first Ethan was not too happy about her leaving him. But he understood that she had to do it. They kept in touch and he flew out to visit her once. It was then that Ethan asked Rachel to marry him. She said yes and they agreed to wait until she returned to the States.

After a year, she returned home to the farm. She had decided not to let anyone know that she was returning. She arrived at the airport, rented a car, and drove the hour and a half to the farm. As she drove around the pond to her house, she felt the calmness return and she knew that this was home. After catching up with her sleep over the next two days, she phoned Brian.

Olivia buzzed Brian and told him that it was Rachel on the line. He smiled and told her to put the call through.

"Hey, Pop. I'm home for good," she said simply.

"Why didn't you let me know you were coming? I would have picked you up," he said.

"I know," she said, smiling mischieviously to herself.

"How was your flight?" he asked her.

"It was good. I am glad to be back on American soil!" She said. "Hey, can you and Lisa bring the children out to the farm this weekend? There are a few things I want to talk to you about. And I want to see my God nephew and niece," she said.

"Let me check our schedule and I'll let you know," he said.

"Sounds good," Rachel said.

They arrived with their two small children Dustin two and Michelle just a year old, along with Queen, on the following Saturday morning, just in time for breakfast. They all sat around the table with Lisa holding Dustin and Rachel holding Michelle, Queen sleeping on the floor. Rachel was happy to see them all.

Lisa filled her in on the antics of the two children and they talked about current events and Queen. Afterwards, Lisa went with the children to lay down for a nap.

Rachel had become a beautiful young woman, Brian thought to himself, of the girl he loved like his own.

"What is on your mind?" he asked Rachel.

"Well, I was thinking about making some changes in my life and I wanted to get your opinion," she said.

"Go on."

"For one thing, while I was in Germany, I noticed that the neighborhood around the house was getting to be a little rough. There were a couple of shooting incidents while I was there. So, what do you think about selling the house?"

"And why didn't you tell me about this before young lady?" he chided her. "Because I knew that you would bring me home and I wanted to finish my training. I'm sorry that I didn't tell you, but I was very careful. So, what do you think about selling it?"

"It might be a good idea. I will check into it."

"Also, I have no interest in living in Alabama. I was thinking that we could donate the property to the church."

"Are you sure that you want to do that?"

"Yes," she said. "Britta would be happy about that."

"Yes, she would," he said proud of the woman that she had become.

"And the most important thing that I wanted to ask you about...." she hesitated.

"Would you give me away at my wedding?" tears welled up in her eyes and Brian's too. He stood up and walked around the table to her and hugged her close. "You know that that is a father's responsibility," he said to her.

"Yes, I know," she said.

"I would be honored," Brian said.

Ethan and Rachel were married at the house in Alabama not long after her return home. She and Ethan decided that since they had met in Alabama and their families were there, that this should be the place. As expected, her parents, Jeanie and Samuel showed up drunk at the wedding. Fortunately there was no trouble and they left shortly after the reception started. Kenneth Jr., along with his new wife Anna, made an appearance and left right after the ceremony.

Brian, Lisa, Ethan and Rachel flew into town the week before the wedding and loaded up the contents of the house onto a moving truck. After the wedding, Brian and Lisa drove the moving truck to the farm in Arkansas and Rachel and Ethan headed to Gulf Shores for their honeymoon. Rachel donated the house, in Britta's honor, to their church where she had been a charter member and Rachel had grown up.

One year later, she gave birth to twin boys. They named them Evan and Elijah. Four years later, she gave birth to a daughter, Cassie. Shortly after Rachel turned thirty-five, she and Ethan learned unexpectedly that they would be parents again.

It was a boy. They named him Simon Russell Reed.

Chapter 8

Rachel was glad to be home. She pulled the van up to the gate that had long since been fitted with an automatic gate opener. It was operated by a solar charged battery. She smiled as she thought of Simon who always commanded "Open Sesame!" when they arrived at the gate. She never got tired of making the drive around her driveway and seeing the picturesque setting of her house on the hill. The string of barb wire had been replaced with a state of the art driveway alarm that sounded in the house and kennel when a vehicle crossed the sensor. She continued past the house and pulled up to the big barn and parked. It was now painted white and had been converted into an indoor/outdoor kennel that housed up to fifty dogs. The upstairs was now an apartment, where Ethan often stayed when she was away on business, to help with the children.

Rachel watched the activity from the van. Simon was leading a German shepherd puppy around by the collar near where Evan and Ethan were working. They were in the training area with a new dog that was in training for herding.

Evan had grown into a handsome young man at twenty, along with his twin brother Eli. Although they were not identical, they both were black headed and brown eyed, Ethan and his Creek Indian ancestry showing through them. Cassie was also black haired and brown eyed, a beauty at fifteen. Simon on the other hand, had taken after her side of the family. He had the golden brown hair with green eyes and had lighter skin. As if he knew that she was thinking of him, the six year old came running towards the van.

"Mommy! You're home!" the boy screamed happily.

Rachel stepped out of the van just in time to for him to throw his arms around her waist nearly knocking her off her feet. She smiled at him and said "Hey, I can't breath here." Zeus jumped out of the van and started licking the back of his neck. Simon released his grip on his mother and started giggling at the dog. "That tickles," he told Zeus as he tried to shrug the dog away. Zeus then started licking his face as the boy grabbed the dog's collar. "C'mon lets go," he told the dog. They started down the hill towards the fenced in training area.

Rachel walked to the back of the van, opened the two doors and started unloading the dogs.

After she finished unloading the van and the dogs were all fed and watered, she went into the house to her study to check her messages. She sat down in her chair at her desk to read them. One was from Tina her old Ellison roommate, Michael reminding her about the Search and Rescue meeting, Brian wanted her to call him, Gustav her contact in Germany for importing dogs and Simon, the little sneak. He had used his father's cell phone and called the house phone to tell her that he was glad that she was home. Rachel laughed. That boy was going to make her gray before her time. He was such a prankster.

She remembered recently the time that she had gently popped his mouth for saying something disrespectful and he ran to his room, heartbroken. A little while later she told him to come out and he walked out wearing his football helmet with the mouth guard attached.

Ethan knocked on the open door. "What are you laughing at?" he asked her. She smiled and played the recording for him to hear. "That's our boy," he said and shook his head.

Ethan sat down in one of the chairs and told her about the progress that Evan was making with Thor and the other training sessions with some of the other dogs.

48

Evan was turning out to be a good handler. Unlike his twin brother Eli, Evan had chosen not to go to college. He wanted to be a part of the family business. He enjoyed working with the dogs.

Eli had just enrolled at Texas A and M. He liked dogs okay but he just wasn't as passionate about them like his mother.

Rachel heard the front door slam shut and then heard Cassie call out to her. "Mom, where are you? Can I spend the night with Chloe tonight?" she yelled through the walls. She walked into her study and plopped down on the sofa. Rachel sat looking at her daughter. "My trip was great, I'm fine...." Cassie didn't let her finish. "I'm sorry Mom! I am glad that your home!" She rose to hug her mother. "So can I go?"

"Yes, but not until after dinner," Rachel told her.

"Goooosh Mom, I was gonna eat dinner with them. They're having pizza," she whined sounding like she was five.

"Tonight, you're having chicken."

"Ugggh," Cassie rolled her eyes and started to leave the room, but collided into Simon and Zeus.

"There are too many people in this house," Cassie yelled, trying to step around Zeus.

"Just a minute young lady," Rachel said to her daughter. "I want you and Simon to tell me about your adventure the other night."

Cassie wheeled around to face her mother. "I'm really sorry Mom. It won't happen again. I should never have taken Max and Simon out in the woods in the middle of the night. I just thought that if...."

Rachel stopped her daughter in mid sentence. "Cassie, I didn't ask for excuses. I just want to know what happened."

Cassie told her mother what had happened.

Simon jumped in with his two cents worth. "We would have never found the road if we hadn't heard those two guys talking." Simon said. Cassie had deliberately left that part out of her story. She decided that she had better cover her self. "Oh yeah, that was creepy Mom!"

Ethan and Rachel looked at each other and sighed.

"What were they talking about Simon?" Rachel asked him.

"I couldn't hear all they said, but they were talking about some guy named Pedro. I'm hungry Mom. When's dinner?" the boy was out the door before she could respond.

Cassie decided that she might better tell them what she heard.

"Those guys were foreign, Mom. I don't know from what country, but not ours. They weren't Mexicans either. They said something about meeting in September with Pedro and something about ammonia." Cassie finished.

"Cassie, I think that you learned your lesson this time, getting lost in the woods. I am not going to ground you." Rachel said to her daughter.

"Thank you Mommy!" she said teasingly to her mother, hugged her and quickly left the room.

Rachel and Ethan exchanged glances, concern showing on both of their faces. Rachel spoke first.

"What were these guys doing on our road in the middle of the night? Ammonium Nitrate? I doubt that they are getting it for fertilizer. Should I be worried Ethan?" she asked him.

"I'll call the sheriff in the morning," Evan said looking concerned as well.

"Brian called you twice while you were gone."

"He left a message too. I wonder what is up." She reached for the phone on the desk, dialed the number and waited. Brian answered on the second ring.

"Hey Pop, what's up?" she asked.

"Hello my girl. Kenneth is in the hospital. He had a stroke."

Rachel didn't know what to say or feel about hearing that her biological father was sick. She hadn't had any contact with the Gleason's in over ten years. None. Not a phone call, letter or email. She had tried to keep in touch, sending cards on birthdays or a phone call to check in. But they didn't seem interested in her, and she was somewhat relieved that she had put her painful past behind her.

"Thanks for letting me know. I just got in, so I'll call you in the morning okay?"

"You better," he said.

She hung up the phone and sat in her chair trying to decide what to do. She knew that she should feel something for him, but the man had never been a real father to her. She decided that she just didn't want to open up old wounds and made a note to send flowers.

"What's up?" Ethan had remained in the room and looked worriedly at Rachel.

He was still in love with her even though he knew that it was over between them. He had really messed up. He had lost the best thing that had ever happened to him. He was just glad that they had been able to remain friends for the sake of the children.

"Kenneth had a stroke." Rachel stood from her chair and walked around the desk.

"I am exhausted. I think that I will lie down before dinner," she said as she started to leave the room.

"I'm gonna head home," Ethan said, standing to follow her.

"Thanks Ethan," she said, before wearily climbed the steps up to the second floor to her bedroom. She walked into her room, switched her television on and reached over to the night table for the remote control as she sat down on the bed. She changed the channel to Fox News.

Of course, the news was not good. It never was these days. The economy was on the brink of collapse, two hundred banks had failed, enemies at our border of Mexico, people out of jobs and losing their homes. Crime was rising as people were becoming hungry and desperate.

She remembered seeing a lot more homeless people while she was on her trip. Fewer people were competing at the dog shows. Most people did not want to wrap their mind around the fact that the good ole U S of A was slowly becoming a socialistic country. The government was taking over banks and had recently added national healthcare.

Rachel was glad that Britta had seen that this was coming. She was even happier that Brian had been able to convince her that she needed to keep the cache that Britta had built. She had replaced the food items over the years, updated the supplies, and Ethan had built a bookcase to hide the entrance to the basement. He had also added another hidden basement in the big barn under the feed room.

She was about to turn the television off when a newscast about the drug cartel in Mexico came on. Nine people had been found dead inside a house just outside of Ciudad Juarez. Their throats had been cut and the three women had been raped and beaten before being killed. The report went on to say that some of the violence had also spread to the Phoenix area, with increased gang activity. She pressed the off button. Just like most Americans, she thought. If you just turn the television off, then the atrocities would just disappear; Poof, gone. But it wasn't gone. There was living, breathing, people that faced these things every day.

She looked over to the opposite wall of her family photos at Britta and Queen, Brian and Lisa with their children, her children's photos taken over the years, Ethan and Rachel's wedding photo. She had chosen to keep it on the wall after they divorced so that Simon would still feel the family connection.

She wondered if she would ever be forced to defend her children, as she stood, walked over to the door and cracked it so that Zeus could get into the room when he made his final rounds in the house.

She returned to the bed, laid back on her pillow and felt the tension from the day leave her body as her thoughts drifted back to the days events and she couldn't help but think about Mitch Carlson.

It had been a long time since she had been attracted to a man, she thought to herself, as she felt her body begin to stir feelings that she had denied herself for way too long. She shook her head and tried to remind herself that her first priority was her children. She didn't need to complicate matters by fantasizing about a man.

Chapter 9

Monday morning brought rain and thunderstorms to the southern Texas town of Crystal City. It was a welcome sight, since a drought had dominated the area for at least nine months.

Mitch Carlson was planning on repairing fences but since the rain had settled in for the day, he decided to catch up on his phone calls. His first call was to Aaron Garcia his ranch foreman, his right hand man, and also his best friend. He was in the barn assisting a mare in foal and told Mitch that he would be up when he finished. That could take hours, Mitch thought to himself.

Mitch was a widower. His wife and daughter had been killed in an auto accident ten years earlier by a drunk driver. He had never found anyone else that could live up to his wife's memory, so he had led a bachelor's life. He was the most eligible man in town and many women had tried their best to catch his eye.

He was born to parents who had met at the Interment camp in Crystal City during World War II. His father was a guard and his mother was an American born German prisoner. Their family was small consisting of Mitch, William and Celia and their parents. Since the death of their father in 1989 and their mother in 1993, they seemed to draw even closer to one another. The three of them lived on the ranch, with Williams house on the east corner of the property and Celia's on the west corner. They had inherited the ranch from their father's side of the family. Following the Mexican-American war, Great Grandpa Carlson had been very successful in purchasing thousands of acres of land. Since then, some of the acreage had been sold off. The remaining fifteen hundred acres had been managed very well and the Carlson family lived on and worked their land. They raised cattle, horses, and some vegetable crops.

Mitch looked at the messages on his desk and was about to start returning some of them when Aaron burst into the office. His rain poncho was dripping puddles onto the floor. He removed his poncho and hung it up on the wall.

"We need that rain," he said, more to himself than Mitch. "We got a nice little colt outta Brandy. She did a fine job."

"No problems, I take it." Mitch inquired about the first time mother.

"Notta one."

"Good to hear."

"The truck with the replacement heifers should be here Wednesday. William can't be here since he has a meeting with the governor," he paused and then said, "Oh, and Celia wants to plan a party for Williams fortieth birthday," Aaron said.

Celia was always taking care of them since their parents had died. She was the oldest of the three of them at forty five, Mitch was the middle child at forty three and William was the youngest about to turn forty. Mitch shook his head wondering how she found the time, when she had a family of her own.

William was in his second term as Mayor of Crystal City and with the mention of the Governor, Mitch was reminded of Rachel.

"Hey, before I forget, I ran into a woman on my way home that is a dog trainer. What do you think about calling her out for a consult?" He and Aaron had talked about purchasing some working dogs for the ranch. It was just luck that Mitch had seen Rachel Reed at the gas station.

"Well, that depends," Aaron said.

Here we go again, Mitch thought.

"What did she look like?" Aaron grinned at Mitch.

"Like she would be a good dog trainer," Mitch shot back.

Everybody he knew was trying to get him married off. Mitch balled up a piece of paper and threw it at Aaron.

Smiling, Aaron stood to his feet with his spurs rattling on his worn cowboy boots.

"I better go check on Brandy. Come over to the house for dinner," he threw over his shoulder as he shut the door.

Mitch thought about it. Since Aaron was single, he had become a pretty good cook, much better than he could do. He might just take him up on the offer.

Mitch thought back to Rachel at the gas station. He had sat in his car watching her take the dogs out of the van and the way that they responded to her. He could tell that she knew dogs as well as he knew horses and cattle. That kind of knowledge comes from experience.

He reached in his pocket for the business card. He dialed the number and waited.

"Reed K-9 Center," Rachel greeted him.

"Hello, Rachel." Mitch recognized her voice. "This is Mitch Carlson. I met with you near Little Rock yesterday."

"Hi Mitch, how are you?" she asked, her heart beginning to race.

"Good. And you?"

"Great, now that I'm home."

Mitch laughed. He didn't like to travel as much as he used to, and could relate.

"I understand what you are saying," he said. "So when would be a good time for me to come out?"

"Anytime after this week is good."

"Alright, I'll check flights and get back with you."

"Just let me know when and we will have someone pick you up at the airport," she said.

"Thank you, Ms. Reed. I'll do it." He answered in his Texas drawl. Mitch hung up the phone and looked out his window at the rain that continued to fall. He decided to go to the barn and see the new colt.

As he walked down the barn aisle, he thought about how many times he had witnessed the foals being born. His favorite part of ranching was the horses. When he was a kid, he would tag along behind their father, climb up on the stall rail and watch the mare give birth. He knew that you could tell a lot about a foal, when the imprint training began on the very first day of life. His father would stay with the mare until the foal was born. He would then begin to help her dry the foal with a towel. At the same time he would run his hands all over the foal, pulling the legs gently, rubbing the ears, face, neck and body of the foal. This accustomed the foal to human handling right from the start. He would then help the foal stand and maneuver the foal over to its mother to nurse. At that point, he would leave the mare and foal to bond and return a few times during the day to touch and handle the foal. Mitch knew that this early imprinting was vital to the training of the foal. The first two years of their life were the most important in development and training.

Mitch walked up to the stall and looked in at Brandy and her new boy. He was still slick but he could tell that he was a dark bay with a stripe down his face. His legs looked good and his rump was already full of muscle. Concert had sired a nice one. May be a replacement sire? Mitch wondered.

Aaron walked up with the feed bucket for Brandy. "What'cha think boss?" Aaron asked him.

"He looks good."

"Yeah, looks like his Daddy," Aaron commented.

He would know since he was the one that had delivered Concert ten years earlier. It was the night that Melissa and Amy were killed, Mitch remembered. He and Aaron were in the barn waiting for the old mare to deliver when he got the call that they had been in a car accident. It was raining that night too. The accident had occurred just four miles from the ranch. Mitch drove past the two cars that had been pulled off the road. The cars were tangled together as one. He knew then that it was bad. When he arrived at the hospital Celia was already there and when Mitch saw her face, he knew that his life was about to change forever. Celia and Melissa were best friends in high school. Mitch knew right away that it was Melissa that was gone, just by looking at Celia. His world began to crumble as he listened to the Doctor tell him about his daughter Amy and that her chance of survival was very slim. They had done everything that they could. The little girl at age four had been a fighter. She clung to life for over two weeks. Mitch never left her side except to go to the bathroom. He held her hand and prayed that his baby would be alright. He finally gave them the word to "pull the plug." He knew she was already gone.

Mitch remembered the nightmare of the following year. He had stayed in a drunken stupor for three months. He just couldn't face the world without his family.

Everywhere he looked, he saw Melissa and Amy who looked so much alike with their long blonde hair and blue eyes. He couldn't shake the memory of their perfect life together. During the week, Melissa was a school teacher. On the weekends they would awaken to their little angel, Amy jumping on their bed.

And on Sundays they all saddled up and went riding after church. Amy was a dream to watch on her oversized mount, with her little legs hanging from the huge saddle. She loved to ride. The old gelding, Scout, was a gentle teacher. Mitch had learned to ride on the very same horse.

A few weeks after his daughter died, Mitch had taken his shotgun out to the barn and shot Scout. He watched the horse fall to the ground. He then walked over to the horse, slid to the ground beside him and tried his best to summon the courage to shoot himself. He was distraught and lost. He had no reason to live.

Aaron had heard the shot and came running into the stall where he found Mitch sitting next to the dead horse, staring into space, his mind closed to the idea of living. Aaron removed the gun from Mitch's hands and called Celia. She admitted him to the hospital for exhaustion. She stayed with him for two days and when they finally released him into her care, she and Aaron brought him home. They removed all of the alcohol and guns from the house. Finally, after a few months, Mitch started to rejoin the living, but he was never the same.

"Oh man, boss I'm sorry. I just didn't think about it," Aaron said to Mitch wanting to kick him self for being such an idiot.

Mitch shook the memory from his head.

"Hey, you saved my ass buddy. Don't be sorry."

Mitch reached into his pocket and pulled his knife out. He reached for the bale of hay and cut the two strings away. He folded his knife, put it back into his pocket and then pulled a couple of flakes of hay for Brandy and tossed them into her hay rack.

"I talked to Ms. Reed. I'm flying out there next week. Think you can hold the fort down?" he asked Aaron.

"This ain't the Alamo. I think I can handle it." Aaron said.

Mitch smiled as he left the stall thinking that, had it been the Alamo, Aaron would have kicked some Texas butt.

Aaron and Mitch had grown up on the ranch together. His mother was the cook for the Carlson family. They lived in one of the old bunkhouses. Aaron and Mitch were like brothers and were inseparable. They went to school together and had many times gotten into fights defending each other. Aaron didn't fear anything. He had once been dared to climb one of the windmills when they were teenagers, by a schoolmate. Aaron had done it and was soon accepted as one of the coolest kids in school. Mitch was glad that it had been Aaron instead of him since he would not have wanted to climb the thirty foot structure.

Mitch looked up to see Celia shut the door to her SUV. The rain had slacked off and Celia ran for the office door. Her umbrella was caught by the wind and pulled from her hand. Mitch ran out to catch it for her. Celia was laughing at him dancing around in the wind and rain trying to catch her umbrella. After he managed to get the umbrella, he and Celia went into the office.

"Thanks little brother."

"You're welcome. I wouldn't want one of my horses eyes being poked out by that thing flying through the air." Mitch teased her.

"So how was your trip?" she asked.

"It was good. The heifers will be delivered Wednesday. I think that they are going to improve our breeding program. Aaron will be here to meet the truck. I hear you're planning a party."

"That is why I stopped by. I want to plan a party for Williams fortieth birthday."

"Sis, his birthday is six weeks away. Aren't you getting ahead of yourself?" He smiled at her. She had done the same thing for his fortieth birthday.

"Well no. You can never be too careful. I don't want to leave anyone out, and I want this to be special for him," she argued.
"Most people want to forget their birthdays. You…. on the other hand, want to make sure they don't," he laughed.

"You're damn right," she said, getting annoyed at him. "Every day is a gift and we can't forget that for one minute," she said as her voice cracked.

Mitch was surprised at her. She wasn't one to cry at the drop of a pin. He walked over to her, knelt down and reached out for her hand.

"Hey sis, what's up?" he asked worriedly.

She shook her head, trying to evade him. "You know how women get. I am entitled, you know."

"Are you sure?" he asked her, not convinced.

"Of course I am." She patted his hand trying to change the subject.

"Okay, if you say so." He returned to his seat behind the desk.

"Would you mind getting me a flight out to Little Rock for next Monday?"

"Is there a problem with the heifers?" she asked him.

"No. I met a dog trainer on my trip home. I'm going out to look at their dogs. Maybe we can get started on the herding dogs and make our jobs easier around here," he said. He didn't mention that the trainer was a woman. He didn't feel like hearing it.

Chapter 10

Mitch stepped off of the airplane tarmac and threw the strap of his carry on bag over his shoulder. When he got to the waiting area he looked towards the windows where people were waiting for passengers to arrive and watching the airplanes taxi down the runway.

When he called Rachel to let her know his flight time, she had insisted on picking him up at the airport and him staying at the farm while he was here. He was looking for her in the airport but he saw the dog first. Zeus was lying down next to Rachel who was wearing khaki shorts and a light green shirt with her company logo Reed K-9 Center. The dog had a service dog vest on. She was kneeling down next to a boy that looked to be around five years old. The little boy pointed at a plane coming in for a landing. His face was lit up with wonder as he watched the planes come and go. Mitch smiled, remembering when he was small and had done the very same thing with his father.

"Hello Ms. Reed," Mitch said to Rachel as he approached her cautiously, mindful of Zeus.

She stood up from her kneeling position and turned to face him. Zeus pushed up to a sitting position watching the stranger, but showed no aggression. A smile spread across Rachel's face as she extended her hand to Mitch. "Hello Mr. Carlson. Good to see you again," she said to him.

"Likewise," he said returning the smile and tipping his hat. He looked down at the little boy who then, as if on cue, extended his hand out to Mitch and said "Hello Mr. Carlson, I'm Simon Reed." Mitch smiled at the boy, amused at his matter of fact way that he had introduced himself.

"Nice to meet you," Mitch said.

"Likewise," Simon replied.

Mitch burst out laughing. This boy would one day be a mover and shaker, he thought to himself.

"Quite a helper you have there," he said to Rachel.

She smiled and said "I hope that you don't mind, but he always asks to come and see the planes."

"Not at all," Mitch said to her.

The three of them and Zeus turned and headed towards the exit, since Mitch had just brought his carry on bag. He noticed that Zeus stayed on the left side of Rachel automatically. She had not given the dog one command since he arrived. The dog watched her like she was a goddess. Mitch could see why. She had a way of drawing you in without her trying to. She wasn't aware of it, but Mitch could see the way that perfect strangers looked at her while they were in the airport. Rachel was oblivious. She was sure of herself and comfortable with anyone that she met.

Mitch loaded his bag into the Suburban that also displayed the Reed company logo.

Simon opened the back door and Zeus jumped into the seat. The drive to the farm was about a fourty-five minute trip. Once they were on the road, Simon soon dozed off to sleep and Zeus laid his head in his lap.

"So Mitch, tell me about your ranch," Rachel invited him into conversation.

My God she is beautiful. He cleared his throat. This is business, he reminded himself.

"We raise Quarter horses, Angus Cattle and some crops. In the past ten years we have had a problem with the illegals growing in

63

numbers and it is staggering. They will often steal crops out of the fields and kill calves and butcher them on the spot. They carry salt with them to put the meat in. When they get a few miles down the road they will cook it on an open fire and then go on their way. And of course, the crime has increased with the drug cartels branching out. The news media is not reporting a lot of what is going on at our Mexican border. We are only thirty five miles from the border. All of our workers carry a gun when they are out working in the fields. My sister and brother agree with me that we need to bring in some dogs. We need some herders, protection and tracking dogs. We intend to track down these thieves and bring them to justice. We are hoping that the word will get out that our ranch is to be avoided at all costs. We have considered selling the ranch and moving North, but this is our family land."

Rachel could hear the concern in his voice. He loved his family and ranch and he didn't want to be forced to leave it. She could understand how he felt. She didn't know what she would do if faced with the same problem.

Yes I do, she thought to herself, whatever it takes.

"Will the dogs be around children?" Rachel inquired. She often "interviewed" people that were interested in her dogs. She wanted to make the best possible match. "No. My wife and daughter were killed by a drunk driver ten years ago."

"I am sorry for your loss," she said and meant it.

"Thank you."

They traveled in silence for a few minutes and then she began to ask him the usual questions. Will the dog be an inside or outside dog? Housed in a kennel or a yard? Who would be responsible for the care of the dog? She continued with her questions until she was satisfied that her dogs would be going into a good environment.

"Excuse me a moment," she said, as she reached for her cell phone to call Ethan. They were ten minutes from the house and she wanted to let them know so that they could be ready for the demonstration.

When they arrived, Rachel pulled the Suburban under the shade tree next to the training area. Rachel let the windows down and turned off the engine.

"Zeus, Stay," Rachel commanded the dog to stay with Simon.

Rachel led Mitch over to the covered sitting area that had an outdoor kitchen, table and chairs and a small equipment room. It sat on a hill overlooking the training area where Ethan and Evan were working with Thor, a Rottweiler that was in training for protection.

Rachel brought a pitcher of sweet tea and glasses to the table as she and Mitch sat down to watch the demonstration.

Evan was wearing a bite suit with a club in his hand and Ethan was holding the dogs lead. Evan began to run away from the dog. When he had gone about fifty feet, Ethan yelled out "Stop! Or I'll send the dog." Thor was pulling and barking excitedly, ready to go. Evan continued to run as Ethan released the dog. Thor jumped forward and with all of the strength in his bulging muscles, covered the fifty feet in seconds. He shot through the air like a torpedo and slammed into Evan. His mouth clamped down on the closest arm of this would be intruder. Evan lifted the dog up off the ground and began to swing the dog around in the air, Thor tightening his grip on the arm sleeve. He then began to hit the dog lightly with the club. The dog bit down harder on the protected arm in the sleeve. Ethan caught up with them, and took hold of Thor's collar and gave the "Off" command. Thor reluctantly released the arm and returned to the ground. He continued to bark aggressively at this intruder that he had captured. Ethan snapped the lead on Thor and began walking him away from Evan. Thor had stopped barking and was still watching the supposed intruder as he and Ethan were walking away. Evan raised the club and advanced towards Ethan and Thor. The dog turned and began to bark aggressively waiting for the command from Ethan to attack, who then gave the word and dropped the lead. Thor again ran at the intruder and grabbed the sleeved arm. Evan repeated the previous scenario until Ethan had the lead and pulled the dog off. They ended the session as Ethan led Thor to the covered kennels next to the training area.

He then went to the next kennel and snapped the lead on a Border collie. The dog began to bark and wag her tail. She was ready to work. In the mean time Evan had taken the heavy bite suit off and had gone to the end of the training area to turn five sheep into the fenced in area. Mitch and Rachel watched the display as Ethan brought the collie into the area with the sheep. He took the lead off of the dog and gave her the command to move the sheep. The dog dropped her head and tail and began stalking the sheep. She glared at the sheep as she went to the right of the group and turned them. She kept the sheep in a tight group and drove them to the end of the training area. She then turned and went to the left of the sheep. She squeezed the sheep into the small pen and dropped to the ground. She continued to watch the sheep until Ethan shut the gate. Mitch watched as Ethan praised the dog and tossed her a treat. She was barking and wagging her tail. The dog was happy that she had done a good job.

Rachel opened her phone and called Ethan.

"Hey, I'm going to send Zeus down for a tracking demo. Let me know when you are ready," Rachel said.

Ethan put the collie back into the kennel. Mitch watched the two men talk and then Ethan headed to the far end of the training area, went into the woods, returned to the fence and back into the woods again. He turned and walked along the fence that surrounded the area. Mitch and Rachel could see Ethan as he leaned up against a tree in the woods and signaled to Rachel.

"Zeus, Here," she called the dog.

Mitch turned to see Zeus jump through the window of the Suburban and come to Rachel and sit in front of her. "Good boy," Rachel praised the dog. She gave the dog a hand signal for him to heel at her side and the dog twisted around to her left side and sat. Rachel began to walk to the edge of the sitting area with Zeus at her side. She stopped and looked down into the training area at Evan who then called Zeus. "Go." Rachel commanded the dog as she swung her arm towards Evan.

Zeus started towards Evan, scaled the fence and when he reached him the dog sat in front, waiting for further instructions. Evan pulled a handkerchief from his pocket and let Zeus smell it. Mitch watched as Evan gave the dog the command to "Find".

Zeus began sniffing the ground until he found the scent. The dog hurried his pace as he sniffed the ground and went into the woods following the trail that Ethan had left. The dog emerged from the woods with his nose still to the ground, followed the fence and then went into the woods again and found Ethan at the tree. Rachel and Mitch watched as Zeus began to bark and wag his tail letting Evan know that he had found Ethan. Evan pulled a ball from his pocket and tossed it into the air in front of Zeus who then caught it, ending the session.

Mitch shook his head. "That was amazing," Mitch said.

Rachel smiled. "Thank you."

"You really like your job don't you?" he watched her, impressed.

"I am the luckiest woman in the world to be able to do what I love. If it hadn't been for Britta, my life would have been very different," Rachel said.

She told him her story about how she had come to love the dogs through Britta and her decision to make this her lifelong career. She explained how she and Ethan had decided to grow this into a family business, as the children began to show interest in the dogs. She also told him about some of the clients and their dogs, her work in Search and Rescue, and some of the service dogs that she had trained. They discussed the training, housing and handling of the dogs.

"Mitch, whoever will be handling the dogs will need to be trained as well. They will need to learn the proper commands in order to get the job done, whatever that may be. I think that it would be best for us to bring the dogs out, get them set up and have a few handling classes in order to teach the new handlers how to effectively work the dogs," Rachel said. "That is, of course, if you decide to go with our company."

Mitch took a sip of his tea. He sat quietly thinking about all that he had seen today. She was a great dog trainer. The dogs were well taken care of and were healthy. He liked what he had seen so far. "How soon can we get this going?"

"Right away," she said as she extended her hand out to shake his.

With their part of the presentation over, Ethan, Evan and Zeus approached them. Zeus came running up to Rachel like an excited child with his toy. The dog dropped the ball in front of her and waited for her to throw it. She reached for the ball and threw it into the distance as Zeus chased after it.

Rachel handed a glass of tea to her son and then poured one for Ethan.

"Thanks Mom," Evan said as he turned the glass of tea up and drank it all.

Ethan extended his hand to Mitch and introduced himself. "Hello, I'm Ethan Reed, and our son Evan," he nodded towards him.

Mitch shook his hand and replied, "Mitch Carlson." And then shook hands with Evan.

"That was an impressive demonstration. How long does it take to get a dog to this level of training?" he asked.

"Thor is two years old, which is a good age to start the advanced protection training," Rachel replied. "Training actually starts at birth, with a technique called imprinting. When the pups are in the whelping box, they are all handled daily and stimulated with touch. Then at around two weeks of age when their eyes open and they are crawling around good, I change out their bedding to a different type surface. At three weeks of age toys are put in the whelping box. At four weeks of age they will begin to crawl out of their whelping box and explore the world outside. We then put obstacles around them to climb over. We hang plastic bags up to blow in the wind. At eight weeks of age they get a collar and leash attached to drag around for short intervals during the day. From that point on, their training becomes a game to them and they look forward to learning."

"We do imprinting on the horses too," Mitch said. "It really enhances a strong bond with people."

Rachel smiled. "Yes, it does." She was glad that she had met a fellow animal trainer and that her dogs would be going into a good environment.

"Mitch, grab your bag and I'll show you to the guest house," Ethan said.

"Nice to meet you," Evan said to Mitch as he stood up to go to the kennel.

"Dinner is at five. Make yourself at home. If you like to fish, there are poles and equipment in the shed next to the pond. If you need anything just call me on my cell phone," Rachel said as she handed him his bag out of the back of the Suburban.

Ethan and Mitch made small talk as they walked along the path from the training area. They arrived at the cottage that was now used as a guest house for clients.

"Come on up to the house whenever you get ready," Ethan said pointing towards the main house.

Mitch opened the door to the quaint, comfortable cottage. He tossed his bag on the couch and went into the kitchenette and washed his hands and face. There were canned drinks in the small fridge, along with a vegetable tray. Fresh flowers were on the table. He got a drink and carried the food over to the couch and sat down. He thought about what he had seen since he had arrived and he liked this place.

He liked Rachel too, maybe too much. He wondered what she was doing right now. Maybe she was taking a shower? He thought about her tall slim body, long hair, her mouth and her green eyes that he just melted into when he looked at her.

"Oh hell, I have got to stop this. She's married," he said out loud to himself as if to concrete it in his mind. Mitch knew that he should stop thinking about a woman like her. She was married and with a happy family. Maybe I'm jealous of something that I know I can't have, Mitch thought to himself. The sooner I get this business deal done, the better.

Chapter 11

Mitch reached over for his cell phone. He pressed the quick dial button for his office. Aaron answered on the second ring. "Hey man, what's up?" Mitch greeted.

"I'm catching up with my cousin Pedro," Aaron answered. "How did the meeting go with the dog trainer?"

"Very good," Mitch responded. "These dogs are trained to the max. We will be finalizing arrangements and I should be back tomorrow around noon. Do we need anything in town on my way back from the airport?"

"No, I picked up the fence supplies this morning," Aaron said.

"Sounds like you have everything taken care of. Enjoy your family reunion and I'll see you tomorrow," Mitch said.

He hung up the phone. He knew that Aaron had everything under control and didn't give the Circle C another thought.

Since he hadn't been fishing in a while and he did have a few hours to burn before dinner, he decided to take a walk down to the pond.

He walked out the back door of the guest house and followed the stone steps down to the small pond. There were shade trees all around the pond with a breeze blowing. Mitch got everything that he needed out of the shed to fish and was about ready to toss the line into the water when Zeus ran up behind him barking. Simon appeared from behind the dog and called him. The dog turned and ran back to the boy who was carrying a fishing pole thrown over his shoulder.

"Can I fish with you Mr. Mitch?"

"Sure you can. Hey, what's the secret to catching a lot of fish?"

Simon thought to himself and smiled a big broad smile with his two front teeth missing.

"You gotta spit on the hook," the boy said.

Mitch laughed at the toothless grin.

"Well let's give it a try," Mitch said, who then spit on the baited hook and tossed it into the water.

Simon and Mitch sat quietly fishing for the next hour saying little, but enjoying each others company. Mitch didn't realize how much he missed his daughter until children were around. And at his age and being single, it wasn't likely that he would be fathering any more children.

When it was time to get ready for dinner, Mitch handed the bucket of fish to Simon to take up to his mother, so that they wouldn't waste.

"See you later Simon, I've got to get ready for dinner," Mitch told him.

"Okay, thanks for fishing with me," Simon said.

*   *   *

Mitch knocked on the door to the main house and waited.

"Hi Mr. Carlson, come in." the girl smiled at him and he saw the strong resemblance to her mother.

Mitch walked into the kitchen to the smell of fish frying.

"Mitch, this is my daughter Cassie," Rachel introduced them and turned back to the skillet that held the fish.

"Hello," Mitch said.

"Nice to meet you Mr. Carlson," Cassie said.

"Dinner is close to ready if you'd like to take a seat in the dining room," Rachel invited him.

Cassie smiled at Mitch as she handed him a glass of sweet tea. "Follow me."

Mitch followed Cassie into the dining room. Ethan, Simon and Evan were setting the table. Mitch looked around the dining room that looked like it had been featured in a home decorating magazine. The room was large with a contemporary table and matching china cabinet. There was a Victorian style rug under the table and oil paintings on the walls.

She has many talents, thought Mitch, as he looked around the finely decorated home.

Rachel entered the room with the tray of fish and handed it to Ethan, who placed it on the table. Everyone sat down to a fine meal of fried fish, hush puppies, cheese grits, baked beans and peach pie for desert. Mitch listened to the children as they recounted their day. He watched the way that Rachel and Ethan interacted with their family and felt a small twinge of regret. His train of thought was broken by Simon telling his story about teaching Mitch how to fish. He smiled as the boy told them how to spit on the bait.

"I really appreciate that Simon. I haven't fished in years and I don't know if I would have remembered if you hadn't been there," Mitch said.

Simon beamed with pride, his snaggle toothed grin.

After dinner and clearing the table, Cassie headed off to her friend Chloe's house to swim and Simon went to play a video game. The adults remained at the table to talk business.

Ethan explained to Mitch how to construct the kennels to house the dogs. In the Texas heat, they would need to be placed in the shade with a roof on the kennels with a concrete floor, if not in a building. They all agreed that, after the kennels were in place, Rachel and Evan would bring the dogs out to his ranch and begin the training of the new handlers. After everything was ironed out and the contract was signed, Ethan and Evan excused themselves from the table.

"Would you like a tour of the property?" Rachel asked.

"Sure. I could stand to walk off dinner. It was very good, by the way. I'm not used to getting a spread like that."

"Surely you have someone to cook for you," Rachel said. As good looking as he is, it was hard to believe that he doesn't have someone in his life, she thought.

"Nope, it's just me," he said. "My sister Celia brings me dinner sometimes when she feels sorry for me."

Rachel led the way out to the kennel house. The dogs began to bark when the lights were turned on. The kennel was clean and had automatic waterers. Rachel reached for a bucket that held treats for the dogs. As they walked down the row of kennels she handed each dog a biscuit thru the wire. After giving the dogs their usual evening treats, Rachel and Mitch quickly left the kennel house so that the dogs would settle down.

They walked to the back of the barn where the loafing shed once was. It had been converted into whelping quarters and housed four bitches that were close to their due dates. The girls were all content to stay lying down and offered a wag of their tail in greeting, but didn't offer to get up in their heavy state.

Rachel led him into the kennel office. It was lined with pictures of Rachel and the dogs of her past and present. There was a picture of Queen and Rachel as a girl with Britta. Mitch remembered Rachel telling him about the woman raising her and teaching her about the dogs. He wondered about her parents, since she hadn't mentioned them. As if reading his mind, Rachel explained how Britta had come into her life and how her parents had left it. She explained that as long as her parents chose alcohol and drugs as a way of life for them, she would not be a part of their lives. They chose their path just as she had. She still prayed for them and hoped that one day they would see what they were missing and give it up.

"God has been good to me," Rachel said, not afraid to admit her faith.

Mitch just couldn't understand how a mother and father could turn their backs on their own children for any reason. He shook his head. "I'm sorry to hear that. My family was very close when we were growing up, and we still are, although our parents are gone," Mitch said.

"Hey, you can't miss what you never had. My mother was Britta. She was there for me when I was sick or well, she celebrated my triumphs, cried with me over my failures, and gave me a reality check when I needed it. She'd tell me that the time for crying was over and to get with it," Rachel laughed thinking back to her childhood.

Mitch nodded his head. "You are right."

"I don't hear that very often, can you say that again?" Rachel teased him trying to break the serious mood.

Mitch laughed and said "You are right."

Their steps began to slow as they walked on quietly, until they reached the main house.

Reluctantly, they said their goodbyes.

"Good night Rachel."

"Good night Mitch. I will be in touch," she said extending her hand to his. She felt the electricity in her body come alive as their hands touched. Mitch held onto her hand and looked into her eyes. She had a feeling that he was about to kiss her, but then he released her hand. She smiled and watched him turn and walk down the path towards the guest house. Then she opened the screened door and walked into the kitchen. She turned around and shut the doors and locked them. She looked out the curtain to see that Mitch had made it to the door of the guest house and she then turned off the porch light. She leaned against the door fighting the urge to go to the guesthouse, throw her arms around him and steal that kiss that she knew he wanted to share with her.

Unaware of his presence, Ethan stood watching them from the window of the dark apartment above the kennel, until they finally said goodnight. He had watched them as they walked the grounds and could see the way that they looked at each other. It was unspoken, but he could see that there was a spark between them. He sat down in the chair and waited for Mitch to make it back to the guesthouse before he quietly descended the stairs and made his way down the driveway to his truck parked at the road.

Chapter 12

It had been a month since Mitch had left the farm. Rachel was in her office trying to tie up loose ends before the trip out to Texas to deliver the dogs.

She reached for the daily mail and noticed something from the Circle C ranch addressed to Mr and Mrs Ethan Reed, c/o Reed K-9 center. She tore it open with her fingers and read it.

It was an invitation to the birthday party of William Carlson that would be held at the country club in Crystal City. She sat back in her chair and reached for her calendar. It was being held the following week after she and Evan would arrive at the Circle C, which was scheduled in two weeks.

Her cell phone chimmed in that she had a text message. It was from Tina. Rachel had texted her the previous week to tell her that she was coming out her way and wanted to try to get together.

"Hey, sorry for not getting back to you sooner," she said. Tina was a district manager for a major department store in Dallas. Her husband had died way too young, two years earlier, and she had decided to return to work after her twin boys, Chad and Ben went off to college. She had an on and off relationship with Ken, an attorney, who lived in Houston. Between work, her sons, and commuting back and forth to see Ken, Tina rarely had time for much else.

"I'm coming to see you. Pencil me in two weeks from today. Friday is good for me. Let me know if this works for you." Rachel sent the text message.

"I will be returning Friday night. It works for me. I'll leave a key in the usual place," Tina replied.

"Great! Talk to you soon." Rachel was happy that it had worked out. She hadn't seen Tina since the previous year when Eli started college. Luckily, he was attending the same college as Chad and Ben, although he was a year younger. The four boys had always gotten along and managed to find things to do together when Tina and Rachel were visiting each other.

Rachel was thrilled to find out that she and Tina both had twin boys. They would often call each other and talk about the difficulties of raising twins. One baby was hard enough, but two was well, two babies. But they both made it through.

She reached for her notebook to make a list of things that she needed to do before they left for the Carlson ranch the following month.

She remembered that she needed to replenish the propane and rotate some of the canned vegetables from the safe room to the pantry. She also needed to tell Ethan about the solar panels that she had ordered. She had been buying them here and there, planning to go off grid when she had enough of them to support their electric load. Her goal was to be self sufficient. With Ethan raising a few head of cows, goats, and hunting every year, their meat supply was well taken care of. Ethan had talked about adding rabbits to his farm, so there would be more meat available. They both planted gardens and had small orchards on each farm.

She and Ethan had moved the livestock over to his farm after the divorce and the farm was operated strictly as a business partnership.

Years ago, Brian and Lisa began to instill in Rachel the urgency of taking care of herself. They felt as Britta did, that one day the United States would implode on itself. They explained to Rachel that if and when that time came, she should be ready. So over the years, Rachel had listened and quietly prepared as if the worst would one day happen, but lived each day to the fullest.

Brian had insisted on teaching Rachel how to handle a gun and how to survive in the woods, just in case she ever got lost.

At first she was afraid to touch the firearm, much less aim it at something and pull the trigger. But with time and experience, she became a fairly good marksman. She even hunted on occasion and could butcher anything that she killed. Now, it was unusual for Rachel to be without a weapon. When she traveled, she carried her 9 mm automatic pistol and her Marlin 30/30.

Rachel and Ethan had decided early on in their marriage, that the children would be taught to handle a weapon as well. They had also taught the children that it was up to them as individuals to protect themselves, and as Americans, they were the luckiest kids in the world to live in a country such as theirs.

In recent years, Rachel had realized that things were starting to get bad, when the economy began to weaken. Anybody with an eighth grade education could see that there was no way to recover from a $180 trillion dollar deficit. The government just kept printing more money. Rachel knew that it was only a matter of time before hyperinflation kicked in and most people wouldn't even be able to buy a loaf of bread much less anything else.

It saddened Rachel to know that her children would be living in a world that might possibly see another depression. She wasn't worried about herself, and she knew that her family wouldn't starve. But she was afraid of what the United States would become. The morals and values that people shared in the 1930's, had long since been replaced with a Gimme attitude. A lot of people today thought that they were entitled to whatever they wanted. What is going to happen when people cannot buy food? When children begin to die of starvation in America? She wondered.

"Thank you, God," she said out loud, grateful to know that she and her family were as ready as could be, if it came to that.

She returned to her list. She put a big red star next to a notation on her list.

"Don't forget boxes for Tina."

Rachel worried about her dear friend. She rarely had food in her house, much less an emergency supply. She knew that Tina would laugh at her. She had often told her that she was just paranoid about the doom and gloom. "And anyway if something happens, I will just come to your house," Tina said, laughing.

Rachel didn't have the heart to tell her that she wouldn't be findable at that point. The only people that knew about the underground rooms and hidden supplies, was Brian, Lisa and her family. She hadn't told Tina the full extent of her cache that she had built over the years. For all Tina knew, Rachel just had a lot of food and could shoot a gun.

Rachel finished her list and decided to go down to the training area to watch Ethan and Evan working some of the dogs. Zeus was right on her heels as she went down the trail. She arrived first at the guest house and thinking about Mitch, decided to go in. She shut the door and walked over to the couch and sat down. She couldn't stop thinking about him. She wondered if he had liked it here, what he was doing, and if he thought about her. She thought about their walk and his cologne and how intoxicating it had been with him. And she wondered why he hadn't kissed her.

She walked into the bedroom and she could still smell a faint scent of his cologne, even after a month. "Don't do this to yourself," she said out loud. She left the guesthouse and continued towards the training area.

She sat down at the table and poured a glass of tea from the cooled pitcher that was there. She pulled her cell phone out of her pocket and hit the quick dial for Mitch. She just couldn't help it; she wanted to hear his voice.

"Hello there," he said, glad that she had called.

They had talked nearly twice a week since he had left, always keeping their conversation about business.

"Hello. How are you today?" Rachel said smiling.

"I'm doing great. And you?"

"I'm doing okay. How is construction on the kennel going?" she asked.

"It should be finished the end of next week, if all goes well."

"Great. We received the invitation and I thought I would RSVP. Ethan will not be able to make it, but since we will already be there, Evan and I would love to come."

"I will let Celia know. She has been planning this for some time now, so it should be quite an event," he said.

"I am sure that it will be," she said.

"I will email you some pictures of the kennels when they are finished," he said.

"I will be on the lookout for them. Thanks Mitch."

Rachel closed her phone, just as Ethan was coming up the hill from the training area. He knew that she had been talking to Mitch. She was beaming.

"Hey Baby," Ethan said.

"Don't call me that!" she snapped at him.

Ethan was surprised at her. He had always greeted her that way, even since the divorce. It was just his way. But today, it just didn't sit well with her.

"I'm sorry. I have a lot on my mind today," she said.

"No problem," Ethan said remembering his place. "You will be happy to know that we have ten new puppies born this morning to Misha," he said knowing that that would make her smile.

And she did. "How is Mama?' she asked.

"Just fine." They both knew that this would be the bitch's last litter. She was Queen's great, great granddaughter. Rachel was planning on keeping a female puppy out of the litter to carry on the line.

"I'm not sure how long Evan and I will be out at the Carlson ranch. I'm estimating three to four weeks. Can you think of anything that I might need to do before we leave?' she asked him.

"No. Don't worry. I'll call John if I need any help," he tried to reassure her. John Asher was their closest neighbor that lived about a mile down the road. His daughter Chloe and Cassie had been best friends since grade school.

"I know that you have it under control," she said.

"Ya'll come on up to the house for lunch. It should be ready, by now," she said standing and going up the hill with Zeus trailing behind her.

Chapter 13

The two weeks passed by quickly. Rachel tried to spend as much time with Cassie and Simon before she and Evan left Friday morning. They went out to eat, shopped for new clothes and Rachel bought a cell phone for Simon so that he could call her anytime he wanted to talk to her while she was gone. This was going to be a longer trip than usual and she was worried about being away from them so long. She even considered flying them out to Texas if the trip turned out to be much longer than expected. She made a note to talk to Mitch about it.

Evan, Rachel and Ethan loaded the van Thursday night with all of the equipment and the five dogs that had been agreed upon. And of course Zeus would be coming along. The three containers for Tina were loaded into the already jammed packed van. Since Rachel and Evan would be leaving before the children were up Friday morning, they said their goodbyes at bedtime Thursday night.

"Mommy, why can't I go with you?" Simon pleaded.

"Honey, it is a business trip. We are already packed to the max as it is. You'd have to ride on top of the van," she teased him.

"Awesome! That would be fun!"

"No, it wouldn't. I don't want to leave you or Cassie either, and this will probably be my last trip for a long time. I'm planning on staying home a lot more after this trip."

"Really Mom?' asked Simon.

Cassie stood in the doorway listening to their conversation and walked over to Simon's bed and sat down next to her mother. She leaned her head over on Rachel and said "That would be great Mom. I hate it when you travel."

"I'm liking it a whole lot less too," Rachel replied, reaching over to hug her daughter, who seldom offered affection anymore.

Rachel, Cassie and Simon said their bedtime prayers together and then she tucked him into bed and kissed his forehead. She kissed Cassie goodnight and hugged her tight.

"Help your father as much as you can."

"I will, Mom," she replied as she walked towards her room.

Five a. m. came early, but since the van was already loaded, there was little left to add, but her suitcase and their bug out bags. If the van broke down, they would have their survival bags if need be. They always carried food and water for the dogs anyway so they would be taken care of. She would hate to break down in the middle of Texas in September.

Relaxed in the seat and with Evan driving, she decided to take a nap. After an hour Rachel awoke to her phone signaling a new text message. She opened it and read:

"I've got an emergency at one of my stores and I won't be home tonight. I'm really sorry! Make yourself at home and we will get together soon. The guys are still coming in this afternoon so ya'll have fun. HUGS"

Rachel read the text with disappointment and responded.

"It is okay. Things happen. HUGS back."

"Well, Tina isn't going to make it home tonight," Rachel said to Evan.

"Drag, what happened?"

She explained that there was an emergency at one of the stores.

"How would you like to have a weekend with the guys? You've been working hard the past few months and you deserve a break. I can drive on down to the Circle C and you can fly in Sunday night." she said smiling at her handsome son.

"Are you sure about this?' Evan asked her, looking forward to spending some time with his brother.

"Yes, I am," she said, opening her phone to make the travel arrangements.

When they reached Tina's house, Evan helped her unload the boxes and grabbed his suitcase. Rachel found the key hidden at the corner of the house under some mulch, and unlocked the door. Copper and Penny rushed out the door. The two golden retrievers were happy to see her, with their tails wagging and excited barks. Rachel had helped Tina find the dogs not long after the loss of her husband. They were in training at her kennel for six weeks and remembered her and Evan.

They brought the boxes of food into the house and started unloading them. The glass jars nearly filled up the small pantry closet. Rachel had made a batch of cakes in a jar and canned some homemade soup and vegetables for her. She felt a little better knowing that her friend had food in her house.

Evan brought the cooler in and they sat down to a lunch of sandwiches, chips, cake in a jar and sweet tea. Rachel was stuffed as she watched Evan continue to inhale the food that she had brought.

"Where are you putting it?' she said to him. He had always liked to eat and had still kept an athletic figure, she thought to herself.

Her phone rang and she answered it.

"Hey Mom," said Eli.

"Hey son. Where are you?"

"I'm still at school. I had something come up and I'm late leaving. Chad and Ben have already left and should be there any minute," he said.

Rachel explained to Eli that Tina had to cancel and that she was going on down to the Carlson ranch.

"I'm sorry that I will miss seeing you. I will stop by on my return trip, okay? Would you mind bringing your brother to the airport on Sunday?"

"Sure Mom. That's not a problem," Eli said.

"Thanks baby. You guys have fun this weekend and I'll see you in a few weeks."

Rachel, anxious to return to the road, hugged Evan and told him goodbye. She flipped her phone open to text Mitch before getting back on the road.

"Hey, we will be arriving earlier than planned. Six o'clock this evening." She sent the text.

"See you then." He replied.

She smiled, started the van and continued on passing miles of nothing but fences and cattle.

White board fence, black board fence, barb wire fence, field fence; stretched for miles down the road until she finally came to the driveway for the Circle C ranch. She turned right onto the asphalt driveway and followed the oak lined driveway until she came to the big main house.

She saw the barn in the distance and continued past the house where she pulled the van under one of the massive oak trees and parked it. She was about to text Mitch to let him know that she had arrived, when he walked out of the barn, smiling.

"Hey, you made it," Mitch said. His face went ashen. "Where is Evan?"

"I dropped him off with his brother."

"You mean that you made that drive alone? What were you thinking? With all of the recent kidnappings, you just drive right on down here?" Mitch looked like he was about to explode. Zeus, growling, watched him as he turned and walked to the back of the van to help her unload, in silence.

Rachel, stunned, was surprised at his reaction. How dare he talk to her like that! She was a grown woman after all. She wasn't helpless. And he wasn't responsible for her. Okay, fine. Let me just get the van unloaded and get away from this jerk, she thought, her anger rising.

They unloaded the van and settled the dogs in the kennel. Rachel was impressed with the setup. There were four large red barns. Three stalls in one of the barns had been converted into dog kennels with top of the line Preifert runs. The runs were indoor/outdoor so the dogs could go out onto a concrete slab if they wanted to be outside. She was pleased to see that the dogs would be well taken care of.

Mitch coldly walked past Rachel and carried the equipment into the tack room where it would be kept.

Aaron walked into the barn and introduced himself.

"Hello, I'm Aaron Garcia," he said, sensing that he had walked in on something.

"Rachel Reed," she said smiling and shaking his hand.

"I've heard a lot about you Miss Reed. It is nice to finally meet you."

"Thank you," she said.

"Aaron, would you show Miss Reed to the guest house?' Mitch all but ordered him with his cold demanding tone. He immediately turned and without saying a word to Rachel, left the barn.

What an idiot I am! Mitch thought to himself. He had totally overreacted. She is a grown woman for God's sake. A married grown woman at that. He went into the house and paced around in the kitchen. What am I going to say to her? She didn't deserve his verbal attack. She probably thinks that I'm such a fool, Mitch thought as he continued to beat himself up. He paced in the house until he had regained his composure.

Aaron led Rachel a half mile past the group of red barns. They came to another large red barn that housed the pregnant mares. The guest house sat away from the foaling barn under another oak tree and was also painted red. It was an old bunkhouse that was once used to house the cowboys years ago, but it had been converted into a quaint little house for guests.

Aaron helped unload her things from the van and then waved as he drove off. She went into the little bunkhouse and fell onto the couch, exhausted. Zeus walked over and laid his head in her lap. She petted the dog and started to calm down.

She thought about the confrontation with Mitch. What was I thinking? Rachel pondered. To think that I could be attracted to someone like him? What was he gonna do, rope her and throw her over his saddle? I don't think so.

She stood up to let Zeus outside to go potty and saw Mitch drive up in his dually truck. She stood in the doorway watching him as he approached her. The anger in his face was gone. The riled up rooster demeanor was also gone. His shoulders were more relaxed. His shoulders..... his arms...his hands... Rachel looked away for a moment and then met his eyes with a defeated smile.

"Can I talk to you for a minute?"

"Sure," she said softly stepping back and letting him walk into the bunkhouse. She shut the door and turned around to face him.

"I owe you an apology. I overreacted to something that wasn't my business. You are a married woman and I shouldn't have...."

Shock registered on her face as she stared at him like a deer caught in his headlights and his words sank in. She understood. He was afraid that something might have happened to her. But that would mean that....he had feelings for her.

"I shouldn't have let my feelings get in the way. I assure you that I will not act on them. From here on out, strictly business," he finished, as his hand gestured a straight line.

Rachel stood watching him. She could feel the heat rising. She walked slowly to him and stood face to face and within inches of him. She reached up and pulled him to her. She kissed him long and hard tasting him, hungry for his mouth, his touch, his body.

She felt his hands move to her arms as he pulled her away. She could see that the kiss had stirred feelings in him just as it had her.

"If you kiss me like that again, I might have to forget that you are married," he said, fighting back the urge to pull her to him again, trying to make himself push her away, but not wanting to.

Rachel leaned forward and wrapped her arms around his neck. She felt his rancher's body hard against hers and whispered into his ear. "I'm not married."

Mitch reached up and gently pulled her arms down from around his neck and stepped back to look at her. Rachel looked into his eyes. He could see that she was telling him the truth. He could also see that she wanted him. He pulled her to him unable to stop himself from devouring her lips. She melted into his body as they frantically moved towards the bedroom, unable to let go of each other. His hands moved underneath her shirt and lifted it up and over her head. She began to run her hands over his chest feeling his muscles built by hard work on a ranch. It was if they had known each other forever and were now being reunited. His body joined with hers as they climbed to heights that neither of them had gone to in a long time.

Chapter 14

Rachel awoke with a start. Looking around the room, she had forgotten where she was at. Then she felt Mitch's body intertwined with hers and remembered. She turned towards him and looked at him in the dim light that shone from the other room. His athletic body stirred her again and she contemplated if she dared to wake him. She lay in the bed for a few minutes and then she faintly heard Zeus at the front door whining to come in.

She slowly and carefully picked up Mitch's arm and tried to move it off of her without waking him, but she felt his arm tighten around her waist.

"Where do you think you're going?"

Rachel smiled and turned back to face him.

"I'm going to let Zeus in," she whispered.

"Hurry back," he said, huskily.

She reluctantly rose from the bed to go let Zeus into the house. She walked naked through the little house and to the front door to let him in before she returned to Mitch's waiting arms.

It was early evening as they lay in the bed, Rachel thought about how Mitch had reacted to her traveling alone. He thought that she was married. What would have given him that idea? She thought back over the past few weeks and realized that she had never told him that she wasn't married. She remembered Ethan introducing himself and Evan as their son. Mitch thought that they were one big happy family. They certainly appeared that way, but it was just a business arrangement. Rachel had never thought about it before, since she had no intentions of starting a relationship with another man. She was content to raise her children and live out her life alone. And she hadn't seen it. How Mitch looked at her, and responded to her presence. Then, as if a light bulb was turned on, she realized that he had been fighting his feelings for her this whole time. She tried to muffle a giggle, but couldn't stop as she began to laugh.

"What's so funny?"

Rachel smiled and thought about tonight. She sat up and leaned against the headboard and looked down at him, smiling.

"What if I hadn't told you?' she wondered out loud.

"What? That you're not married? Baby, I'm glad that you did," he said stroking her leg.

Rachel sat forward and twisted her body on top of his. She sat looking down at him. "Are you really?" she asked him. She could feel her body pressing against his. He could feel it too. He pulled her off him and twisted his body onto hers. "I think you know the answer," he said as he pinned her arms down on the bed. "Do you want me to tell you again?" he asked, his voice thick. She was unable to speak. It had been four years since she had been with a man and the closeness of him made her head spin. "Do you?" He asked her again as he began to kiss her neck. "Yes, tell me again," she whispered intoxicated by his smell and his hands touching her.

And he did. After they were spent, he kissed her gently and sweetly on the lips and they drifted off to sleep.

Rachel awoke to Zeus pressing his cold nose under her hand, as he always did in the mornings. She rose quietly and went into the living room for her suitcase. She retrieved her robe and slipped it on and then let Zeus outside. She was suddenly hungry as she went into the little kitchen to find some food. Celia had stocked the small refrigerator with everything one might need. Rachel cooked some bacon, eggs, toast and grits and then set the table, since she couldn't find a tray.

She walked over to the large window in the living room and opened the curtains to an already hot summer day. The view was picturesque from the window. The misty fog lingered around the foaling barn and the turn out paddock with mares and foals at their sides, grazing in the green grass. She could hear the shrill whinny of the foals as they called to each other. To the left was the asphalt driveway lined with oaks and into the distance was the main house, where Mitch lived.

She turned and went to her suitcase to get her clothes and running shoes. She walked back into the bedroom and quietly as she watched Mitch sleep, she changed her clothes. When she finished dressing, she sat down on the bed and leaned over and kissed him. "Wake up sleepy head." She watched him as he came awake, stretched and then smiled at her sleepily.

"Hey. Where are you going?" he asked her as he reached out for her hand.

"I'm gonna run down to the kennel and check on the dogs. I won't be long." She promised him. "Breakfast is on the table," she said.

"I'll wait for you," he said, watching her leave the room.

Rachel left the little house and set out at a slow jog as Zeus fell into place next to her. They jogged the half mile to the barn and rounded the corner to see Aaron's truck parked outside at one of the other barns. Rachel felt awkward since she hadn't expected to see anyone so early in the morning. She walked into the newly remodeled kennel/barn to check on the dogs. The dogs were glad to see her as they barked their greeting at her and Zeus. Rachel smiled and reached into one of the buckets next to the kennel and got a handful of the treats. She began to hand the treats out to the dogs, and they quieted down crunching on the dry biscuits.

"Good Morning," Aaron called out to her as he entered the barn. Zeus snapped to attention and began to bark at him. "Okay." Rachel released the dog, who then began wagging his tail and approached Aaron.

"Good morning," she returned the greeting.

"The dogs look good this morning," Aaron commented.

"They settled in nicely," Rachel nodded in agreement.

Aaron began to ask her questions about the dogs. What their names were, their jobs, and the feeding schedule.

"If the dogs are not worked they will need to be exercised, or they will become like children and start misbehaving," she explained to him.

He laughed and said "Yeah, same with the horses."

Rachel put the last fresh bucket of water in the kennel and turned to leave. "See you later," she said as she waved goodbye, anxious to return to Mitch. She and Zeus set out on their slow jog back to the guest house.

Aaron watched them until they got to the guesthouse and Mitch opened the door for them to come in. "It's about time," he said to himself. He was glad to see that Mitch was happy. Over the past few weeks he had watched the transformation from someone drifting through life to someone coming alive again. Aaron could see Mitch's face light up when he talked to Rachel on the phone. He was in love. He just didn't know it yet.

He was dressed when she returned and he smelled fresh. She came in and he instinctively reached for her. "I'm all sweaty," she said, holding her hands up to him and running around him to the bathroom. "Hold that thought, I'll be right back," she called out to him from the other room. She hurriedly peeled her clothes off, climbed into the shower, and was finished in two minutes flat. She threw on a sundress and went into the kitchen. She smiled a big beautiful smile. "Good morning."

He stood from the table and wrapped his arms around her. He deeply inhaled the smell of her, pulled her close and kissed her. "My god, you are beautiful," he said to her.

"Down boy," she said, trying to fake a stern face. "Let's eat." Rachel didn't think that she had ever been as hungry, as she ate a full plate of food and reached for more eggs. Mitch watched her as she ate more than he did. He wondered how she kept her body so hot, eating like that. But it was good to see a woman eat instead of pick at her food.

"I saw Aaron at the barn," Rachel said. "That was awkward."

Mitch told her all about Aaron and how he had saved his life when he was at his lowest.

"I'm glad that you have someone like him in your life," she said softly.

"Evan will be arriving tomorrow night. So what would you like to do?"

"Well, since we don't have much time, I say that we take full advantage of the day," Mitch said, reaching over for her hand and standing up.

"So what do you have planned for today?' Rachel asked.

"Baby, after last night those plans went right out the window."

She smiled at him, as he led her back into the bedroom.

They spent the day and the rest of the night in bed making love and talking about their lives. Rachel told Mitch about Ethan having an affair, and how it had ripped her apart. Mitch told her about the accident that claimed Melissa and Amy, and the days after when he nearly ended it all.

"I am so sorry that you had to go through that," she said to him with a heavy heart, as she stroked his face and pulled him closer to her.

"It seems like a lifetime ago. The pain has lessened over the years. It makes me appreciate where I am now, here with you," he said picking up her hand and kissing it.

"You may not be ready to hear this," he said, "but I loved you the first day that I saw you at the service station. I felt it, even then," he said. "When I met your family, I could hardly stand the thought of you being married, untouchable, out of reach," he said gently stroking her arm. He lifted her chin up to his face and looked deep into her eyes as he said, "I have lived for the past ten years in a fog. You rocked my world last night. If you think for a minute that I will let you out of my arms, my life or my heart, you are crazy."

Tears began to roll down her face. She kissed him and then she let her body answer him. When she finished, he had no doubt that she felt the same way.

They would occasionally come up for air, let Zeus out and go to the kitchen to get some food to refuel. And then, back to the bedroom they would return.

Sunday morning came bright and early. Mitch was cooking breakfast for them and she was enjoying a rare treat of not having to cook. She sat at the table watching him with a towel wrapped around his waist, moving around the kitchen. His clothes were drying in the dryer. He had not wanted to leave her for one minute since she got here and since he hadn't needed his clothes until now, he was using a towel.

94

Rachel smiled at the sight of him. She had never been happier. They ate their breakfast and were having coffee when Mitch broke the quiet.

"What do you think about moving into the main house with me? There are enough bedrooms for you and Evan to move in there." He reached for her hand and kissed it.

Rachel thought about it. What would she tell Evan? Rachel pulled her hand away from Mitch, as she considered the implications of her actions. She began to shake her head back and forth. "No," she answered simply.

She had been so swept up in the passion and her new found love that she hadn't thought about it. She wouldn't be setting a good example for her children and she just couldn't do it, no matter how badly she wanted to.

"I can't move in with you," she cried out. "I can't lie to my son, myself or my God, but I love you and I don't want to hurt you," she said pleadingly for him to understand as she stood up from the table to leave. He stood and started towards her and she held her hand up. "Don't," she said as she began to cry.

"Stop crying," he said, reaching for her again and not taking no for an answer as he held her while she cried into his chest. "Hey, its okay," he said softly stroking her hair. She nodded her head against him trying to catch her breath.

She pulled her head back and looked at him. "Do you know what I meant when I said…." He put his finger to her lips and nodded, "Yes. I do," he said sadly knowing that he had caused her pain. He should have taken it slower, he thought to himself.

He led her into the living room and they sat down on the couch facing each other.

"Look, its okay. I'm not going anywhere. You and Evan will stay here and I will stay in the main house. We will take one day at a time and we will figure it out as we go along," he said gently. "Okay?"

"Okay," she said nodding, starting to feel better.

She leaned over on his shoulder and they sat together holding hands, unwilling to get up.

Mitch knew that he had to leave her before Eli arrived. He kissed her forehead and stood to go get his clothes out of the dryer.

He returned fully dressed and he reached for her. She tightened her grip on his hand and stood up with him. "Why don't you go lie

95

down and take a nap," he motioned with his head towards the bedroom.

"Good idea," she said smiling.

"I'll text you later," he said as he slipped his boots on and watched her go into the bedroom and lie down, before quietly leaving for the main house.

She slept for two hours, before her phone woke her to a new message.

"I will be there in twenty," Evan texted her.

"K," she answered.

Rachel got up and went to make coffee. She quickly looked around the room and straightened up before her son arrived. Then she went into the kitchen and put the dishes in the sink.

She looked out the front window and saw the rental car pull in and park. She opened the door of the little house and let Zeus out. She stood on the porch and watched Evan get out of the car and stretch. Zeus ran around excitedly glad to see him, as if it had been a year since he had seen him last.

"Hey Mom," he said. She smiled. "Hey son."

They sat down at the little kitchen table and she listened as Evan told her about his weekend with the guys and the new girl that Eli had met. "It sounds like he's got it bad for this girl," Evan said. "He left early this morning to get back to school, or should I say Jessica," he said, sounding angry.

Rachel smiled at her son. "Don't worry about your brother. He will be okay," she said patting his hand. "Hey, come on down to the kennel and see the setup that Mitch has put together," she offered trying to take his mind off it.

They began the short walk towards the barn with Zeus following along.

Evan liked being here. He had always liked animals anyway, but he especially liked horses.

"So I see that you had company while I was away," Evan said.

Rachel continued to walk as she considered how to answer her son.

"Yes. Mitch came over for dinner last night," Rachel explained, not telling him everything.

"And breakfast too?" Evan asked smartly. "I saw the breakfast dishes Mom."

Rachel stopped walking and turned to look at Evan.

"Mom! The guy likes you. I saw it when he came to the farm. Go for it, Mom. It's about time you were happy," he said starting towards the barn again.

"When did you get so grown up? Thank you Evan." She said as tears came to her eyes. She explained that she had been agonizing over this new relationship and she didn't know how her children would react.

"I think that the others will be okay with it," Evan said. "Simon is still young and he likes Mitch."

They walked into the barn, to see Mitch talking to Aaron down the aisle..

"Hey, man," he said extending his hand to Evan. "Aaron, this is Evan Reed. He's gonna help teach us a thing or two about dogs."

They shook hands and Aaron said, "Hey, let me show you around."

Mitch watched Aaron and Evan walk from the aisle of the barn. When they were out of sight he leaned over and kissed Rachel. He felt like a teenager about to get caught kissing in school.

"Evan just told me that he is okay with us seeing each other," she said, smiling happily.

Mitch picked her up off her feet and swung her around happy himself. "One down, three to go!" Mitch put her back on her feet and stepped back smiling. He knew that the approval of her children was most important to her.

"Celia and William will be over in the morning. They would like to meet with you and Evan around eight."

"Okay. I'd like to do a demonstration for them before the meeting.

"You are gonna knock their socks off. Just like you did mine," Mitch said.

"Well, not exactly," she said without thinking.

Mitch cleared his voice and looked away as Aaron and Evan walked back into the barn.

"We will see you in the morning then," Mitch said watching Rachel and Evan as they left the barn.

Chapter 15

Mitch had tossed and turned all night thinking about Rachel. He wanted her in his bed next to him. Now that he had found her, he could feel the emptiness when they were apart. It was 1:00 a.m. and he texted Rachel.

"I can't sleep without you here."

"Me too." She texted him back. "I am going to look a fright for the meeting in the morning!"

"Never."

"Sweet dreams," she finished and flipped her phone shut.

William, Celia, Aaron and Mitch arrived as scheduled at eight a.m. to meet with the Reeds. Mitch had explained to them that they had planned a demonstration for them outside the barn. He had never once let on that one of the Reeds was a woman, so when Celia walked out and saw Rachel standing in the shade holding Thor, she cast a glance at Mitch that said "What's up?" He deliberately ignored his sister as the demonstration began.

Evan, wearing the bite suit and looking like the Michelin man, moved towards his mother. Thor alerted to the threat advancing towards them and began to bark excitedly. Evan waved the club in the air, as he advanced towards them.

In a frenzy, Thor was ready to go. Rachel had planted her feet and was holding Thor back with every ounce of strength in her arms, her muscles taut and straddling the dog. Evan turned and began to run away from them. Rachel had a cap gun in her hand and she fired the gun into the air. "Stop! Or I'll send the dog! She yelled out to Evan who kept running away. Rachel dropped the cap gun, released Thor and then she began to follow behind the dog.

The Carlson group stood mesmerized as Thor covered the ground and sailed into the air at Evan. Rachel finally caught up to them and pulled Thor off of him, completing the demo. Rachel commanded Thor to down and stay, which he did. She dropped the lead and walked over to Evan and started helping him take off the suit. Thor laid on the ground watching, ready to spring into action if called on.

Since it was already hot, Rachel and Evan had decided to just do a short presentation.

Rachel opened her phone and called Mitch.

"I'm going to do a short obedience demonstration so sit tight."

"Will do." Celia saw Mitch's face light up when he talked to Rachel and suspected that there was something going on.

The Carlson group watched from the barn area as Rachel walked over to Thor. She gave him the heel command and the dog stayed right by her side as she walked, ran, turned and then stopped quickly. Thor sat. Rachel gave the down command and Thor lay down. She commanded the dog to stay and she stepped forward and walked ten paces, stopped and turned around to face the dog. Rachel gave the command for him to come and he ran towards her and sat sharply in front of her. She gave a hand signal for him to finish and Thor ran around behind her and sat again next to her side, waiting for the next command. She again gave him the heel command and began walking towards the waiting group as Evan fell in beside her and Thor. The dog continued to heel next to Rachel and just before they got to the group Rachel gave him the down and stay command. He dropped to the ground and Rachel never missed a step as she and Evan continued walking towards the group. Rachel saw the group of people shaking their heads in awe as they walked up. She ignored Thor while she and Evan were introduced to the group. She then turned back to the dog and gave him a hand signal to come to her. The dog ran forward and sat. Rachel praised him and tossed a ball into the air praising him for a job well done. Thor mouthed the ball and began going to each person for them to throw it.

Celia reached down to pet the Rottweiler and get the ball to throw it.

"He's beautiful," Celia said to Rachel. "Outstanding job," she said to Rachel and Evan. Celia glanced at Rachel's hand and noticed that she wasn't wearing a wedding ring.

They returned to the barn office to finish up the meeting in the air conditioned room. After the meeting was over Rachel, Evan and Thor excused themselves from the group. Mitch had not taken his eyes off Rachel since the demonstration. He saw her in a whole new light. What a woman, he thought to himself.

Celia, William, Aaron and Mitch were standing around talking about the Reed's and how fortunate they were for Mitch to have stumbled upon them.

"I noticed that Rachel wasn't wearing a wedding ring," Celia said to Mitch.

"You are right." Mitch was becoming aggravated at his sister. "But I am about to remedy that situation," Mitch said matter of fact and turned to walk away from his family. Celia, William and Aaron's mouths dropped open and with wide eyes they trailed after him.

"Wait a minute brother," William said.

The three of them caught up to him and William started first.

"You can't just say something like that and walk off. Let's hear it."

"All of it," Celia threw in, crossing her arms.

Aaron stood back with a smile on his face. He was thinking about their childhood and the last time that Mitch had ambushed them.

"I have known her less than two months and I love her. She is the most beautiful, smartest, funniest, hottest, woman that I have ever met and I am going to marry her. I don't want to hear anything out of any of you about it," Mitch said his look dared them to say a word. "Now, get back to work." Mitch commanded them and stomped off.

Celia with raised eyebrows looked at William, William looked at Aaron and Aaron said, "You heard the man. The boss said to get back to work." He started to walk away, smiling.

"Oh no, you don't. Celia and William ran after him. "You know something. Spill it."

"I know the same thing that you know," Aaron laughed shrugging his shoulders. "You gotta admit that it's good to see him happy."

"Okay, that's it. I'm going to talk to Rachel." Celia said throwing her arms up in the air.

"Celia, stay out of it," William warned her. "He will tell us when he wants us to know."

Celia knew that her brother was right and although reluctantly, she gave up.

"Do you think that he's serious or is he just jerking us around?" Aaron heard Celia ask William as they walked towards their cars.

The week started with Rachel stopping by the main house in the mornings after her run, to have breakfast with Mitch. Following breakfast, Rachel and Evan held the training class for the Carlson group. She insisted on keeping her relationship with Mitch professional as she taught them how to handle the dogs. By the end of the week, everyone had come to know each other and was comfortable with the new additions to the ranch.

Celia was surprised that she liked Rachel. She had watched her interact with Mitch and realized that they were perfect for one another and she liked seeing parts of the old Mitch emerge when he was around Rachel. They were making good progress, so they decided to take off Friday to get ready for the party on Saturday at the Country Club.

On Saturday morning, Mitch texted Rachel before she could leave for her morning run and told her that he had an errand in town and he would be back later. She was disappointed, but instead of sitting around the guesthouse all day, she decided to go for a ride.

She sent Evan a text message.

"Do you want to go for a ride and take a couple of the dogs out with us?" she asked.

"Yes! Let's go."

"I'll be down in a few."

So after clearing it with Aaron, they saddled up and started out with Thor and Zeus following the horses.

After riding over a mile south of the ranch, they stopped in the shade of a tree to get a drink of water. Still mounted and the horses standing quietly, Rachel saw movement in the brush as two men tried to sneak along on the other side of the over grown fence line. She pretended that she hadn't seen them and since they couldn't hear her from where they sat, she told Evan, "Don't let on, but there are two men south east of us about a hundred feet." She smiled.

The dogs were in the down position resting, after their mile hike.

"Lets start moving towards them slowly and you watch my back." Rachel said to her son. They had brought their rifles and pistols. Rachel and Evan moved forward on their horses and the men began to run. Rachel raised her pistol and fired into the air. "Stop! Or I'll send the dogs! Rachel knew that the horses couldn't jump the overgrown fence. The men kept running and Rachel gave the dogs the command to go. Thor and Zeus shot out together, scaled the fence and brought both of the thugs down onto the ground. The dogs stood guard over the two men barking and growling. The horses were dancing around with all of the excitement going on. Evan and Rachel had their pistols aimed at the two men. Rachel yelled out, "Get up and come here." The two men just lay on the ground.

"Mom they probably don't speak English," Evan said.

"Great, we don't speak Spanish." Rachel said.

Evan yelled out to them. "Hey! Get up," he said as he gestured for them to stand up. The two banditos turned and looked at him. They then looked at each other, and back at the dogs, who continued to bark at them. They slowly stood up trying not to antagonize the dogs and the two men waded thru the brush. The dogs continued to bark and watch the men even after they had reached Rachel and Evan, who then motioned for the two men to fall in, walking in front of them.

They had walked a short distance, when Rachel saw a jeep in the distance heading towards them. She and Evan readied their pistols, and pulled the horses up.

"Watch it," Rachel commanded the dogs.

When the jeep got closer, she saw that it was Aaron and Mitch.

Rachel and Evan relaxed and she told them what had happened.

Aaron and Mitch searched the two men and found a gun, knife and some cash, but nothing else.

Aaron told the two men to get in the jeep. Mitch sat in the front seat of the jeep and kept his .357 magnum pointed at them, as Aaron drove back to the ranch.

"Wow! Mom, you were something. Would you really have shot those guys?" Evan asked her.

"Don't point it, if you ain't gonna pull the trigger," she said in her worst red neck southern drawl ever.

"I'm just glad that I didn't have to shoot anyone," she said, still shaking.

"The dogs were awesome!" Evan continued, as he twisted in the saddle. "They didn't hesitate at all, Mom." He was proud that he had helped to train them and he talked all the way home about how cool it had been to capture these guys.

Rachel was just glad to get back to the ranch since her lower half was beginning to ache, what with all the extra activity with Mitch and now horseback riding.

Mitch and Aaron arrived back at the ranch at the same time that Evan and Rachel rode up to the barn. Mitch reached up and helped Rachel down from her horse.

"Are you okay?" Mitch asked her.

"Yes, fine. Just a little sore." she said.

Evan was more interested in where the two men were at.

"Where are the two guys at?" Evan asked.

"We returned them to the border," Mitch explained to him. He didn't tell him that he had given the guys a message to take back to Mexico.

Aaron announced that a mare was about to foal and that he had to leave.

"Hey, can I help?"

"Sure, come on," Aaron told him.

Mitch and Rachel were finally alone.

He reached out and pulled her to him, wrapping his arms around her.

"So can you rope cattle too?" he teased her.

"I sure can. But I'd rather rope you." she teased him leaning against his body. She felt the attraction building, and pulled away from him.

"I'm sorry Mitch," she said. "I shouldn't tease you like that. It is just so darn easy with you." She shook her head and turned to walk back to the guest house.

"Let me give you a ride home," Mitch offered. "Come on Rachel, you can hardly walk." He went over to the tethered horse and pulled her rifle from the holster and put it in the back of the jeep. She turned and slowly walked back to the jeep.

"It is your fault, you know," she said teasingly glancing at him.

"I didn't hear any complaints," he shot back at her, smiling.

She was glad that the jeep had a roll cage so that she could use her arms to pull herself up and gently lower her body into the seat. When they arrived at the guesthouse Mitch walked around and helped her out of the jeep, before kissing her on the cheek.

"See you tonight," he said smiling like a kid in a candy store.

Rachel hobbled into the guest house and went to run a hot bath. How am I going to dance like this? She wondered to herself as she lowered her body into the tub. She sat in the tub for over an hour and started to feel some of the soreness leave. After her bath, she rose out of the tub and suddenly feeling very tired, she decided to take a nap before getting ready for the party.

Chapter 16

"**M**om, wake up. It is time to get ready for the party," Evan said. Rachel felt like she had just closed her eyes, but she had slept for three hours. I must be feeling my age, she thought to herself, still tired.

She went into the kitchen, started coffee and grabbed some ice for her puffy eyes. She went into the bathroom and turned on the cold water before emptying the tray of ice into the water, as well as a washrag.

Rachel had told Mitch that they would meet him there, and she and Evan arrived right on time. She couldn't help but admire her son in his tuxedo as he walked around the van to open the door and help his mother out.

She had chosen a full length, formal, emerald green halter dress, with sequins on it. It had a slit up the right side of her leg. She wore emeralds to match the dress and her eyes. She had pulled her hair up onto her head and a few curls framed her face. Rachel and Evan gave the host their names and waited as he checked the list.

"Enjoy your evening," the man said, as he let them pass.

"Thank you," Rachel said smiling.

She walked into the room and looked around. The only person that she wanted to see was Mitch, but everyone in the room turned and looked at her and her son standing in the doorway.

Rachel's eyes finally fell on Mitch as he stood watching her as she entered the room like she owned it. She had achieved the desired effect. The site of her made him weak in the knees. Their eyes met and he smiled his approval at her. He crossed the room to her and held out his hand for her to take, and he led her over to a group of people to introduce her and Evan.

Off to the side of the room, Brian and Lisa stood watching Rachel as she entered and her eyes found Mitch. Lisa leaned over to her husband and asked, "How long has this been going on?"

"I have no idea," he said, happy to see Rachel and Evan.

"Let's go over and see our girl," he said reaching for his wife's hand.

Rachel caught sight of Brian and Lisa as they approached. Her face lit up when she saw them. "I didn't know you would be here!"

"Well, you would, if you called more often," Brian said to one of his favorite people. He kissed her on the cheek and hugged her.

"You look stunning," Lisa said, hugging her.

Brian held his hand out. "Mitch," he said shaking hands with him and then greeting Evan. "Howdy, my boy."

"Hey Granddaddy," Evan said.

Rachel was glad to see them. It had been a good six months since they had been together and although she talked to them on the phone often, she still missed them.

Mitch reached for her hand and asked, "Would you like to dance?" The band was playing a slow, romantic song.

"Of course," she said feeling like she was in a fairytale as he led her onto the dance floor.

Rachel felt like she was floating as Mitch held his arms around her and they danced slowly back and forth, unaware of anyone else.

"You really shouldn't have worn that dress," he said looking deep into her eyes.

Rachel, disappointed, leaned away from him to see his face unable to believe that he had just said the words.

"You just upstaged every woman in here," he said, looking at her like he wanted her all to himself.

"Mission accomplished," she said smiling. The people around them whispered amongst themselves, asking if Mitch Carlson had finally been won.

Rachel could feel all eyes on them as they swayed back and forth to the music and she leaned her head over on his shoulder and closed her eyes. She felt his face close to hers and the warmth of his breath.

"Marry me?" he asked.

She lifted her head to search his face to see that he was sincere and pleading with her.

"My pocket," he said and released one of her hands. She watched his face as she moved her hand down to his pants pocket and reached in to retrieve a ring box. With their eyes locked and his arms around her waist she brought the little black box up between them and still clutched in her hand, she smiled and nodded her head yes. Suddenly all motion in the room stopped and a quiet fell over the crowd as they watched her open the box and her eyes dropped to the biggest diamond she had ever seen. Mitch smiled and leaned forward to kiss her, staking his claim as all watched and then the crowd of friends and family began to clap, whistle and hoop it up, Texas style.

She looked around the room to see Evan, Brian and Lisa watching her. They were smiling at her.

She looked back at Mitch. The room began to spin and she felt dizzy. Before she could speak, her knees buckled and her body collapsed into his arms.

"Rachel, Baby? Rachel?" Mitch slid his body carefully to the floor still holding her. All of a sudden, the room full of people crowded around them. His face was full of fear as Aaron and William made it over to his side. They lifted Rachel up and then someone in the crowd helped Mitch stand. They carried her into an adjoining room and laid her down on a table. One of the waiters brought Mitch an armful of table cloths and they placed them under her head.

Brian, Lisa and Evan pushed their way through the crowd towards Rachel. "Let us through!" Brian bellowed out. They finally reached the room as Rachel was coming around.

Evan rushed to her side. "Mom?"

Rachel slowly blinked her eyes. She felt like she had been in a deep sleep. She saw the people around her and she slowly remembered. "I'm fine," she said, sitting up, with Mitch pulling her into a sitting position carefully, as if she were glass.

"Baby, do you feel okay?" Mitch felt like he was reliving a nightmare.

"I'm okay," she said dreamily. "I think that you have something for me," she said.

Mitch smiled nervously, reassured for a moment. "It'll wait. Are you sure that you're okay?" he asked worriedly.

"Really, I'm okay. Everyone, please return to the party." She smiled at her son nodding her head.

They watched as everyone left the room so that they could be alone.

"You scared me, you know," he said as he opened the box and removed the ring before sliding it on her finger.

"I'm sorry. I haven't eaten anything all day. Really, I'm okay."

"So how did you do this?" Rachel looked at the ring.

"I talked to William first. I didn't want to steal his glory at his birthday party but he loved the idea. So then I talked to Evan and told him that I loved you and asked him if he would mind if I married you. He said it was "tight," whatever that means."

Rachel laughed. "That means good," she said amused.

"So, will you marry me?" he asked her again.

"Yes, I will," she answered him happily.

"Are you sure you're okay? I don't want you to answer under duress or anything," he teased her taking her hand in his.

"I am perfectly fine."

He leaned over and kissed her. "Yes, you are," he replied and she smiled. "Let's get you some food so that we can celebrate," he said.

"Oh yeah, time for a party!" she said stepping down from the table and leaning into him as he put his arm around her and they rejoined the party.

It lasted well into the following morning. Mitch and Rachel were the hit of the party. William didn't mind it. He was just relieved to see that his big brother was happy. Their family had mourned the loss of Melissa and Amy long enough.

Rachel and Brian danced and caught up on the happenings of the past few months. He told Rachel about the lack of concern in Washington in regards to the illegal immigrants. He told her to be extremely careful even moving around on the Circle C. The kidnappings had become more numerous and the thugs were expanding their territories.

When the party was over, Rachel rode home with Mitch and Evan followed in the van. Mitch pulled his truck up to the guesthouse and parked. He and Rachel sat quietly as they watched Evan go into the guesthouse.

"Did you have a good time?" Mitch held her hand and looked at her delicate fingers.

"Yes. Did you?"

"The best night of my life… So….when do you want to tie the knot?"

"I don't know. Do you have a date in mind?"

"Tomorrow," Mitch said kissing her hand, and began to work his way up her arm.

Rachel laughed a throaty laugh. "In a hurry?"

"Yes, as a matter of fact, I am. Life is too short. I know all too well that we are not promised tomorrow. I don't want to waste one second," he said seriously watching her face.

Rachel kissed him. "I don't want to wait either. But we don't even have a marriage license," she said.

"I can take care of that Monday morning," Mitch said. Rachel sat up straight in the seat and turned to face him.

"You're serious."

"Yes, I am."

She sat back against him, quiet as she thought about what he had just said. What about her children, her business, her home? She couldn't see taking the children away from Ethan and moving them out here to live. She loved the ranch, but she wouldn't feel safe here wondering if her children would be at risk, living so close to the border.

"What about my children? I can't just leave them. And I can't just move them here away from their father," Rachel said, suddenly thinking that this was happening too fast.

"I understand that," Mitch said. "Our schedules are pretty flexible. What do you think about us living at your farm six months out of the year and six months here? Cassie and Simon could come out here for their summer vacations." Mitch looked worried. What if she changes her mind?

"Rachel, this is my home, but you are my family now. I don't care where we live, as long as we do it together. You know that I would never ask you to leave your children, right?"

"Of course I do." She knew that he was not that kind of man.

"You tell me when you want to get married and I will be there baby," Mitch said.

She kissed him, thinking how lucky she was. "I want to make a trip home. I need to bring back some equipment anyway and I'd like to tell Ethan face to face. Then Ethan and I can tell the children together," Rachel said. "Evan can stay here and finish up the training."

"Okay. Do you want me to come with you?" Mitch asked.

"I would love for you to, but I think that it would be better if I went by myself."

"I don't like the idea of you traveling alone," Mitch said.

"I won't be alone. I'll have Zeus with me," Rachel replied.

"You have a point, but I still don't like it. I guess I had better get used to it, since I am about to marry an independent woman," Mitch said.

"I have been independent my whole life, only because I have had to be. I don't want to anymore," Rachel said, kissing him. "This is where I want to be," she said as she pulled his arms tighter around her.

They sat in the truck for a while holding each other, thinking about the party and their new lives together. Rachel finally kissed him goodnight. She pulled his coat tighter around her and stood on the porch watching him as he turned the truck around, before calling it a night.

Evan was still up, when she went inside. "Hey Mom. Wild night, huh?"

"Yes, pretty wild."

"Mom, Mitch asked me if I would be interested in staying on here and heading up the canine unit. What do you think about it?"

"I think that it is a wonderful opportunity for you, but ultimately it is your decision," she paused for a moment and then asked, "What do you think about me marrying Mitch?"

"I have never seen you this happy Mom. I say go for it."

"Thank you, son," she said. "Hey, don't say anything to the others just yet okay?" She wondered how her other three children would react. She hadn't let on to any of them that she was involved with Mitch.

"Of course Mom," he said.

Rachel reached over and hugged him tight and kissed him on the cheek. "I'm gonna turn in. Good night."

"Night Mom," he said.

Rachel slept in the next morning. When she awoke, she lay in bed looking at her engagement ring. She reached for her phone.

"Hey. Where are you?" she texted Tina. She knew that she was most likely going to be home on a Sunday, or with Ken in Houston.

"Waco. I'm opening a store next week. What's up?"

"I'm planning a trip home, and I'd like to see you! Can I meet you in Waco?"

"Sure! I'll pencil you in." Tina said.

"I will let you know when I get into town," Rachel texted, closing her phone and tossing it onto the bed. Rachel stretched and thought about how lazy she felt. She didn't want to get up but she knew that she had a lot to do before leaving for Waco. She dressed for her morning run and left the guesthouse with Zeus following. She continued past the barns, and went immediately to the main house. The door was unlocked and she went in. Mitch was in the kitchen cooking breakfast for them both.

"Hey, I wanted to surprise you this morning, but you beat me to it," she said.

"I don't want a repeat of last night, with you falling out in the floor. So, it is now my job to make sure that you eat and eat plenty," Mitch said handing her a glass of orange juice and pulling out a chair for her.

"You are so good to me," Rachel said after sipping her juice.

"Get used to it. I intend to take care of you for the rest of our days," he said kissing her. He tasted the orange juice on her lips and thought about how badly he wanted to spend the whole day in bed with her.

"I'm heading home in the morning," Rachel told him.

"That was a fast decision," Mitch said, surprised.

"It just worked out that way. Tina is in Waco, and I want to see her. I can't wait to tell her the good news!" she said smiling, as she looked at her new ring. "Besides, the sooner I make the trip, the sooner we can start our lives together," she said as she walked over to him and sat on his lap.

"I think that I still need convincing," Mitch said, pretending to be aggravated with her.

Rachel kissed him and began to unbutton his shirt.

"You do know that in my heart, I am already married to you," she said. She smiled at him, stood up and began to walk backwards away from him teasingly.

Mitch sprang from the chair. Rachel startled, screamed and turned to run, but he was too quick for her. He reached out and pulled her to him. He reached down, scooped her up in his arms, carried her into his bedroom and with his left foot he kicked the door closed.

Chapter 17

"Turn it a little to the right. A little more, and pull it towards me. Good." Tina motioned with her hand for her assistant to stop. They had just finished setting up the display. She looked at her watch. "Come on Rachel," she thought to herself as her stomach growled.

She thought of her best friend Rachel and how they had met and how she had in the beginning, dreaded going to boarding school. After getting kicked out of the last of the local schools, her parents had decided that she needed a wake up call. Little did they know that it was the best thing that they could have done for her, when they sent her six hundred miles across the country to attend the Ellison Institute.

She had expected the next two years to be hell, but it had turned out to be just what she needed. She felt free. Free from her parents constant watchful eye, expecting her to fail them once again.

She had managed to stay out of trouble and excelled in her classes. Her new roommate soon became her best friend and they were inseperable. Tina had decided not to return home on holidays, but chose rather to stay at Ellison. Here parents were disappointed but had agreed, since she was doing so well at this new school, they didn't want to rock the boat.

Near the end of their senior year at Ellison, Tina met Kyle and it was love at first sight. He was a local boy and worked in his family store, while at the same time, attending his first year of college.

Tina's cell phone buzzed, shaking her from her thoughts. She reached for her cell phone and looked at the number displayed as she walked into the manager's office and closed the door before she answered the call. She entered the room looking all chic and trim. Not a hair was out of place and her nails were finely manicured. She looked like she had just returned from the beach, looking all tan.

"Can't you drive faster than that?" Tina smiled, looking forward to seeing her friend.

"Hey, you know that I can!" Rachel said.

"Where are you?" Tina asked.

"I'm in town. I'm famished! Can we eat Mexican today?" she asked.

"Sure, I came prepared. I brought my Mylanta," Tina laughed.

"Are you sure? I don't want to cause any digestive upset." Rachel teased her. She knew that Tina liked to eat Mexican food, but her stomach wouldn't tolerate it.

"I'll just wash it down with a great big margarita," Tina said.

"Sounds like a plan. I'll text you when I get into the parking lot."

"Hey, why don't you spend the night tonight?" Tina invited.

Rachel, tempted, considered it and then said, "Okay," thinking that it would be nice to spend more time with Tina and then get an early start the following morning.

"See you in a bit," Tina said, ending the call, rising from the chair and opening the office door to go back out onto the floor. Startled, she stepped back.

"Surprise!" Rachel threw her arms up smiling.

"You are too much!" Tina said, hugging her friend. "You look wonderful!" she said, noticing a happy glow on her friends face.

Zeus, wearing his "service dog" vest, sat whining, waiting to be released from the sit stay command.

"There's my boy! Tina exclaimed. She knew that she didn't dare try to go to the dog, so she waited for Rachel to release him.

"Okay."

Zeus barked and jumped forward to greet Tina.

"Hi Zeus!" Tina said, as she kneeled down and hugged the big dog. The office workers looked on at Rachel, Tina and Zeus, smiling.

"Marcia, we are going to lunch. I have my phone, if you need to reach me," Tina said to the store manager.

"Yes Ma'am."

Tina and Rachel walked through the store and out the doors to the parking lot. Zeus followed faithfully.

Tina reached into her purse for her keys.

"Let's take my car," she said sheepishly.

"Okay, be my guest. I'll be driving enough for both of us tomorrow," Rachel said wondering what she had up her sleeve.

Tina pushed a button on her key ring and pointed it at a brand new red BMW convertible parked two rows over. The top began to raise and then neatly recede into the fold at the back of the car.

"I just got it last week. My present to myself, because I can," Tina said smiling broadly.

"You go girl!" Rachel said, celebrating with her friend. "Nice car!"

Rachel remembered the clunker that Tina once drove and was happy that she had done so well for herself.

"Do you want me to put Zeus in the van?" Rachel asked, not sure if Tina would want a dog in her new car.

"No. We will drop him off at the hotel and then go eat," Tina said.

They fastened their seat belts and with Zeus in the back seat, Tina wheeled the car out of the parking lot with a screech of the tires and shifted the car into the next gear. She drove the car a mile to the Clarion. "We're here."

With their hair flying Tina pulled the car into the hotel parking lot. They were smiling, carefree and glad to be together again.

Once inside, the clerk didn't question Rachel about the dog being there, since service dogs were allowed nearly anywhere a person might go. Tina approached the clerk and asked for a second key card for Rachel.

When they got to the room, Rachel noticed a doggie basket that Tina had purchased for her two dogs. It held two new collars, a few chew toys, and two extra large femur bones.

"Hey, I couldn't help myself," Tina said as she began to tear the plastic off of the basket, and reached in and pulled out one of the bones. She tossed it onto one of the beds for Zeus to chew on.

He jumped up on the bed and picked the bone up in his large powerful jaws wagging his tail, before lying down to work on it.

Rachel picked up her cell phone to call Mitch.

"Hey Baby," she said.

"Hey back," he said. "Did you make it to Waco okay?"

"Yes I did. But there has been a change of plans. I am going to spend the night with Tina and leave in the morning. We're staying at the Clarion," she said.

"Good," he was glad that she would be breaking up her trip some, instead of driving all the way through.

"So, I am really going to miss you tonight. I guess I will have to cuddle with Zeus," she said.

"That is alright. You just remember that I'm waiting for you here and I intend to make up for lost time when you get back."

"I'm going to hold you to it," Rachel said. "We are on our way to lunch. I'll call you later."

"Bye, Baby," he said.

Rachel flipped her phone shut and smiled big as she brought her left hand up to her cheek and flashed her new engagement ring.

"OMG! Where did you get that?" Tina's face registered surprised shock. "Are you engaged?"

Rachel was beaming. "Yes, I am."

"You just met this guy! Are you sure about this?" Tina said, concerned now about her friend.

Rachel smiled at her. "I have never been more sure about anything. We fit. When I am with him, all is right with the world," She said suddenly wanting to turn around and go back to the Circle C.

"Then I am happy for you!" Tina reached over and hugged her friend.

"Tell me how it happened! Did he get down on one knee?" Tina asked excitedly, wanting to know every detail, feeling like they were back in school.

Rachel told her how Mitch had proposed to her at the party.

"Man, it sounds like he is a romantic. You better hold on to him!"

"You will never guess who was at the party." Rachel said

"Who?"

"Brian and Lisa. I was surprised to see them," Rachel said.

"How are they? I've not seen them since I bought my house," Tina said.

She had retained Brian as her attorney years ago. She attended a lot of the parties that the Governor threw, and she had met Ken at one of those parties.

"They look great, and they were just as surprised to see me at the party," Rachel laughed. "So, what is going on with you?"

Tina rolled her eyes and sighed. "Work, work and more work! I am so tired sometimes that I just want to run away. But then I get bored. I just can't seem to find a happy medium," she said.

Rachel looked at her friend, not wanting to say what needed saying as they made their way to her car. "Do you think you might possibly be running from something that you don't want to think about? Like the fact that Kyle is gone?" Rachel asked her carefully.

"Every day," Tina said. "I guess that if I stay busy enough, the pain wont catch up to me. I miss him so much," she said sadly. I don't think that I will ever love anyone like that again," she said.

Rachel reached for her hand. "You will love again." Rachel nodded her head at her. "Kyle would want you to," she said.

A young boy with red hair and freckles, turned the corner to see them holding hands and blushed. He looked to be all of eighteen. He knocked on a door and announced "Room service," as Rachel and Tina walked by. They both made a face at each other and dropped their hands suddenly realizing that he thought that they were a couple. They waited until they had turned the corner of the hallway before bursting out laughing, feeling like teenagers once again.

*   *   *

Rachel and Tina were seated in the back of the local Mexican restaurant a few blocks down from the Clarion. They had, as usual, filled up on salsa, chips and a margarita before the waiter brought them their main course. They had decided to get a take out box and were waiting for the waiter to return.

"I'm gonna go to the ladies room," Tina said standing. Before Rachel could reply, they heard a loud explosion and the windows in the front of the restaurant shattered from their frames and glass flew through the air. Some of the people sitting next to the windows had been blasted from their chairs and were now bleeding with glass shards sticking from their bodies. Others were not so lucky, and were lying dead in the floor. People began to scream and some ran from the room. The blast had shaken Tina in her standing position and Rachel had felt her chair shake from the blow, but they had escaped injury.

"What was that?" Tina asked Rachel looking at her with big eyes.

"Some kind of explosion," Rachel said. "Let's get out of here."

Rachel grabbed Tina's hand and watched as the people in the restaurant begin to panic.

Rachel and Tina made it out to the parking lot and stood looking around as smoke began to rise into the air. There were fires burning sporadically throughout the city. The smoke was thickening and Tina began to cough. Sirens were ringing all around.

This is not good, Rachel thought.

"We have to hurry," Rachel said. "Take me by the hotel so that I can pick up Zeus," she said, going into Search and Rescue mode.

Rachel dialed her cell phone as Tina started the car.

Mitch answered on the second ring.

"Hey Baby," he said.

"Mitch! There has been an explosion! We are on our way back to the hotel. There are fires everywhere. Call Brian and find out what is going on!"

"Are you hurt?" he asked, trying to remain calm.

Rachel could feel her heart begin to pound in her chest. She could hear Tina talking to Chad next to her. Tina had turned the car onto the road as they headed towards the hotel.

Rachel could see the hotel from a block away.

"We're okay. Oh my God, Mitch!" she cried into the phone. "The hotel is on fire!" She screamed at him. "Zeus is in there!" she cried out. "I'll call you back."

She flipped the phone shut and threw the door of the car open as she stumbled from the car and ran towards the mangled burning structure, before Tina could even stop. The back part of the hotel was gone and there wasn't much left of the front. The office stood eerily untouched and out of place.

Rachel could feel her body begin to shake as she looked at the scene before her. There was no way that Zeus could have survived that, she thought. What was left of the service station next to the hotel was on fire and there were sounds of sirens in the distance. People were screaming and some were bleeding and body parts riddled the pavement. There were bodies in the parking lot. Rachel recognized the delivery boy's red hair, but his face was gone.

Tina had caught up to her and was walking around in a daze looking at the destruction, unable to grasp the enormity of what had happened.

This doesn't happen in America, Tina thought.

Rachel stopped for a moment. Get a grip, she thought. What do I do? Okay, I've done this before, search and rescue. Analyze the situation. Then what? Organize. Take a breath. She brought her shaking hand up to her mouth as she walked towards the mangled heap of debris.

"Tina, are you okay?" she asked looking at her friend who was holding her phone to her ear. She was just standing there in a daze looking around. Rachel could hear Chad screaming through the phone "Mom! Say something! Are you okay?" Rachel reached out and gently removed the phone from her hand.

"Chad, this is Rachel. She is in shock but she will be okay. I will take care of her. Call Eli and tell him that I am okay. Tell him to call his father. You boys stay put and I will call you back as soon as we know more," she said hanging up.

"Tina, can you hear me?" Rachel asked her friend as she gently squeezed her shoulders.

Tina blinked her eyes a few times and then focused on her face. She nodded her head that she had understood her friend. "Yes." Tears began to roll down her face as she looked at Rachel.

"Listen to me. Are you listening to me?" Rachel said, gently shaking her friend and trying to make eye contact.

"Yes." She said again nodding her head.

"We are okay. But I need your help. Can you help me?" Rachel asked.

"Yes," she said, this time more aware of her surroundings.

Rachel hugged her friend glad to see that she was coming to her senses.

"Okay," Rachel said tearfully. "We have got to get to my van. All of my equipment is there. Can you drive us?" Rachel asked her, hoping that she was okay to drive.

Tina nodded and Rachel grabbed her hand and said, "Let's go."

She and Rachel got to her car that she had left parked in the road. It was blocked by debris and she couldn't get it into the parking lot.

"Tina, do you have your gym bag in your car?" Rachel asked.

"Yes I do," she replied like a zombie.

"Change your shoes," Rachel instructed her as if she were a child.

"What about Zeus?" Tina asked as she began to cry. "We can't just leave him, she said crying harder.

"He's gone, honey." Rachel said as she began to cry as well, as they got into the car.

My beloved Zeus, she thought. She had bred the litter herself, and he was her pick of the litter. She thought back to his puppy hood. At two weeks in the whelping box, before his eyes had even opened, he had crawled to her hand and laid his body over it. Every time she visited the litter he would make his way to her and lay by her side. At three months of age he would gaze at her as if to ask, "Well, when do we start?" When she did start his training, he knew his commands by the third or fourth session. She thought of the children at the schools that had come to know and love him, being introduced for the first time to a German shepherd dog. Rachel knew that many children, after meeting Zeus, would go on to develop a love for the breed. She thought of the many lives that he had saved in their work of search and rescue.

Rachel wiped the tears from her face. Pull yourself together, there will be time to mourn later, she thought to herself, as Tina turned the car around to return to the store.

Chapter 18

Mitch flipped his phone shut and immediately opened it to call Evan. He didn't even let him answer his phone before saying, "Come up to the house right away." He ended the call and scrolled down to Brian's personal cell phone number that Rachel had programmed into his phone.

"Brian Russell."

"Brian, this is Mitch. I just talked to Rachel. She is in Waco and..."

"Is she all right?" Brian asked.

"Yes, she was heading back to the hotel to find Zeus. She said that he was in the hotel room when an explosion hit. She asked me to call you. What has happened?" he asked as he made his way into the living room and turned on the television to the local channel.

"Mitch, this is a terrorist attack. They hit us nationwide, with explosions all over major cities. I suspect this is just the beginning. Keep trying to reach Rachel. Tell her that the dog is barking. I would suggest that you and your family load up and come on up to my ranch. Don't wait Mitch. Evan knows the way." Brian said.

"I'll let you know after I talk to Celia and William," Mitch said.

"We may not have communications much longer. I can tell you that Rachel will come here, since I am the closest for her to travel. Just be careful Mitch whatever you decide," Brian said.

Mitch hung up the phone as Evan burst through his front door.

"What is going on?" he asked his face full of fear and his cell phone in his hand.

"All circuits are busy," he said holding his phone up.

Mitch explained the call that he had gotten from Rachel and his conversation with Brian.

"At least she is in Waco. She is less than a hundred miles from Brian's ranch," Evan said. "She will go to his place when she figures out what happened."

Evan pushed the quick dial button for his mother and waited for the phone to ring, but he got the same message.

Mitch looked at the boy trying to be a man, and wondered how he could sound so sure about what his mother would do in this horrible situation.

Mitch picked up his handheld radio that they used on the ranch and called for Aaron.

"Come in Aaron," he said.

"Yeah, Boss," he said.

"I need you to come up to the house right away. Call Celia and William and have them meet us here."

"Yes sir, boss," Aaron said.

Mitch turned the volume down on the radio.

"Evan, go pack your things. Then go to the number four barn and start loading tack in the gooseneck trailer parked behind the barn. I should be finished by then and I will join you down there. We're going to Waco."

"Yes sir," Evan said as he turned towards the door.

Mitch reached for his cell phone and tried to call Rachel again. He got the same "All circuits are busy" message.

He threw the cell phone across the room, put both hands on the kitchen counter and leaned over to bow his head. The adrenaline came rushing into his chest, and his legs began to shake.

"God please keep her safe," he prayed for the first time since he could remember. I can't lose her too, he thought to himself, as he heard Aaron knock on his door and walk in.

"Hey boss, what's up?" Aaron asked, unaware since he had been in one of the barns working.

Mitch stood up straight and tried to compose himself.

"There has been a nationwide terrorist attack. Rachel is in Waco and I am taking Evan to find his Mother," he said.

Aaron could see the fear in his eyes. Not of a terrorist attack, but of losing Rachel. Before he could respond, Celia and William came in with worried faces. They had been listening to the news and knew about the explosions. They also heard Mitch telling Aaron that he was going to Waco to find Rachel.

"I wanted to tell ya'll while we are together. I spoke to Brian and he urged us to come to his ranch. He thinks that this is just the beginning and he thinks that it is too dangerous for us to be so close to the border. I wanted to ask ya'll what you want to do. Ditch this place and head north or stay and fight?" He asked. "You have my answer already. I have to go find Rachel."

"We decided in the car," Celia said. "We're staying to fight for what is ours. Just as your going to fight for what is yours," Celia said, walking over to her brother and putting her arms around him. She began to cry as she hugged him tight.

"Watch your back brother," she said. She released her grip, turned and walked out the door. She knew that she couldn't keep him there, since he had finally found love again. They were racing the clock and she had to let him go, no matter how much she wanted to scream and beg him not to.

William walked to his big brother and stood looking him in the face. His eyes held fear, love, and anger. "We will try to keep it together. If we get overrun, we will head north." William held his hand out to his brother, their eyes held all of the words that were left unspoken. Mitch reached out and pulled him to him. "Take care of Celia." William nodded and turned to leave. Mitch watched as he closed the door behind him.

Aaron was standing with his hands on his hips, looking at the floor. Mitch knew what that meant. "Its okay brother," he said to Aaron. "This is your Alamo."

"Yes, but you can bet your ass that there will be a different outcome," he said angrily.

"Can you give Evan a hand down at barn four?" Mitch asked.

"Sure Boss," Aaron said as Mitch watched as he walked towards the door.

After Aaron closed the door, Mitch stood in the kitchen alone for a moment before going into the living room to search for his cell phone. He picked it up and tried to dial Rachel again, but still couldn't reach her. He put his cell phone in his pocket and went into his room to start packing. He pulled his suitcase out of the closet and started throwing clothes in. He grabbed his toiletries bag and tossed that in as well. He zipped the suitcase up and walked to the closet and pulled a Rubbermaid container out and dumped the contents out on the floor. He tossed the container and lid into the hallway. He turned and looked around the room, wondering if he had forgotten anything when he saw Rachel's nightgown on the bed. He reached for it and tried to stuff it into his back pocket. Just this morning he had held her in his arms. He wondered if he would again.

He pulled his rolling suitcase into the kitchen and walked over to the living room wall and began taking down photos to put into the Rubbermaid container. After he had finished, he picked up the suitcase and the Rubbermaid container and walked through the kitchen to his truck parked in the garage. He put the two containers in the back seat and went back into the house. While he was in the garage he reached up above his head, pulled a large cooler from one of the shelves and went to his chest freezer for a five gallon bucket of ice to pour into the cooler. He returned to the kitchen and started putting items into the cooler to take with them. After he finished packing food, he went into his study to the gun safe and took a 30/30, 20 gauge, 12 gauge, and his fathers old M1. He carried them to the truck and placed them in a blanket on the back seat. He returned to the gun safe, and got all of the ammunition that he owned. He carried eight ammo boxes out to the truck two at a time. He returned to the safe one last time. He lifted the wire rack off the door that held his pistols and carefully carried it to the truck and placed it on top of the suitcase in the back seat of his truck, as he tried to think about what he might be forgetting.

Pressed for time, he stood at the garage door looking into the kitchen trying to memorize every detail, feeling in his gut that this would be the last time that he would stand there. He reached for the doorknob and pulled the door closed.

He backed his dually out of the garage and turned towards barn four. He drove around behind the barn and backed the truck up to the goose neck trailer. He got out of the truck and went into the barn. Aaron was leading one of the mares around to the trailer to load her. Evan was carrying some of the pack equipment.

Mitch went into the tack room and looked around. They had already loaded most of the equipment. He went to one of the closets and opened it to retrieve two back packs, but they had already packed those too. Aaron and Evan came into the tack room. They were keeping their heads, but they were worried.

"Boss, we loaded three of the pack mares and two of our best trail horses. You have everything you will need to camp for two, maybe three weeks. And we put four cans of gas in the bed of the truck," Aaron said.

"Thanks, Aaron. Do we have enough room for a couple of the dogs?" Mitch asked.

"There is room in the back of the truck," Evan replied.

"Let's get them loaded then. And bring one of the tracking dogs. Did you pack already?" He asked Evan.

"Yes sir," Evan replied.

"Okay. I am ready to roll when we get the dogs on board," Mitch said.

Evan turned and started towards the kennel building.

Mitch and Aaron started walking to the truck. They felt like their whole world had been picked up, shaken and thrown back down. Their lives had been changed in just a matter of a few minutes by some idiots that reeked of hate. Now all that they could do was to try to make the best of a bad situation.

"Did you pack the first aid kit?" Mitch asked, suddenly remembering the one thing that he had forgotten.

"Yes," Aaron replied, hoping that they wouldn't need it.

The two men watched Evan running towards the truck with an equipment bag, and the two German shepherds following him at a brisk pace.

He tossed the bag into the back of the truck and let the tailgate down for the dogs to jump into the back.

129

Evan reached his hand out to Aaron, but Aaron pushed it away and pulled the boy to him in a bear hug. "You watch your back," Aaron said and then pointed at Mitch, "And his."

"Yes sir, I'll do my best," Evan said, nodding his head, swallowing hard and trying not to cry. He turned and walked around the front of the truck and got into the passenger side.

Mitch and Aaron stood looking at one another. Mitch spoke first. "Aaron, don't be a hero. If it looks like ya'll can't hold it here, head for the Governor's place."

"If I can, I'll try to defend it until you return," Aaron said, shaking his hand and then hugging the only brother he had ever had. Mitch knew that he may never return and that Aaron would die trying to defend the ranch.

Mitch shut the door to the truck and turned the engine over. He put the truck in gear and felt the bump as the truck and trailer lurched forward. It had taken the men thirty minutes to load the truck, but it seemed like a lifetime.

Chapter 19

Ethan startled awake, reached over to the alarm clock and pushed the snooze button. Five a. m. had come way too early this morning.

Since Rachel and Evan had left for the Circle C, most of the work had fallen on him. Running two farms was hard work and he was exhausted. He lay in the bed thinking about Rachel and wished she were here, next to him in the bed. But he knew that that ship had sailed. What he wouldn't give to have his family back like it was before, he thought.

He rolled over in the bed and opened one eye to see Raven and Minah, two of the German shepherd dogs from the kennel looking at him. Their tails began to thump against the hardwood floor as they sat looking at him waiting for him to get up. Minah, woofed at him.

He closed his eyes and groaned. He knew that if he didn't get up the woofing would get louder. The two dogs began waging their tails and whining.

Ethan threw back the covers, sat up in bed and reached over to turn off the alarm clock. The two dogs started towards the door and turned back around to make sure that he was coming. Their tails wagging ninety and their claws clicked on the wood floor as they danced around.

He had been sleeping in the downstairs guest bedroom. Since the divorce, Rachel had thrown everything out of the master bedroom and redone it to her liking. It was her room now. Not a trace of him was left there except their wedding photo that hung on the wall, and that was for Simon's benefit. He reached the kitchen door and opened it as the dogs darted out barking to announce to the kennel dogs that they were coming.

Sleepily, he reached for the coffee pot that Cassie had set for him the previous night and poured a cup before returning to his room to get dressed.

He had put Cassie in charge of kitchen duty. She was in charge of cooking and cleaning, and in exchange she earned some spending money.

Simon was responsible for cleaning kennels and helping Ethan feed, water and exercise the dogs.

Ethan usually arose first and let the children sleep in. His first task was to go into the kennel, hose down the runs and make sure all of the dogs had water.

He emerged from his room dressed and ready to go. He opened the door of the kitchen to see the sun coming up. It was a little cool out and it would make for an easier day of work he thought to himself, as he made his way down the stone pathway to the kennels.

After he finished in the kennel, it was time for him to return to the house, start breakfast and wake the kids for school. He remembered to let Sadie out of her kennel, to take her over to his farm, since they were separating goats today. The Border collie began to bark, ran to the truck and jumped up into the bed of the truck.

After breakfast, he drove the ten miles into town to drop Simon off first and then Cassie before stopping at his farm to start his work there.

He knew that Ryan would have already started with the chores by the time that he got there. The twenty year old was friends with Eli and Evan. Over the years, he had helped out at the kennels and when he graduated he had decided to go to the local college. So, for room and board and a small salary, he lived in the barn apartment and worked for Ethan. He's a good kid, Ethan thought to himself. Ryan would sometimes come over to the kennel and help out without being asked. Ethan had seen him looking at Cassie on occasion but she had made it clear that they were just friends.

Ethan pulled his pickup truck into the driveway and parked in the front yard near the house. Sadie, ready to go to work, jumped out of the truck and began to bark at Ethan.

"That's enough," he scolded her harshly. It was just too early for her barking he thought. The dog dropped her head sadly and crept over to lay down next to the truck. Ethan reached for his daily planner and noted that they were to move the goats into pasture one, deworm and tag the kids. He was going to have a busy day before returning to the children and the work there.

He was glad that Rachel was on her way home. She had said little in their conversation, except to indicate that she was picking up equipment and returning to the Circle C. Ethan made a mental note to ask Ryan if he wanted to earn some extra money by helping out at the kennel.

His farm was a modest sixty acre spread with a small farmhouse and a few barns. It suited his needs for his bachelor life and it was comfortable. The main barn near the house held six stalls with turnout areas for the quarter horses. Upstairs there was a small two room apartment that Ryan lived in.

In the summer he ran his Boer goat herd with his red Angus cows on a rotation schedule, into the four different pastures. The herd was rotated every three or four days to a new pasture. There was a loafing shed in each pasture for the goats, since they didn't like getting wet. The bottom half of the door was cut out just for the goats. Sometimes a calf or two would go in with them, but by the time they were a month old, they couldn't fit through the opening and soon tired of trying. In the fall, the nannies that were due to kid were separated out into a pasture with hay and grain, so that the cows didn't hurt the newborn kids.

He had recently built a small rabbit house. Ryan had picked up the ten Californian does and one buck just the day before. Ethan walked into the small room and turned on the lights. The fluorescent lights lined the roof of the building. Cages hung from the rafters that housed the white rabbits. Each cage had a tray for waste that slanted towards the back and would be taken weekly to the compost pile. Then in the spring it would be spread in the fields to fertilize the crops.

Ethan walked the aisle to inspect the rabbits and was pleased that they were all healthy. The automatic waterer was set up and he checked some of the nipples to make sure that they were working properly. He added food to the feeders before leaving the building and, reached for his radio to call his helper.

"Come in Ryan," he called.

"Yes sir," Ryan answered.

"What's your location?"

"Pasture three. One of the nannies is kidding."

"I'll be right down. Over," Ethan said.

"Over," Ryan said.

Ethan arrived to see Ryan sitting on the ground with his boot pushing on the hip of the nanny to hold her in place as he leaned back and pulled a kid out.

"Looks like a good twelve pounder," Ryan said proudly as he pushed the buck kid to the front of the doe for her to begin the bonding process.

Ethan reached into the kidding bag and tossed him a towel to wipe the slime off his hands. He then reached into the bag and got the iodine and dental floss to tie off the newborn kids cord.

The nanny had gotten to her feet and was "talking" to the kid, muttering "mah ah ahh" as she cleaned him. She then raised her head, yawned and began to paw at the ground. She walked around the kid and lay down. Her tail was raised and she was pushing at the ground with her back feet as she began to strain with another contraction. Ethan and Ryan watched as the nanny raised her head with her eyes wide, screamed, and successfully birthed another big kid. This time it was a doe. Both were the traditional color with a white body and a red head. Their long ears hung low like a Bassett hound and their heads were rounded.

Ryan waited until the nanny had stood up and was cleaning the kid before he put his arms around the nanny in front of her udder and gently squeezed and lifted her off the ground to check for more kids.

"She's done," Ryan said.

"Nice kids. I'm glad that we bought that Ryals buck in the spring," Ethan said. "I brought Sadie over to move the goats into pasture one."

The two men left the doe to bond with her kids and returned to the house for Sadie and the two four wheelers that they would use to move the goats.

Once Sadie had moved the herd into pasture one, Ryan went into the small barn and poured out a little feed to draw the herd of goats in. When the herd was finished with their feed, Ethan and Ryan proceeded to vaccinate, tag, and worm the new kids.

The morning was gone before they knew it. The two men returned to the house for lunch before setting out to start another job.

As he walked into the kitchen, Ethan reached for his phone that was vibrating a new call, from Cassie.

"That girl is gonna get in trouble for using her phone at school," Ethan said out loud before answering it.

"What are you …" Ethan was cut short by his daughters frantic wail. "Dad!" she screamed into the phone. "Turn on the TV. They're letting us out of school, something about some explosions… Dad, what is going on?" she asked.

Ryan heard Cassie through the phone, and started for the TV.

He and Ethan stood watching the local television station as a broadcaster, Kathy Sullivan was reporting on the chaos.

"…And not just Little Rock, these explosions have occurred nationwide, leaving Americans stunned that we are no longer safe on our own soil," she finished.

The camera panned to fires burning throughout the city of Little Rock, buildings reduced to rubble and terrified people running in the streets. Some were bleeding, some covered in ash, and some were lying dead in the street.

Ethan turned to Ryan, whose face had drained of all color.

"Ryan, can you pick up Cassie for me?" Ethan asked, still holding the phone to his ear.

"Yes sir," he nodded.

"Cassie, Ryan will pick you up at the gazebos on the south side of the school. It's gonna be okay," he said to his daughter, hoping that he was right. He flipped the phone closed and then texted a message to Simon. Ethan was glad now that Rachel had bought the boy the phone, although he had not liked the idea in the beginning.

"I am coming to get you. Meet me behind the cafeteria. The dog is barking," Ethan texted him, letting him know that they were about to play a "game", as he walked to his truck. He was also glad that Rachel had taught him to read before he went to school.

Ethan and Rachel had played the "G I Joe" game with the children, many times. It began by using the signal phrase. The older children knew now that if and when the signal phrase was used that the "stuff had hit the fan" and it was time to drop everything and come home. But Simon was only six, so this was just a game to him. He would find out soon enough about the realities of the world.

"Cool!" he sent back.

"Go now," Ethan said, already in his truck and about to turn onto the road.

He was at the school within five minutes. He turned on the road that led behind the school and to the cafeteria. He saw Simon sitting behind the dumpster and he pulled the truck up to it. Simon smiled at him, stood up and looked around to see if anyone had seen him, before darting towards the truck.

Chapter 20

Startled, Rachel reached for her cell phone that was ringing, just as Tina wheeled the car into the parking lot of the store.

"Brian?" she asked, sounding like a lost little girl, as she shut the car door. Tina started towards the door of the store as Rachel talked to Brian.

"Baby its time. The dog is barking. Come home. Are you okay?" he asked.

"Yes. We just got back to the van. Zeus is dead," she said to her surrogate father.

"I'm sorry honey. Now listen, remember what I taught you. This is for real. There are fires burning all over the United States and I am afraid that this is just the beginning. Get Tina and come home. Eli, Chad and Ben are on their way here. I told Mitch and Evan to head this way. I am still trying to reach Ethan and the children, but you know that they are safe where they are," he said.

Rachel nodded her head, and said "Okay. We will stop at Tina's first and then head there."

"Be careful and stay alert," Brian said.

"I will. And Brian... I love you," she said.

"I love you too, honey. Now get going," he said.

Rachel looked up in time to see Tina coming out of the store wearing her gym clothes and sneakers. Their eyes made contact and she glanced at the phone before flipping it shut, wondering just how long it would be before the phones went out. She blinked back the tears and looked at Tina as the realization hit her that this was the day that Britta and Brian had feared. Brian had told her years ago, that if she ever got a call from him and he used the phrase "The dog is barking," it meant that "the end of the world as we know it" was now at hand and to drop everything and go into survival mode.

Rachel went to the back of the van and opened the doors before stepping up into it and pulling her Search and Rescue bag out. She then reached in and pulled out her steel toe boots, a map and a gun. Tina watched as she continued to dig in the bag until she pulled out a can of spray paint, dropped it and she sat up against the van to hurriedly change her shoes. She walked around the van to the nearly empty parking lot and began spraying the paint on the pavement. Tina looked at her like she had lost her mind. "What are you doing?" she asked.

Rachel finished, stood up to check her work and read the message that was spray painted in red.

"GONE TO TINAS, BRIANS. HWY 31."

Tina read the message and then looked up at Rachel.

"It's bad, isn't it?" she asked her friend.

"Yes. Our country is under attack. We are running out of time and we have got to hurry. Chad and Ben are with Eli and they are on their way to Brian's now. Evan and Mitch are on their way as well. It's not safe to wait for them," Rachel said shaking her head.

Tina listened to her friend. Rachel could see that she was working it out in her mind.

"Let's go then. I will follow you," Tina said finally.

Rachel started to explain to Tina that is wasn't a good idea to take her car, but decided against it, as she walked to the back of the van. She knew that she had to hold onto some semblance of normalcy, at least for now.

"How much gas do you have in your car?"

"About a half of a tank."

140

"That should be enough, and I filled up before I arrived at the store."

Rachel reached into the bag and pulled out the .38. She held it out for Tina to take, who looked at her wide eyed. "No way," she said shaking her head violently back and forth.

"Tina, if something happens to me you may have to protect yourself," she said as she reached for Tina's hand to press the gun into it.

Tina pushed it away, wide eyed. "No!"

Rachel was becoming agitated. "We are not leaving until you take this gun," Rachel said as she held the gun out to her friend again.

Tina thought for a moment and then looked down at the gun and reached for it.

"I wont use it," she said, angrily, waving it in the air as if an afterthought.

"Just point and pull the trigger," Rachel said looking at her friend who was horrified at the mere idea.

Rachel took a deep breath. She opened the map and spread it out on the floor of the van, to plan their route to Tina's house.

"We need to avoid any towns that we can, and take back roads. It will take longer, but I think that it will be safer," she explained.

"In that case, I know some good back roads to take just West of Athens," Tina said, tracing the route with her finger.

"When we get closer, you take the lead," Rachel said, folding the map and reaching out to Tina to hug her.

"Keep your eyes open okay?" she said, as she slammed the door, suddenly missing Zeus who would have been sitting right next to her.

"I will."

She watched Tina push the button to put the car top back into place. As she waited she looked around at the fires still burning in the distance, with thick black smoke beginning to fill the air. She could hear the sound of sirens, people screaming, and cars horns. That meant that more people were trying to do the same thing that they were, get out of dodge. It had only been twenty minutes since the explosions.

Rachel reached down to turn on her CB radio and turned the dial to channel nineteen. She listened to a couple of truckers talking about the best route to take to get out of Waco, as she and Tina waited to get into the line of traffic.

141

"Thank God for cell phones," Rachel said to herself, knowing that a lot of people had ditched their CB's with the invention of the little phones, which meant less trash talk on the radio. She reached for the microphone and keyed it as she announced herself.

"KDQ 2097 come in BLR 227 over," she said. She didn't know if she would be able to reach Brian from this distance, but it was worth a shot. She tried a few more times, before she turned the volume down and turned on the van radio.

Rachel leading the way, finally turned the van onto highway 84 and headed Northeast until the road split onto highway 31. She looked back in her rear view mirror to see that Tina was right behind her. The people in their cars looked panic stricken as they gripped their steering wheels, wide eyed and white knuckled. The traffic was stop and go until they got outside of Waco, and then it was very little traffic going away from town.

They made good time and finally reached Corsicana where the traffic became thick again for a few miles and then thinned out again as they continued on towards Athens.

Rachel saw the sign that read "Malakoff 1 mile."
Everywhere Rachel looked, there was smoke in the distance. Rachel was watching the road ahead and listening to the radio, when Tina came around the van like a bolt of lightning, to take the lead. She saw the blinker on the little car indicating that Tina was exiting at Malakoff and she did the same. She followed Tina as she turned and maneuvered past the town of Malakoff and onto a dirt road that finally brought them out at highway 175. Tina turned onto a paved road, then another dirt road, and something that looked like a pig trail that finally brought them out north of Athens, onto Highway 19 where they continued north towards Canton.

The broadcasts on the radio reported that it was still too early to tell who was responsible for the attacks. Thousands of cities had been hit and the number of dead was rising rapidly. The terrorists had targeted hotels, gas stations and malls. National Forests had been set ablaze.

Rachel shuddered to think, grateful that Simon and Cassie were in school. She prayed that their forest had been spared, as she tried the CB again.

"KDQ 2097 come in BLR 227 over," she said.

She repeated the call a few more times and was about to turn off the radio when she heard a response.

"Copy KDQ 2097, go ahead." Rachel smiled, it was Brian.

"We're proceeding to Canton on Highway 19, copy," Rachel said. She decided to ignore all protocol and talk normally.

"Ten-four."

"Any word on Mitch or Evan?"

"No," Brian replied.

"Copy that."

"Orders are for you to stay put in Canton. Rescue is on the way, copy?"

"10-4. KDQ 2097 out." Rachel ended the call. She knew that there were other people trying to get information on their loved ones and she didn't want to tie up lines. She had let Brian know her whereabouts and that was important.

She wished that she knew where Mitch and Evan were. She desperately wanted to hear his voice, so she flipped her phone open and hit speed dial. She was surprised when it began to ring and then she heard his voice. "Rachel?" he inquired.

"Where are you?" she cried out, desperate to know, and now beginning to feel the fear.

"We are on our way baby. Are you alright?" he asked.

"Yes," she nodded through the tears. "I love you. Tell my boy that I love him. Please be careful Mitch," she begged him, more afraid of losing them, than her own life. "You are coming to Brian's right?" she asked.

She knew that she was doing the right thing by going on to Brian's. She had to make sure that her children were okay and then maybe Brian would send out a team to find Mitch and Evan.

"Yes, I love...." she heard him say and then the vans engine quit and everything went silent. She struggled to hold onto the stiff steering wheel of the van with one hand but she couldn't. She dropped her cell phone and reached for the vans steering wheel. With power gone, she struggled to steer the heavy van to a successful halt.

"Mitch!" she screamed as she reached for her cell phone that lay in her lap, hoping that he was still on the line. She held the phone to her ear, as she looked up into her rear view mirror to see cars and trucks slowing and then stopping as if they were bumper cars and the ride was now over. The phone was dead.

Ahead of her, she watched a large tractor trailer rig weaving from side to side of the road. "No," she said out loud. "Don't do it," she begged in her mind. She watched the rig turn and tip onto its side and then slide a short distance in the road before colliding into the small BMW. Rachel, horrified, looked ahead at Tina's car that she had managed to steer off to the side of the road, but she hadn't been able to move away from the large tractor trailer rig. "Noooooo!" she heard someone screaming, and realized that it was her. She opened the van door and vaulted out. She heard a whistling sound as she watched in horror as a 747 airplane descending from the sky, down, down, down, as if in slow motion. The huge plane made contact with the ground, broke apart and exploded. The thick black smoke began to spread into the sky to darken the once blue horizon. She screamed as she looked on in horror knowing what had happened. She looked up and down the road at the cars and trucks that were now at a standstill, forever stopped in their tracks.

Her body began to shake as her legs of rubber tried to run towards the small crumpled car that held her friend. They failed her miserably as she fell to her knees and struggled to catch her breath. She had hoped that she would never see the day when an Electromagnetic Pulse would push the United States back to the eighteenth century but she suspected that it had happened. On all fours, her head began to spin as she watched the driver of the rig climb out of the cab of the truck on the driver side, closest to the sky. His head was bleeding and it looked as if his arm was broken. Please help her, she thought. And then slowly she felt her body leaning towards the ground as she joined the pavement.

Chapter 21

Lisa stood leaning against the wall, with her arms folded and looking out the picture window of the ranch house. The view was peaceful and soothing as she watched the goats graze in the nearby pasture. Their small two hundred acre ranch was home to a hundred head of black Angus cattle, a hundred head of Boer goats, forty quarter horses, chickens, rabbits and six German shepherd dogs. She turned to the wall on her right to look at the blue ribbons and trophies that her children Dustin and Michelle, had accumulated over the years showing livestock in 4-H. They had a successful operation that had allowed them to purchase the best genetics in the country. She was suddenly saddened by the thought of the life that they had lived for the past thirty some odd years, was about to come to an end.

She had been in the office, arranging for transport for ten of their best show does to go to Mississippi for breeding to the National champion, when her second line rang. It was Brian. She put the man on hold and answered her husbands call.

"The dog is barking," he said.

Her heart began to race. Shocked, she tried to remember what she was suppose to do next as she replied, "I'll bring him in."

She ended the call with her husband, and sat in her chair trying to regain her composure and slow her racing heart. They had practiced this a hundred times, but still the fear she felt was real. She knew what to do. She took a deep breath and prayed, "Give me strength Lord." She sat up tall and reached for the phone.

"Mr. Ryal's, I'm afraid that I have an emergency. I will have to call you back," she said, knowing that she wouldn't.

"I understand. If there is anything that we can do to help, please let us know," he said simply. He had always been a man of integrity, and Lisa felt she had to say something, to forewarn him that his world was about to change.

"Mr. Ryal's, when you hang up this phone, turn on the television, gather your animals and your family, and pray. Pray hard," she said and hung up the phone.

She now found herself looking out the window. She knew that Brian would have called the children and started the ball rolling on what they had to do next. As practiced, he would leave his office and arrive at the ranch within two hours, if all went well. Dustin and Michelle both lived locally, so they didn't have far to come. Her job was to begin to secure the ranch.

She turned from the window and went to the gun cabinet and removed her revolver and clipped it onto the waistband of her jeans. She ran her hand across the wood of the cabinet that their son Dustin had made for them four years earlier. It was made out of cedar. She leaned her face against the cool wood and smelled the sweet pine and smiled.

She pulled away from the gun cabinet and walked over to her desk. She picked up the phone and called down to the main barn.

John picked up and answered "Rocking B." She wondered if this would be the last time that she would hear him say those words. He had worked for them for eighteen years and had started out cleaning stalls at nineteen years of age. After several years, it became apparent that John shared the same concerns for the country as they did. He had been "interviewed" and once Brian was satisfied that he

147

was okay, asked him to come on board. He had worked his way up on the ranch and was now foreman.

"John, the dog is barking," she said softly. "God speed."

There was a pause on the line, as he processed the information. He cleared his throat before speaking.

"Yes ma'am," he said.

She heard the click of the line as the two phones disconnected and she knew that John would drop what he was doing and go home to gather his family, before returning to the Rocking B and the safety of their group that they had formed.

She wasn't in a hurry. She knew that most everything was in place and she just had a few things to do to get ready to greet the families that would soon descend upon the ranch.

They had practiced the procedure until it was ingrained in her mind. Brian made the call to her, she made the call to John, and John made the call to Phillip. John and Phillip contacted some of the remainder of the group, and Brian contacted the rest. Everyone should be in place within two days. They had at least thirty five people that would defend the ranch plus their families. Brian and Lisa had planned for a maximum of a hundred people, just in case.

The three barns would be converted into living quarters for the families. Each family was assigned an area in a barn, and knew what they were allowed or required to bring.

Some of the families had livestock that would be brought to the ranch. Each of the groups families were required to have a years worth of food stored up, along with their own personal choice of firearms, medical supplies and the agreed upon camo uniforms.

The first shift of security would move into place at the perimeter of the ranch. Ten guards per three eight hour shifts would allow for easy rotation to begin with.

Lisa walked to the bookcase and removed the four three ring binders that held SOP, Logistics, Housing and other miscellaneous information that they had developed over the years. She placed them on the desk and turned to go into the kitchen. She removed five extra large crock pots, plugged them in and turned the switch on high.

She went into the adjoining garage to one of the freezers. She began to take out half gallon size containers of homemade beef stew that had been saved just for this day. She placed them in the small wagon that was kept in the garage and wheeled them into the kitchen.

148

She placed some of them into the crock pots and the others she placed in a bathtub full of hot water to thaw. She would remove them in an hour and start a large stock pot with the contents of the containers. She then went into the large spare bedroom that had been converted into a pantry. She reached for two five pound bags of yellow corn meal and a large Rubbermaid container on wheels and returned to the kitchen. She gathered the ingredients for her corn bread and placed them on the counter so that she would be ready to start it when it was time.

She opened the Rubbermaid container that held the "picnic" essentials for a large number of people and reached for the itemized list, scanning it to make sure that nothing had been removed.

She looked around the kitchen and satisfied with her work, she went into their bedroom closet to remove one of the large metal trunks that held the two way radios and a solar panel hookup that was used to charge the batteries. She grasped the handle and wheeled the heavy trunk to the French doors that led out onto the covered patio. Victor and Hammer, two of their six German shepherds, were wagging their tails ready to come back inside. She thought of Rachel and wondered if Brian had reached her. She remembered that she was on her way back home today and was going to stop in Waco to have lunch with Tina. Lisa looked at her watch. She released the handle of the trunk, let the dogs into the house and turned to go back into the kitchen to phone Brian.

She got the "all circuits are busy" message and hung up. She closed her eyes and prayed, "It's in your hands Lord. Please keep her safe." She opened her eyes to see the two dogs sitting in front of her looking at her. She knew that they sensed that something was up.

"Come on boys, lets get to work," she said as she walked back to the patio doors. She pulled the trunk out onto the patio, released the handle and started for barn one. The two dogs bounded off in front of her.

When she arrived at the barn, she slid the carriage style doors open and went inside. Each barn was constructed of concrete block, had concrete floors, held twelve stalls, an office with a bathroom, tack room, feed room and wash rack. The first barn was used for sick animals and fortunately was empty. Lisa reached for the broom and began sweeping the aisle. When she got to the end, she inspected each stall to make sure that they were swept and clean. After she finished, she went into the two other barns to determine what would need to be done to house the families. She inspected them and made a list for the members to start on once they began to arrive. John was thorough, so it wouldn't take long for the barns to be converted into housing, she thought.

After she finished inspecting the barns, she decided to return to the house to wait for Brian to arrive home. As she headed towards the house Victor and Hammer began to run and bark aggressively at a car that had pulled into the driveway.

When she rounded the corner of the barn closest to the house, she saw a white car. It was empty. She reached for her pistol on her hip, just as Eli, Chad and Ben appeared from around the front of the house. She was happy to see them and glad now that she wasn't alone. She waved at them from across the yard. Eli broke into a jog and threw his arms around her when he reached her. "Hello Gram," he said. "Are you okay?"

"Yes, honey. Any news?" she asked him, as Chad and Ben walked up. She reached for both of their hands.

"I talked to Grandpa. He said that Mom asked Mitch to call him. She said that she was in Waco with Tina when the explosions hit and that they were okay."

"Thank God," she said. She turned to look at Chad and Ben.

"Don't worry about your Mother, she is safe with Rachel. We have trained for something such as this," she said.

"Thank you, Gram," they said in unison.

"You're welcome. When Brian gets home, we will talk more, but in the meantime, can you boys go down to barn two and get it ready? Eli, there is a list on the desk in the office."

"Yes Ma'am," he said, kissing her on the cheek and dutifully turned towards the barns.

When Lisa arrived at the house, she looked out the front window to see Brian's black suburban coming up the driveway faster than usual. She could see him talking on his cell phone as he drove. Then he pulled it from his ear, looked at it, mouthed a curse word and threw it on the dash. He looked up in time to make eye contact with Lisa and his face softened. As if their thoughts joined as one, they knew that as long as they were together, they could survive anything.

Chapter 22

Cassie reached for the cast iron skillet to turn the potatoes. Sweat trickled down her back as she stood cooking dinner on the propane stove. She glanced over at her now useless cell phone that was on the counter and then reached into her pocket for a hair band to pull her hair into a pony tail, just as Simon came into the kitchen.

"When is dinner?" he whined. His face was flushed from the heat and working with Dad and Ryan.

Cassie thought back to just this afternoon. She couldn't believe it. One minute she was sitting in class and the next, her country was at war. Chloe had hitched a ride with them. She and Chloe waited at the Gazebos just as she was told. The two girls piled into Ryan's truck and both remained silent as they rode in the truck wondering if they would be in trouble on Monday for skipping school.

Just before turning onto Dads driveway, the EMP struck.

"Damn it!" Ryan said. He had just fixed the alternator on his truck the previous week and he was not happy that it had croaked again. Chloe and Cassie looked at each other as Ryan maneuvered the truck over to the side of the drive so as not to block it. Still holding their books, they started the walk towards the house.

Dad and Simon were outside sitting on the patio that was shaded by an oak tree as the three of them walked into the yard. Simon saw them coming and ran to meet them.

"Cassie! We're playing G I Joe. Do you want to play?" he asked excitedly.

Chloe and Ryan exchanged glances.

"Let's see what Dad has to say first, okay?" Cassie said as they walked towards him.

"Daddy, my phone doesn't work and the truck quit…. my watch is dead…?" she sobbed looking at her father. She wanted him to tell her that it would be okay and soon the phone would chime a message and she would wake from this nightmare. He pulled her into an embrace as Ryan, Chloe and Simon looked on.

Ethan swallowed a lump in his throat. The anger was rising as he thought about the fools that had done this. How dare they, threaten his family, his life, his country, he thought to himself. He thought of Rachel and the boys in Texas.

Simon interrupted his thoughts, "Cassie, its okay. We're just playing a game," he said.

Ethan walked Cassie over to a chair and helped her sit down as he watched her legs begin to shake with fear. She looked like she was five years old again.

He knelt down in front of her and took her hand in his. He turned to Chloe, Simon, and Ryan and said, "You kids sit down." He motioned with his head to the chairs on the patio.

He turned his face back to Cassie.

"Baby, you know what has happened," he said. "I can't change it," he continued, "And you know that we are in a much better position than most people in this country right now. Do you remember the G I Joe games that we played over the years? It was just in case something like this ever happened. Now, I may be wrong. The power could come back on any minute now and this will just be a false alarm," he waved his arm in the air.

Cassie looked at her father. She knew that it wasn't a false alarm. She had read the article on her Mother's desk about the Electromagnetic Pulse.

Cassie nodded her head and said, "Okay Daddy."

She looked at Chloe, terrified, crying and with big eyes.

Ryan looked like he suddenly realized the enormity of the situation and Simon was sitting in the chair swinging his foot back and forth waiting for the game to begin.

"How am I gonna get home?" Chloe asked. "Take me home, please. I want to go home," she said out loud to no one in particular.
Cassie rushed to her friend and hugged her. "We are gonna be okay," Cassie said. Simon sat in the chair looking at them and then walked over to Ethan.

"Daddy, why are you and Cassie crying?" he asked, beginning to frown.

Ethan stepped back, took a deep breath and looked down at his youngest son. He knelt down again but this time to his son.

"Simon, do you remember the smoke in the sky when we were coming home from school?" Ethan asked.

"Yes sir."

"Well, that means that some very bad people have bombed our cities and there will not be any school for a little while," Ethan said.

"For real? He asked excitedly. "So we get to have a longer summer?" Simon asked happily. "Cool!" he said. "So can I go play with Sadie?" he asked.

"Sure." Ethan smiled as he watched Simon run towards the barn.

Ethan turned back to the older kids.

"C'mon, sit back down now," he said.

After they were all seated, he began.

"Chloe, honey, we are going to get you home. Don't worry. Ryan, you can saddle up one of the horses if you need it to get home," Ethan said.

Ryan shook his head. "No sir. My parents are on a cruise. Would it be alright if I just stayed on with ya'll?"

"Of course son," Ethan said somewhat relieved to have the extra help.

"Now, we need to get a few things done first. We may not be able to come back here so we need to get a plan together. Cassie, you and Chloe go inside and start packing the fridge and pantry into Rubbermaid containers. Ryan, you start getting the rabbits ready for transport. I'm gonna see if I can get old green to start," he said standing and heading towards the barn.

He sat in the seat of the 1972 Chevy truck that he had inherited from his father twenty years ago. It had been stored in the barn for years. He would on occasion take it for a spin into town just to keep it in running order.

He knew that the EMP generally fried the newer vehicles that had electronic chips and he was hoping that the old truck would start.

He turned the key and the engine roared to life.

"Yes! Thank you God!" he yelled out loud.

The children came running towards the barn, as he backed the truck out and let the engine idle.

"You did it Daddy!" Cassie said.

They were all smiling, thankful for the transportation.

"I can't pull the livestock trailer with this truck, so we are gonna have to make more than one trip," he said. "We have a lot of work to do. I want to load up as much as we can on the truck and take it with us. We are gonna take the rabbits and some of the goats. We will come back for the cattle and the horses," he said, still sitting in the truck.

"Ryan, get in. I need you to help me rig up a few cattle panels on the truck to hold the goats. Then, we can tie the rabbit cages on top of the cab of the truck," he said starting the truck.

Cassie, Chloe and Simon returned to the house to finish packing the pantry.

"It doesn't seem real does it?" Chloe said as they two girls put cans of food in the containers.

"No," Cassie replied quietly, sighing. "I hope my Mom and brothers are okay."

"I hope so too."

"So why did the truck and our phones quit working?" Chloe asked.

"An electromagnetic pulse. It fries anything with a chip in it," Cassie tried to explain it easily to her. She wondered if she should tell her the full extent of it.

"It could take years to get back to normal," she said.

"What the hell! Are you serious?" she asked.

"I am afraid so."

"No electricity or phone, or computer?"

"No air conditioning."

"You mean like the 1800's?"

154

"Pretty much."

Cassie and Chloe continued on with their work in silence, as they each considered the implications of what had happened.

When they were finished loading the goats and rabbits onto the truck, Ethan loaded up Cassie, Chloe and Simon into the front seat of the truck, with Cassie holding Simon in her lap as they headed back home. Ryan stayed behind to start saddling up the horses.

They drove the five country miles back to the kennel. With the four of them packed into the front of the cab and no air conditioner, their bodies were sticky. They passed people walking on the road but continued on.

Ethan turned into the neighbors yard to drop Chloe at home. He turned off the engine and got out of the truck, looking around for Chloe's parents, John and Susan. The front door of the small frame house was thrown open to Susan and John rushing out with frantic faces.

"Chloe!" she screamed running to her daughter and engulfing her in her arms. "I was so worried. Thank God you are okay."
John approached Ethan and extended his hand. "Thank you for bringing her home," he said.

"Man, she's like one of my own," Ethan said shaking his hand.

"What the hell is going on?" John asked. He had been on the tractor in the one of his leased fields a few miles away when the EMP struck. It had taken him over an hour to walk home.

"I believe that our country has been hit with an EMP," Ethan explained.

"What?" he asked incredulously.

"Let's just say that we have just been set back into the eighteenth century," Ethan said.

John turned and put his hands on his hips.

He turned back around to face Ethan. "You mean that we are at war?"

"Yes," Ethan said it feeling sick to his stomach. "John, I am going to be moving my livestock back home, and I could use some help. If you will give us a hand, you and Susan are welcome to some of the stock."

John looked at his wife who nodded, grateful for the offer. John hadn't raised livestock in a number of years since deciding to grow crops on his land. They both knew that they needed the animals, if they were to survive.

"I'd be glad to," John said.

"How soon can you be ready?" Ethan asked.

"Ten minutes."

"Okay, I am gonna drop this load off and I'll be back in about twenty minutes."

"We will be ready," John said.

Ethan and the children loaded back into the truck and drove home. He pulled the truck up to the gate of the training area and waited while Cassie got out and opened it. He drove the truck through the gate circled around in the lot, pulled the truck back through the gate and turned off the truck. He got out, dropped the tailgate and opened up the gate panel for the goats to exit. They didn't hesitate to free themselves from the jam packed truck and formed a group in the middle of the training area. Their heads and tails were held high as they sniffed the air and looked around.

Ethan, Cassie and Simon were glad to be home. The propane generator had kicked in and the house was cool when they walked in the door. Ethan walked to the kitchen sink, poured a glass of water and turned it up to drink it all.

"Cassie, you and Simon pack us some sandwiches, snacks, water and Gatorade to take back," he instructed. "And go turn that air conditioner off," he said. "I am going to get Missy and check on the rest of the dogs." He knew they would need more that one dog to move the livestock.

I hope it works, he thought to himself, wondering if they would be able to move the cattle five miles back home. He had always had the security of the fences on his farm and the thought of moving the stock without borders was scary. With seven people and the two dogs, they just might be able to pull it off, he thought to himself.

Susan didn't ride, so she would drive the truck behind the herd with three riders on each side of the herd. They would try it with a small group of twenty, and if it went well, they would return and move a larger group.

Ethan and the children returned to pick up John, Susan and Chloe. Cassie, Chloe, Simon and Missy the dog, got into the back of the pickup for the ride back, and John and Susan rode in the front with Ethan. Missy began to bark happily, ready to do her job.

Chapter 23

Rachel opened her eyes to see the man who had been driving the big rig. He looked to be in his early fifties, sported a beard and mustache and sadly needed to lose about fifty pounds.

"Where is she?" she asked, standing up shakily. She looked around for Tina, but she wasn't there. She began to move towards the small car, when the older man stepped in front of her.

"Ma'am, I'm sorry, she didn't make it," the burly looking older man said. "You don't want to go over there."

"Get out of my way," she snarled at him with a fighting look. Suddenly, with renewed strength, she ran to the little car.

The mangled car and the big rig had become one as they had collided into one another. The smell of diesel fuel was strong and began to burn her nose and eyes as Rachel was stopped in her tracks. She caught sight of her friend in the car. A piece of metal was sticking from the side of her skull and her eyes were fixed. Rachel heard herself screaming and then felt the man's hand on her arm.

"I'm so sorry. I tried to stop it. It was just too much of a load. It just wouldn't stop. I'm so sorry Ma'am," he said.

Rachel turned to look at the man and he reached out to try and comfort her. She cried into his shoulder for what seemed like an eternity, before realizing that he was a total stranger. She caught her breath, and stepped back. "I know that you did," she said to him nodding her head. "I saw…." She began to cry again and turned to walk towards her van.

"How long was I out?" she asked, coughing from the gas fumes.

"Just a few minutes," he said.

"Oh my God! All of those people in that plane!" She cried out.

"It has happened! I can't believe it! I never thought…"

"What has happened?" he asked. "I'd really like to know. This is the craziest thing that I have ever seen."

Rachel didn't answer him but instead turned to go to the back of the van. She tried to open the doors but they were locked. She returned to the driver side, climbed into the seat and then made her way to the back of the van doors. She reached for the door lock knob, manually pulled it up, and pushed the two doors open. She turned around and pulled the carpet up from the floor to reveal four long compartments.

She removed her rifle and leaned it against the van. She turned to reach up towards the packs hanging on the wall of the van. One was Evan's and she wondered if he had what he needed, fighting the urge to lose it. She rechecked the packs and after she was satisfied that nothing had been removed, she tossed them out onto the pavement. She stepped out of the van and shut the doors.

The man stood watching her, shocked to see the beautiful woman pulling guns out of the van.

Rachel lifted Evan's pack. "Turn around," she instructed, as she held the pack up for the man to put his arms through as he favored his injured arm. "There is enough food and water in here for three days," she said and turned to lift her pack onto her back. She knew that she couldn't carry two packs so she might as well help someone while she still could.

She reached for the strap of her rifle and swung the gun over her shoulder before walking to the driver side of the van and looking in to see if she might have left something. She reached for her purse, threw the strap over her other shoulder, grabbed the map and slammed the door of the van shut.

"Goodbye," she said to the man and turned to leave.

"Ma'am, don't you think that you should wait for the authorities to get here?" he asked. "You can't just leave the scene of an accident…"

Rachel stopped. He couldn't really believe that could he? She wondered. She turned back to look at him, mortified.

"Mister, in case you didn't notice, our country is at war. The authorities are not coming. That was an EMP that struck earlier. We now have no phone, no electricity, no transportation, nothing. I would suggest that you go home," she said and turned to leave. The man continued to protest that it wasn't safe for her to be walking alone and that she needed to reconsider, as she walked towards the entangled mass of the big truck and the little car.

She came to the little BMW that now entombed Tina. She stopped at the wreckage and looked inside the car to see if she could see her .38 that she might be able to reach it easily. It was lodged between the passenger side door and the seat. Rachel tried to open the door but it was jammed shut. She slid the strap of the 30/30 down her arm and used the end of the gun to smash the window. She reached into the car, retrieved her gun and quickly clipped it on the side of her waistband.

She closed her eyes to the tears and choking on the words said, "Goodbye my friend."

She opened her eyes to look north up Hwy 19 at the vehicles now dotting the freeway. People were standing around their vehicles trying to decide what to do next. Suddenly she wondered if the man had been right. Maybe she should stay with the van. Canton was a little over fifteen miles. Surely, Brian would send someone looking for her if she didn't show up in Canton. She shook her head. "No. Don't change the plan now," she said out loud to herself.

Nervously, she started to walk north on highway 19. Everywhere she looked, she could see smoke billowing into the sky. There were four stranded cars nearby and she continued to walk towards them with caution. She walked past the stranded motorists and didn't speak. She looked straight ahead and avoided eye contact.

One young girl, who looked to be in her early twenties, with a three year old boy tried to engage her in conversation asking, "Where are you going? Wait, please, can we go with you? Please!" she asked frantically.

Reluctantly, Rachel stopped. With her right hand, she reached behind her and opened one of the zippered compartments in her pack. She removed a vacuum packed bag containing a days worth of food and a bottle of water and returned to face the young woman. She handed her the package and the water.

"Where do you live?" she asked the girl. Underneath the blackened tear streaked face, Rachel suspected that she was a beauty.

"Athens," she replied. "I was on my way to work," the young woman said.

Rachel looked down at the little boy sitting on the ground playing with a truck. "Do you have any family?" Rachel asked.

"Yes," the girl replied.

"Take the boy and go home. Good luck." Rachel said walking away.

"Wait! No! Don't leave us here! Please!" she screamed as Rachel resumed walking. Tears were streaming down her face as she walked. She hadn't thought about how hard it was going to be to get past the panic stricken people. Why did they look to her for help? She had a backpack and her guns. Did that make her a leader in their eyes? I am no leader. I am just a woman who wants to go home to her family. A sob escaped her. Just like these people, she thought.

It was a little after four o'clock and she had walked almost five miles. She had lost count of the stranded people that she had passed. Some of them had fallen in behind her to make the trek north as well. She ignored them as she walked, determined not to be swayed from her goal. She still had nearly ten miles to go to reach Canton and the safety of Tina's house.

She was grateful that she had continued to do aerobics three times a week, especially now. But with the weight of the backpack she was getting tired quickly. She knew that she would not be able to reach Canton before dark. As she put one foot in front of the other and at the same time tried to observe her surroundings, she thought of her family. She wondered where they were and if they were safe. She knew that Ethan would take care of Simon and Cassie. They had anything that they might need thanks to the preparations that she and Ethan had made over the years. And Eli was with Brian. Thank God, she had reached Mitch just in time. My God, she thought, will they make it to

161

Brian's? The time between the first explosions and the EMP had been exactly an hour. That meant that they only had an hour to pack up and get ready to go. She ran the scenario in her mind. Okay, thirty minutes tops, to load up. So that would leave thirty minutes of driving. From Crystal City they might have made it thirty or forty miles before the EMP. So they would be near Uvalde. Rachel calculated in her head. It was close to four hundred miles from Uvalde to Dallas. If they walked ten miles per day, that would mean that it would take them over a month to get to Dallas.

That was if all went well, if the weather was good, if all of the bridges were intact, if angry mobs didn't accost them, if they could even find food. She blocked the thought from her mind.

She looked up the road to see another group of stranded motorists and just didn't want to deal with another crowd. She walked to the side of the road, turned and watched the people walk past her as they continued on their trek north as if they were zombies putting one foot in front of the other.

After the people had passed her and were well up the road, she turned and walked down the side of the road into the thick woods. She reached up for the straps of her pack and let it fall to the ground, before sitting down on top of it, still holding her 30/30 in her arms. She was trying to decide if she wanted to make camp or keep moving, when she heard movement in the brush behind her. She slid down the side of her pack and brought her gun up to rest on top of it. She was motionless except for her eyes as she scanned the woods in front of her. Then, she saw it. A rabbit hopped forward and then sat back on its haunches looking at her and sniffing the air.

She closed her eyes as she breathed a sigh of relief. She laid the gun down next to her and opened one of the zippered pouches to find another vacuum packed bag of food, a bottle of water and a small pocket knife. She turned and leaned up against the pack. She used the knife to cut the bag open and then slid it into her pants pocket. She opened the bottle of water and drank half of it before pouring the contents of the bag of food into her lap.

She had made up hundreds of these little bags that held a meat source of protein, high calorie snacks, water and condiments. She looked over the contents and chose to eat dessert first, as she tore open the four small chocolate bars.

She felt energized after finishing her meal and relieving herself. She moved the pack into place and picked up her gun. Determined to make it to Canton before morning, she walked on.

Chapter 24

The road was crowded with stranded motorists as far as the eye could see. Some of the people had formed groups and had decided to wait for help to arrive. Rachel prayed for them as she passed by them. She suspected that these were the type of people that would eventually panic when no help came.

The cars and trucks were now large metal heaps, and since none had been immune to the effects of the EMP strike, crowds of people snaked through the obstacle course of metal as they walked. A woman pushed a wheelchair that held her husband and what few belongings they had were piled in his lap to hold. A mother pushed a stroller with her baby as her two other young children walked along side. Some people pulled wheeled suitcases behind them. Others carried their belongings in their arms. Occasionally, a bicycle would streak past the crowd.

Rachel stayed to the right side of the road and for the most part walked in a straight line until she would come upon a vehicle whose driver had managed to pull to the side of the road when the strike hit.

She knew that every step that she placed was precious, since her legs had begun to burn within the first few hours. She walked through the pain until her legs became numb. Stopping every thirty minutes to rest, each time, it was harder to begin the walk again.

Some of the vehicles that had been brought to a permanent halt were intertwined with others, when their drivers had been unable to avoid it and crashed. Nearby, injured people were bleeding, crying and screaming for help. Some, like Tina, had been less fortunate and still sat in the vehicles that had become their caskets.

She tried but it was difficult not to look, when she would hear a child cry and her heart would sigh with the sadness of it all.

She reached into one of the pockets of her pack that held the headlamp and moved it into position on her head, as darkness would soon descend upon them.

The hours passed and soon Rachel reached the turnoff towards Tina's. She turned to the right and left the mass of people behind her. A few people turned off with her. Rachel was relieved to see the familiar surroundings of a small convenience store and gas station that was well lit with camping lanterns hung throughout the store. Three armed men were inside the store as four people at a time were allowed in. She continued past it knowing that she would soon be at her destination. And finally, there it was. In the darkness she could see the entrance to the subdivision. She could smell food cooking and some of the houses had candles burning inside for light. He stomach began to churn for something to eat, even though she didn't think that she could eat a bite. It was close to midnight as she walked around to the back of the house to find the key to let herself into Tina's house. The two dogs were in the fenced in back yard, and began to bark at her intrusion.

"Penny, Copper, its okay. Good boy, good girl," she praised the dogs for doing their jobs, as she laid her gun on the patio table and removed the heavy pack. Their tone changed to greeting her familiar voice, as she walked to the fence and reached over to pet them both.

The dogs jumped around her with their tails wagging, happy to see her. She approached the back door and as she put the key in the lock, she heard a click behind her as a man cocked his shotgun.

She froze in place.

"I wouldn't do that if I were you," the voice said behind her.

She slowly raised her hands above her head as her heart began to pound in her chest. She could feel the pressure pounding in her ears as she waited. "My name is Rachel Reed. Tina was my friend and I am here to meet Chad and Ben. Please don't shoot!" she said quickly.

"What do you mean that she was your friend?" he asked.

Rachel slowly turned around to face the man and brought her arms to her side.

"She died in a car accident on our way back here," she said unhappily.

The man lowered the barrel of the gun. He looked at Rachel sadly, believing her. She could barely make out his features in the dark, but she thought that he must be the neighbor that was taking care of the dogs, that Tina had described to her.

"Are you Joe?" she asked.

"Yes," he answered with sadness in his voice.

He walked to the patio table and chairs to sit down. Rachel did the same, suddenly relieved to rest her weary body.

"I am sorry for your loss," Joe said meaning it. He wondered how he was going to tell his wife Judy that Tina was gone.

"So am I," she said.

"You are welcome to come to the house and get a bite to eat. The power is out so we are trying to cook and save the food in our freezer," he said.

"I have just walked fifteen miles and I am exhausted. I just want to get some rest, but thank you," she said.

"I understand. There is no radio or phone service. Do you have any idea what might have happened?" he asked.

"I believe that our country has been attacked with an Electromagnetic Pulse," she said simply, too tired to explain further.

"I suspected as much," he said.

Rachel remembered Tina saying that he was retired military and that he could be an ass sometimes. But right now he looked like a man defeated, as did so many others.

"We will talk in the morning. Get some rest," he said standing from his chair.

"I will. Goodnight," she said as she watched him turn, walk around the corner of the house and go home before she opened the door and brought her pack and gun inside. She leaned up against the door to close it and slid down to the floor. Exhausted, she began to sob and cry for her friend, for her family, and for her country. Her body rocked as she let it go. She tried to catch her breath as she cried uncontrollably. Her arms ached for her children and for Mitch.

She heard a knock on the door and she tried to compose herself before turning onto her hands and knees and then stand.

"Ms. Reed, I'm Judy, Joe's wife. Please let me in," she said.

She opened the door, to see Judy holding a bag with a plate of hot food and a cold bottle of water. She stepped forward and reached out to Rachel, hugging her and balancing the food in one hand.

"I'm so sorry. She was my friend too," she said holding Rachel as she cried. Rachel pulled away, grateful for the kind words.

"Thank you," she said.

"Come on honey, sit down," the older woman said leading her to the kitchen table and lighting a candle. She removed the plate of food from the bag, sat it down in front of Rachel and removed the lid. She went to the drawer in the kitchen and brought her a fork, before sitting down across from her.

"Tina talked a lot about you," Judy said watching Rachel as she covered the food back up and push it away.

"She talked about you too," Rachel replied. "She was very fond of you."

"What happened to her?" Judy asked.

"We were on highway 19 when the EMP struck. I was following her in my van. She managed to pull her car over to the side of the road. A tractor trailer was coming towards us and the driver was fighting for control of it but it turned over on its side and slid right into Tina's car," Rachel managed to finish, before breaking into tears again.

Judy shook her head, sickened at the thought of her friend dying in such a terrible way. And now her boys were orphans.

"And you walked fifteen miles alone? You are a strong woman," Judy said smiling.

"No, I'm not," Rachel sobbed shaking her head. "I am just afraid to be without my family. And Ben and Chad are going to need us now. I didn't have a choice but to come here."

"It takes a strong woman to decide that. Don't sell yourself short. I think that you have what it takes to handle just about anything," Judy said nodding.

Rachel was suddenly very tired. It was close to one a.m. and she just wanted to get in a warm soft bed.

"Thank you for the food. Forgive me but I just don't have an appetite right now," she said.

"You are welcome," Judy said standing to leave. "Get some rest and we will talk tomorrow, okay?"

"Okay. And thanks for your kind words. I can see why Tina cared so much about you," she said walking her to the door.

"Goodnight," Rachel said shutting the door.

She reached for her headlamp that hung around her neck, blew out the candle, made her way into the guest bedroom. She threw herself across the bed and within minutes she was fast asleep.

Chapter 25

Rachel turned over in the bed. It was hot in the room and she heard two dogs barking. "The dog is barking! The dog is barking!" Evan was screaming at her. He was in the back seat of a Jeep and it was speeding away as he continued to scream at her "The dog is barking!"

She awoke with a start and sat upright. With sweat streaming down her face and her heart racing, she looked around the room and remembering that she was at Tina's house, as she lay back on the pillow.

She thought about the previous day as she had cried her tears away before being replaced with emptiness. She didn't want to get up. She just wanted to stay in the bed and wait for someone to come and take her home. She didn't want to face the worries that were about to become a new way of life for her. She turned over on her side and tried to go back to sleep, but she couldn't. She thought of Mitch, her fiancé, the love of her life, the man she wanted to spend the rest of her life with. Would it really happen now? Would she ever see her children again? What about Ethan? What if something had happened to him. Who would care for Cassie and Simon? She wondered before, finally, she rose from the bed.

She went into the kitchen to make coffee and realized that Tina had all electric appliances. She opened the cabinet to see if she had any instant coffee. No, but she had tea. It would do.

She was glad that Tina had always insisted on drinking bottled water. She opened the door to enter the garage for a case of it and stopped in her tracks. She stood looking at the 1967 Mustang that Kyle had worshiped. She could hardly believe her eyes. For some reason she thought that Tina had sold the car when her husband died, but there it sat. She walked to the driver side, opened the door and sat in the seat. No key. She got out of the car and shut the door. It would wait until the rescue team got here, she thought, if they got here. If they didn't, she would look for the key or learn to hot wire a car.

Caffeine, she needed lots of it. She carried the case of water into the kitchen and shut the door back. She removed a handful of tea bags and put them into four of the bottles of water and put the lid back on. She carried them outside to the patio and sat them in the sun, before her eye caught a shiny new grill in the corner of the patio. She hadn't seen it until now and was relieved to see that it was gas operated with a new tank and everything.

The dogs began to bark at her wagging their tails. They were glad to see her; their trainer, their other master. But they would have to wait. She turned and went back into the house. She opened the pantry to see the shelves lined with the cakes in the jars, and the vegetable soup that she had brought on her way down to the Circle C. She did have a couple of dozen cans of soup and broth, crackers and cereal. She shut the pantry door and went to the refrigerator. There was a hint of cold inside and she leaned her head into it for just a moment to feel the coolness as she looked to see what was there. There was wine, soda, butter, sour cream, and coffee creamer in the carton, but that was about all. Rachel shut the fridge quickly to retain the coolness for as long as possible. She then opened the freezer to see a couple dozen frozen dinners, ice cream, and some melting ice in the ice maker. She took the box of chocolate ice cream and a spoon and started eating it as she walked into the living room to open the blinds and windows to get a breeze coming into the house. She had slept until nearly noon according to the angle of the sun, and it was already hot.

She returned to the kitchen to open the window above the sink and noticed that the dogs were looking towards the neighbor's house with their tails wagging. She carried the box of ice cream with her and started next door.

Joe and Judy were sitting outside on their patio grilling lunch.

"Good morning," they greeted in unison. "Have a seat," Judy offered.

Rachel sat down and held the box out to them, but they refused.

"Did you get any rest?" Judy asked.

"Yes, I slept all night and half the day, from the looks of it."

"I'm sure that you needed it," Judy said.

"Yes. And then some," she tried to smile.

"Rachel, we are having a neighborhood meeting at two o'clock this afternoon. I would like for you to be there, if you wouldn't mind," Joe said.

"Sure Joe, but I don't know if I will be of any help," she said.

"You walked fifteen miles yesterday, you had an army backpack on when you arrived, and you were carrying a 30/30. You knew what you were doing. I have a feeling that you will have something to offer."

She thought for a moment before she spoke. "I just don't know if your neighbors are ready to hear the truth," she said.

"Then they damn well better get ready. I am afraid that we are in this for the long haul. If we are going to survive, then we are all going to have to work together," Joe said.

"You are right about that," Rachel said. "I will be there. I guess that I had better go finish up before the meeting," she said standing.

When she got back to the house, she opened the gate to let the dogs into the house. They were happy to be in, but after finding out that it was cooler outside in the yard they were soon at the door barking to get out.

Rachel had taken inventory of the food and water. She had enough food to last her for a month if she was careful but had only enough drinking water for a week or so. She had decided to take the water out of the toilet tanks and boil it. That would mean that she had enough water for nearly two weeks. She would use a five gallon bucket that she had found in the garage for a toilet, and with the gas grill outside, she would be able to cook. So, food, water, shelter and defense were taken care of for a short while.

173

The dogs had a fifty pound bag of food, so they would be set for a good ten days. They also had a five gallon bucket of water that was full so they would have water for a few days at least.

With the essentials taken care of for the time being, she decided to go next door to wait for the meeting to start.

There must have been forty or fifty people in Joe and Judy's yard. The smell of sweat and food intermingled and produced an aroma all its own.

There were couples, couples with small children, couples with older children, and a few elderly people. They all wore the face of fear. Not knowing can have a devastating effect on ones mental state, and these people were worried.

Joe motioned to Rachel to come over and she did. She stood next to Judy, as he started the meeting.

"Hello. Thank you for coming," he said. "As you all know, yesterday our lives changed drastically. But what you don't know is how it was changed. I believe that our country was attacked by an EMP. For those of you that don't know what that is, it is an electromagnetic pulse. It pretty much fries circuits in anything electrical. Now, we are left with the aftermath of an attack on our country. We have been pushed back to the horse and buggy days, literally. We are going to have to take care of our basic needs, of food, water, shelter, and defense of our community, at least until we hear from our national leaders. We don't know when that will be. I called this meeting today to see where everyone stood. I propose that we all work together to make sure that everyone has water, food and a way to defend ourselves. Give me a show of hands if you are in favor," he asked. Nearly every hand was raised with the exception of two men that looked on.

"Well it looks like a majority to me. After we are finished here, if you are interested in joining a planning committee, get with Judy to sign up," Joe said.

"I have one more thing to bring up. Last night, Rachel Reed joined our community. She was a friend of Tina Douglas who was killed yesterday as they made their way here. Ms. Reed walked fifteen miles to get here and I would like to welcome her to our neighborhood," Joe said. He turned to face her and began to clap his hands. The people in the neighborhood joined him in welcoming her.

Their faces showed their sorrow for her loss as she looked over the small crowd.

She tried to step up on the chair that Joe offered her, but her legs were too tired and sore from her hike the previous day. Joe reached out for her arm and helped her step up.

"Thank you for that warm welcome. Yesterday morning, I left Crystal City Texas on my way home to Arkansas. I met Tina for lunch in Waco and it was wonderful to see my old friend," she said trying to remain composed. "Just after lunch, an explosion blew out the windows of the restaurant that we were sitting in. So began the end of the world as we knew it. We managed to get out of Waco and as we were traveling on highway 19, the EMP struck and a tractor trailer collided with Tina's car. She was killed instantly. I am thankful that is was quick and that she did not suffer," her voice broke with emotion.

"I am sure that my story is not the only one. Each and every one of you here have your very own story to tell. But first we must survive. I think that if we all work together, we will not only survive, but prosper as well, with Gods help," she nodded her head and turned back towards Joe, who walked over and helped her step down from the chair.

He resumed his place back up on the chair and was about to make another announcement when the sound of an engine broke the crowds concentration. Two army jeeps startled the crowd as they entered the subdivision. Rachel turned to see Eli, Chad, Ben and three armed men in the jeeps. They parked the two vehicles in Tina's drive and Rachel struggled as she ran to her son. She threw her arms around him and hugged him close. "Thank God, Thank God," she said stepping back to look into his face. Relief flooded over her to know that he was okay, that her son was standing before her.

Then she dropped her head. She prayed for the strength and the words to tell Chad and Ben that their mother was gone. She raised her head and turned to look at them. They were scanning the crowd for their mother, but when they didn't see her, their gaze returned to Rachel.

Her face told the story. The tears streamed before she could utter a word. "I am so sorry..." she said as she reached out for them both. They looked at one another trying to let it sink in. Then they looked back at Rachel, horrified.

The crowd looked on as Eli and Rachel led the boys, now men, into their house and closed the door to the rest of the world. The three armed men stayed outside to guard the two vehicles. The crowd moved towards them and began to question the men. They didn't answer but stood ready to defend the property if need be.

Chad and Ben listened as Rachel told them how their mother had died.

"She was killed instantly," she explained.

"Where is she?" Ben spoke first.

"Honey she is gone now. There was no way to get her body out of the car," she said.

"I want to know where she is at," he demanded, rising to his full six foot four stature.

"Fifteen miles south on highway 19," Rachel said.
He stood and started towards the door, but Chad stepped in front of him. "You are the last of my family and I will not let you do this," he said.

The two brothers who looked so different but had shared the same womb, faced off. Ben, mad at the world, looked at his twin. He knew that he was right. It was too risky. Ben pulled his arm back and smashed his hand into the wall in front of Chad. His brother didn't flinch as Ben worked out his grief on the wall. And then Chad reached out and pulled his brother back away from the wall. Eli and Rachel looked on knowing that there were no words to say to them. They turned and quietly walked out the door.

Rachel approached the three men who were guarding their transportation.

"I am Rachel Reed," she said and held her hand out to the first soldier.

"Ma'am, I'm John Smith." He nodded

"Paul White," the second soldier said.

"Ron Martinez. My condolonces ma'am," the third soldier said to Rachel, who nodded.

She turned back to her son. "I am so glad to see you," she said.

"Did you hear from your father or Evan?" she hoped that he would say yes.

"No, I didn't."

"Did you bring my bag?"

"Yes ma'am."

He walked to the back of the first jeep and pulled out the black duffle bag and handed it to her.

She turned to go back into the house with her bag.

Eli stayed outside with the soldiers watching the crowd. A few people tried to ask them questions and some were becoming irritated that they were not answering them.

"I guess we better give them some answers," John said to Eli and the two other soldiers.

He stepped up into the seat of the jeep and stood holding his automatic weapon across his chest, looking out over the crowd, waiting for them to quiet down.

"We are here to retrieve Ms. Reed and return to an undisclosed location where Governor Russell is waiting. All that we can say at this time is that we can confirm that a foreign enemy has launched an attack on our country. We do not know who is responsible at this time. Help will be disbursed as soon as possible," he finished and then jumped down from the jeep.

Rachel walked back into the living room, wearing her fatigues, army boots, and her two pistols clipped on the waistband of her pants. Chad and Ben were sitting and talking, as families do when someone they love has died. Rachel walked over and sat down next to Ben and put her arm around his shoulders. She was the adult and was supposed to have the wisdom to share with the younger ones. Still, she felt at a loss for words for the boys.

"When I was sixteen and had lost pretty much the only person that had ever truly loved me, your mother was there. She became my dearest, best friend, my confidant, my partner in crime," she smiled as the tears flowed. "I know what if feels like to be an orphan. The only differences are that my family chose to leave me, and I was left alone to face the world. You two have each other. And now, you have me and my family, like it or not, you're stuck with us," she said looking at the two of them.

Ben leaned over and kissed her on the cheek and said, "Thank you."

Chad's eyes held the words but he didn't say them, but nodded.

"You guys know that we are running out of time. The longer we stay here, the worse it is going to get. Are you going to return to Brian's with us?" she asked, hoping that they would say yes. She couldn't bear the thought of them staying here alone.

They exchanged looks and without talking it over, turned back to Rachel and said "Yes."

The power of twins, Rachel thought, smiling. She had always been amazed at the connection between her own boys and the unspoken words that they had always shared.

From conception they had had to learn to share the womb with another, to survive. And now they would learn to share the world, to do the same.

"Would you like to say something to the neighborhood before we leave?" she asked looking between the two of them.

"I think that we should," Chad said. "It is getting bad out there."

"Lets do it," Rachel said feeling the urgency come upon her as she stood and started for the door.

Chapter 26

Rachel motioned for Eli to come with them as they made their way next door. The group of people was still gathered as Rachel, Eli, Ben and Chad arrived. Rachel stood back and watched as the two boys went to talk to Joe. Then he nodded and Chad walked over to the chair and stepped up.

"We have just come from North of Dallas. Conditions are not good. People are dead, hurt, hungry or desperate," he said. His eyes looked over the crowd, thinking that he owed it to them to tell them the facts. His voice held authority as he spoke and they listened.

"Dallas is burning. I am sure that many cities all over the country are burning also. There are no firetrucks. People are fleeing the cities. This neighborhood is right in the path. It would be wise to set up a perimeter around the subdivision and post guards. You must hurry to prepare for the bands of people that may try to force their way in. It will only get worse as time goes by. I urge you to come together to work as one," he said.

He started to step down from the chair, but a man from the crowd spoke out.

"Does that mean that you will not be staying to help us?" the man asked angrily.

"That's right," Chad replied. "Our orders are to return to our base of operation."

"You can't just leave us here!" a woman screamed out from the crowd.

The voices in the crowd began to rise as they began to talk between themselves.

"Listen to me," Chad yelled out.

"We will be of more service to our country than we would be here," he said. "If our country falls, we are all doomed." He looked out over the crowd. His words brought the crowd to a hushed silence as they considered his words.

"It is time for each of us to draw on our strengths, and work together," he said stepping down from the chair.

"Well done," Joe said. He would miss the two boys that he and Judy had watch grow into manhood.

Rachel turned to Eli. "When do you think that we should leave?" she asked.

"First thing in the morning," he said. He and Rachel said their goodbyes and left Chad and Ben to visit with their friends.

Inside the sweltering house, Rachel and Eli were drinking a bottle of water trying to catch up. "Brian sent us out first thing this morning to find you," Eli said.

"Mom, things are really bad. It looks like what you would see on TV, countries at war. I never thought that it would happen here. People are dying on our own soil Mom," he said.

All that she could do was to nod her head. She thought of the young girl with the little boy, and wondered if she had made it home.

"Son, this is what we have been trying so hard to prepare for. Your father and I have watched this country deteriorate over the past twenty years. Britta and Brian saw it, even before then. All that we can do now is to gather our family together, pray and trust in God," she said. "I am really torn. Part of me wants to go look for Mitch and Evan and the other part of me says to go home to Cassie and Simon," she said looking lost.

"And Dad," Eli said.

She didn't speak, but held her hand up for him to see the ring on her finger.

"Mitch asked me to marry him and I said yes," she said. She waited for a response from him and watched his face as it registered anger, hurt, disappointment and then it softened.

He swallowed hard as he thought about how cruel fate could be. His mother had been devastated when his Dad cheated on her. She had thrown herself into work over the past four years but she had never truly recovered. He noticed a glimmer of happiness in her eyes and it looked like she had finally found love again. And now it had been snatched away in a mere second. He reached for his mother and hugged her.

"Why don't we wait until we get back to Grandpa's before we decide anything?" he asked.

She nodded. "You're right."

The door opened and Chad and Ben came in.

"I have warmed up some food if you are ready to eat," she said.

She had warmed up the vegetable soup and cake on the grill. She caught a whiff of the aroma of the chocolate and realized that it was near dinner time.

She went into the kitchen and got some food and soda for the guards outside and carried it out to them as Chad, Ben and Eli sat down to eat. She noticed that the crowd of people had left and returned to their homes. The smell of food cooking on grills hung in the air. The aroma would have made a satisfied man hungry.

"Thank you ma'am," John said passing out the food to the others.

"Sure. Thanks for coming to get me," she said.

"Our mission isn't complete yet ma'am."

"I have faith in you. Brian wouldn't have sent you if he didn't think you were up to it," she said.

"Yes ma'am," he said.

She returned to the house to join the boys. She sat down to eat the soup that she had canned three months earlier. She knew that she must eat although she still didn't have an appetite.

"I don't guess that we will have room to take anything back with us in the Jeep," Ben commented.

Rachel remembered the mustang parked in the garage.

"Wait a minute," Rachel said. "Do you have a key to the mustang?" she asked.

"Yes," Chad and Ben answered in unison.

"Why?" they asked.

"I'd like to see if it will start before we leave," she said.

The two looked at each other confused.

"Older cars don't have electrical chips," Rachel explained.

Ben stood, pushed his chair back with his legs and walked to the kitchen drawer. He pulled out a set of keys and held them up for all to see, smiling for the first time since they got there.

They followed him into the garage and watched as he opened up the driver side door and got in.

"Say a prayer," Rachel said.

Ben put the key in the ignition, turned it and the engine made a muffled sound but didn't start. He tried again and finally the car roared to life.

"Yes!" Eli yelled out and the three of them hi-fived each other.

Ben smiled at his brother. "Nice." Starting a car held a whole new meaning for them now.

Rachel and Eli helped Chad and Ben pack up what few belongings that they could fit into the back of the Mustang. Their family pictures, winter clothes, the remainder of their mother's jewelry and their father's coin collection all fit into just a few boxes. The four of them carried the last of the boxes out to the mustang and squeezed them into the back seat, before they all decided to turn in.

Rachel was restless and couldn't sleep. Nighttime was the worst. Stillness brought on the worry. She paced the room unable to sleep.

Where were Mitch and Evan? Were they hurt? Did they have enough food? She sat down in the chair, but she couldn't stay still.

She stood anxiously to her feet and reached for the candle. Quietly she crept into the living room to find her pack that held her map. She sat the candle down on the coffee table and removed the map. On her knees she laid the map out on the table in front of the candle to better see the small lines. She wished now that she had chosen to have the procedure to correct her vision, as she leaned back away from the map and squinted to see the small print.

Her eyes went to the bottom of the map to the small town of Crystal City and then traveled north up highway 83. She looked at the map and sat back on her heels, feeling the soreness in her thighs.

What route would I take if I were in their shoes? Avoid the cities, keep a low profile, and travel off road as much as possible. She leaned forward again to look at the map. Okay, I'd go North on 83 up to Junction. Then I would turn northeast and head for Copperas Cove and then on to Fort Hood. She smiled. That was the most likely route that they would take, she was almost sure of it. Evan would do the same. They had played this game before. Only this time, it wasn't a game.

Rachel folded up the map, put it back in her pack and reached for the candle. She crept back to her room, sleepy now with her mind at ease. Tomorrow, she'd be a step closer to home.

Chapter 27

From the outside looking in, a person wouldn't even know that the lives of the eighty six people that inhabited the Rocking B had been changed by the EMP strike, just six weeks earlier.

They had electricity, although it was being generated by other means than an electric grid. They had jobs, and although not being paid in a form of currency, they were being compensated with a form of security and community that was priceless, as they worked to rebuild and restructure a new way of living. They had communications which was effective but slow as they tried to reach the outside world.

In the communications room, there were five tables set up with equipment that was powered by solar and wind powered batteries.

Table one was a charging station for the forty hand held CB's that were rotated out on a regular basis. Members could come in and exchange a CB whose batteries were dead and get another radio with a fully charged battery

On table two was two ham radios operated by Rachel and Marie, one of the other group members.

Table three and table four held old manual typewriters for written correspondence that was sent by riders on horseback as a new form of pony express took shape.

Table five consisted of two computers that were set up and monitored for signs of life on the outside, but as of yet no connection.

Brian had stored this equipment in large Faraday cages that he had made some years back and it had survived unscathed.

They had an adequate defense, as the perimeter of the ranch was patrolled with posted guards. The schedule was running even better than expected as more people were added to the compound and integrated into the workforce.

Jim James had worked for the Department of Transportation. He and two helpers had been put in charge of moving throughout the area to retrieve the solar powered units that had previously been used along the roads to monitor traffic. The small solar panel and battery was then recycled into use for generating more power at the ranch.

Rachel and Marie worked tirelessly day in and day out to reach areas in the outside world. They had managed to make contact with a man in Germany who reported that the retaliation had been swift.

Iranian and Mexican guerillas had joined forces and were responsible for the attack. Iran was now an even bigger dust bowl. Mexico and Venezuela were now trying to take over the United States. China had yet to stake its claim on the country that it had owned for decades.

Rachel and Marie had just recently made contact with three new hammers across the United States. They were located in Wyoming, West Virginia and Georgia. Reports were not good.

The President was dead and the vice President remained unaccounted for. The south had been taken again by groups of Mexican resistance that had been in place for years. Mississippi, Alabama, Georgia, Florida and parts of Tennessee were now being controlled by the new Mexico Republic. Americans were fleeing the major cities and trying to escape the tyranny, as the tidal wave of people slowly moved westward.

Rachel had seen horrific things on the return trip back to the ranch, as order was soon replaced with desperation.

In less than forty eight hours after the EMP, people were being killed for water. In the small towns that they were forced to go through, looting was rampant. Store owners were being shot, and orphan children were crying along side the bodies of their parents. People stood on the side of the road as they passed, begging for help, food or water as they offered something of value in exchange. Rachel could hardly bear it. She knew that as time went on, travel would become extremely dangerous. She was torn between waiting for Mitch and Evan or returning home to Arkansas and her children. She knew that the longer she waited, her chance of making it home to her children became slim. After talking to Brian and considering it, she had decided to wait, and with each passing day, her concern grew.

She looked up to see that her relief Sandra had arrived and she stood to leave for the day.

She was tired as she walked from the house to the back patio, where she knew she would find Lisa at the twenty solar ovens that had been put in place.

"Hi." Lisa smiled.

"Hey," she said as she sat down at one of the tables. She reached for the pitcher of lemonade, poured a glass and sighed heavily, before putting the pitcher back down.

Lisa knew that Rachel had something on her mind since she rarely stopped to talk. She sat down across from her and joined her in a glass of lemonade.

"What's up?" Lisa asked.

"They should have been her by now," she said forlornly, leaning forward and resting her elbows on the table.

Lisa could see the strain on her face and knew that she was having a hard time. She had been battling nausea and had lost weight, but she still looked beautiful.

"Have faith honey," she said. "Evan is a strong, smart young man. Just look at Eli," she said.

Rachel nodded. "And he has Mitch, so he's not alone," she paused. "I just want my family back together. I want to go home. I want to hold my boy Simon on my lap and listen to Cassie complain about school," she said swallowing a lump in her throat.

"Hey now, none of that, suck it up soldier," Brian said as he appeared on the patio. He winked at Rachel and leaned down to kiss her on the forehead, before pulling up a chair. He sat down next to her and his expression became serious. He looked over at Lisa, placed his hand held radio on the table and reached for her hand.

"I've got to go to Fort Hood," he said. "A helicopter will be here in the morning to pick me up."

Lisa looked at him, terrified and unable to speak.

"The Mexican Republic has taken San Antone and they are advancing towards Austin," he said.

Rachel and Lisa looked at each other. Up until then, Lisa's family had been safe and together on the Rocking B and now she felt the fear that Rachel had felt for the last month and a half. She had known that it was only a matter of time before she would be forced to watch her husband leave. She closed her eyes and prayed silently. Keep him safe God, please, keep him safe.

The hand held radio interrupted her thoughts.

"Come in Brian," Jim asked.

"Copy, Jim," he replied.

"Aaron Garcia is at post four asking for Rachel, over."

Before Brian could reply she was on her feet and running for the yard.

"Rachel." His commanding voice stopped her.

She turned to look at him panic stricken, her eyes pleading and her heart racing.

"Wait," he said and returned to the radio.

"Copy that. We will be right down," he replied to Jim before joining Rachel and reaching for her hand.

"Let's go," he said.

Lisa watched them, as they quickly walked to one of the jeeps parked next to the house, and then sped out of the yard to post four.

"Brian, what does this mean?" she asked him as he maneuvered the jeep down the dirt road leading them to the border of his property.

"I don't know kiddo." He didn't want to speculate or get her hopes up, so he kept quiet. But if Aaron had made it to the ranch, why hadn't Mitch and Evan? And if they weren't with him, then where were they?

As the jeep approached the barrier at post four, Rachel could see Aaron sitting down on the ground and there was a man sitting next to him.

Brian pulled the vehicle to a stop and Rachel jumped out, running through the gate and falling to her knees at Aaron's side.

189

His leg was bandaged and he was sweating. He looked as if he had been shot. She reached out to feel his forehead and confirmed that he had a fever.

"Aaron! You are burning up," she said.

"Before Mitch left he told us to come here if we were overrun," Aaron said looking at her weakly.

He inclined his head towards the man that sat next to him, and said, "My cousin, Pedro."

Brian and two men walked over to them.

"Let's get him in the jeep," he said.

Pedro stood and one of the other men helped lift Aaron up and carry him to the jeep and deposit him in the back seat, as Rachel slid into the seat next to him. Pedro carried the two back packs and put them in the back of the jeep before getting into the front seat next to Brian.

"Aaron, when did you see Mitch and Evan last?" she asked him.

"The day of the strike, I helped them load up five horses and equipment. They were headed to Waco to find you," he said.

"I stayed with Celia and William to defend the ranch, but we couldn't hold it. They were killed," he said nervously glancing at Pedro.

Her heart dropped as she listened to Aaron. Mitch and Evan could still be alive and on their way here, she thought to herself, unwilling to believe anything else. She listened as Brian radioed ahead to the house and asked them to be ready to transport Aaron to the medical unit.

Eli had heard the conversation on the radio and was waiting when they returned. "Eli when you finish, please go find Michelle and Dustin. Ask them to come to the house for dinner tonight," Brian instructed before turning to go into the house. "Yes sir," he said.

Rachel and Eli watched as Aaron was taken into the hospital ward, with Pedro following behind.

"Hi Mom," he said. "Did he have any news on Evan or Mitch?"

"Just that he helped them load up to leave on the day of the strike," she said sighing. "Brian just got word that a helicopter is picking him up in the morning to take him to Fort Hood. The MR has taken San Antone," she said feeling strange saying the words. She

190

thought of the Alamo, and wondered if the outcome would be different this time.

Eli turned away from her to avoid her eyes and brought his hands to his hips. He turned back to face her not wanting to see the pain in her eyes that he was about to inflict on her.

"Mama, I want to go with Grandpa," he said. "I want to join the army."

Her heart began to race. No way in hell, she thought. Not gonna happen, she fought with herself. Her mind returned to the past remembering when Eli and Evan small at age two, at age six going off to school, graduating from high school and then Eli left home for college. And now he was a young man wanting to defend his country. Tears came to her eyes. She knew that she couldn't keep him from it.

She nodded her head afraid that her voice would betray her with words that she wanted to scream at him. She reached out for his arm and slipped hers through his.

"Walk with me," she said as he slipped his arm around her shoulders and they walked towards the barns to find Michelle and Dustin.

By dinner time, word had spread throughout the community that Eli, Chad, Ben, James, and Owen would be accompanying Brian to Fort Hood to join up.

Dinner was somber as the family considered the consequences. Rachel had decided to stay at the Rocking B for a little while longer to help Lisa. With six of the members gone, they would have to adjust schedules to compensate.

The following morning, the families gathered as they waited for the helicopter to arrive. Around nine a.m. they heard a once familiar sound in the air as the roar slowly descended and landed near the house. The families watched their boys go off to war and, as the six men ran to board the aircraft, Lisa watched as her husband went with them.

Chapter 28

The horses' shrill scream of terror pierced the quiet as the mare reached for the sky pawing the air, her eyes wide. Mitch was nearly unseated as he leaned forward in the saddle and pulled his pistol from his holster. He managed to get a clear shot at the rattlesnake that had startled his horse as she returned all four feet to the earth. He tried to hold her steady as she danced around with fear, while he dismounted. His hand went to her neck as he tried to quiet her. Her head was lifted high, her ears forward and nostrils flared as she tried to determine the strange smell. She soon relaxed and dropped her head although still breathing fast and heavy.

Evan watched the scene in front of him, unsure of what to do. He sighed with relief when Mitch announced that they would make camp, and he held up the four foot long snake and said, "Dinner."

"Yes sir," he said and leaned to the right in the saddle to prompt his horse to turn off of the road. Her ears flickered back to him and then forward again as she moved towards a patch of woods.

Evan guided his mare to a tree, dismounted and tied her, before turning back to loosen the girth. He walked to the first pack mare and began to remove the panniers. Their supplies had dwindled, so there were only two of the horses carrying packs. The third pack horse carried a saddle with the pack empty. They rotated the horses daily to give them a rest. They had held up well under the pressure of daily traveling, although they were used to working on the ranch for a few hours, not full time travel.

Mitch and Evan sat around the campfire sipping on weak coffee. The nighttime sound of the woods was soothing as they waited to eat. The two German shepherd dogs were lying between them. Allie was stretched out on her side and Axel was lying on his belly watching the snake cooking on the fire, anticipating a morsel.

Mitch pulled the tattered map and a small pen light from his pocket. He opened up the map and turned on the light. His eye immediately went to his hometown of Crystal City. He wondered if he would ever see the ranch again and he remembered the last day that he was there.

When Rachel called him in a panic from Waco, setting this whole course in motion, he never imagined that he would be traveling across Texas by horseback. His time with Rachel felt like a dream, one that he was not willing to let go of. It hardly seemed real now.

He had been holding his cell phone talking to Rachel, when it went dead and his truck came to a standstill north of Uvalde. There had been no flash, no sound, no warning, just quiet. Mitch would never forget the look on the boys face. He was terrified.

"EMP," he said. Mitch had watched as Evan reached for the door handle, jumped out and ran to the back of the trailer. The dogs had begun to bark at his excitement.

"We have got to hurry Mitch. There is no time to waste," he said as his fingers fumbled with the latch of the trailer door. When his fingers failed him he turned to Mitch.

"You do it," he said frantically, as the dogs continued to bark and when he could stand it no more, he screamed "Shut the hell up," he commanded the dogs. He couldn't think with the noise of their barking.

Mitch watched Evan struggle with himself trying to calm down. He began to pace towards the front of the truck and then to the back, like a caged animal.

194

"Take it easy son. Everything is going to be okay. Settle down," he said reaching over to touch his shoulder. The boy looked like he was about to jump out of his skin. He turned on him, slapping his hand away.

"You don't get it! Our country is at war. Some son of a bitch just pulled the plug on our lives! We have got to do something!" he yelled at him. "How can you stand there so calm?" he asked.

Mitch folded his arms across his chest and waited for the boy to finish.

"Listen," Mitch said watching the boys face as sweat began to bead on his forehead in the heat and slowly trickle down the side of his face.

"I don't hear anything," he yelled.

"Exactly. There are no bombs going off or bullets being fired, or airplanes overhead about to attack. The people that did this, meant to bring our world to a complete halt. Our lives are not in immediate danger. But how we decide to react to this could get us killed. Now think," Mitch finished.

Evan had stopped his pacing and was listening to him. The fear was leaving his face. Mitch watched as the boy considered the situation. Mitch reckoned that he was thinking the same thing that he was.

"What now?" Evan asked.

Mitch smiled and reached out and patted him on the back.

"Now, we have a long ride ahead of us," he said as his fingers worked the latch on the back of the trailer and his sick stomach was hidden well from the boy who needed his strength.

Mitch and Evan unloaded the five horses and tied them to the trailer.

"You need to learn how to do this," Mitch said as he carried the pack equipment out to one of the horses. "If something happens to me, you will need to know how to do it."

Evan watched as Mitch saddled one of the horses and then brought out the pack that fit right over the western saddle. They would be able to carry a lot of gear with the three extra horses.

Mitch instructed Evan on placement of the pack and told him how the weight needed to be distributed evenly and balanced comfortably on the back of the horse in order to prevent sores and tiring the horse.

When they had saddled all of the horses, Mitch began to go over the gear that Aaron had packed and thanked him silently to himself. He always took care of everything he thought.

Mitch removed the large tent and the camp stove to save on space and reduce the weight of the pack. They would make due with tarps and cook with the small portable propane stove. He continued to lighten the loads of the horses that they would be required to carry. Aaron had not anticipated that the trip may take longer than a few weeks and Mitch was trying to save the energy of the horses and simplify things.

After making more space, Mitch went to the truck to determine what they could take and what should stay. He reached into one of the Rubbermaid containers and removed a few garbage bags and set them to the side. He looked at the pictures and removed the majority from their frames and put them into a gallon size freezer bag and set them to the side as well. He emptied one of the containers out on the seat of the truck and tossed it outside on the ground. He knew that they couldn't carry everything with them and decided to make a cache just in case they were ever back this way, or if some of his family came this way, saw the truck, and would look for something left behind. He buried the container twenty feet from the road and marked it with one of his handkerchiefs tied to a stick.

Mitch could see only a few stranded cars on the road ahead of them as they left the truck and trailer behind and started their journey north with the dogs following at their sides. Mitch felt more assured with the dogs along, although he didn't know why.

Their trip had been quiet as they passed people by and continued on. They had passed other people on horseback, bicycles and older jalopies that traveled down the road.

Most of the people just looked up at them and continued walking. A few had asked for a ride or a drink of water, but they ignored them and just kept going.

When they were two miles south of Junction the number of refugees grew as did the stench. The smell of dead bodies and feces hung in the air. Mitch reached into his pack for a bandana and tied it around his face and then handed one over to Evan.

He looked like he had stepped back in time, mounted on his horse wearing his black Stetson and a bandana around his face as they

196

pushed through the crowd. They managed to get across Interstate 10 when four men started moving towards Mitch.

"Hey mister, can you spare a drink of water?" one of the men asked as he proceeded to walk towards him. Evan was riding behind Mitch and saw the man continue towards Mitch. He called the dogs to attention. "Watch him," he said. Allie and Axel ran towards the four men and began to bark aggressively with their feet planted and their tails up.

The man who had spoken, raised his hands and Allie lunged forward and stopped in front of the man rocking forward on her front feet as she barked her warning.

Mitch pulled his pistol and aimed it at the man.

"Back off," he yelled over the dogs.

The four men began to back away as he and Evan pushed the horses into a trot with the dogs watching the strangers as they went. Evan gave a whistle and the dogs turned and ran to catch up with them.

"Good boy, Good girl," he praised them from atop his horse.

Planning their route had proved to be a difficult task as they tried to avoid people as much as possible. Their days, over the past month, had become routine and they rarely spoke now.

They had arrived at Bend Texas and had successfully crossed the Colorado River just before coming upon the snake, which was slowly roasting over the fire.

Mitch opened the tattered map to look at it again, as he did every night. His penlight traced their planned route from Bend to Lometa and then on up the west side of Fort Hood and Waco where they would proceed north towards Greenville. He calculated the distance left to go at around 250 miles. He closed the map and slid it back into his back pocket. He leaned back against his saddle and took a sip of his weak coffee. He reached for the stick stretched across the fire that held their dinner. He checked the meat for doneness and reached for their plates.

He handed one to Evan and watched as the young man tasted the delicacy and then devoured the rest.

"Good stuff," Mitch said.

Something that could have cost him his life was now his nourishment. He thought about the old west and how people had made due with what they had. He imagined that a lot of people would be learning to do the same from here on out.

Mitch and Evan sat looking into the fire after enjoying a fine meal of rattlesnake. The dogs had eaten a few pieces and licked the plates clean before Mitch and Evan washed them and returned them to the packs.

Evan had drifted off to sleep and Axel was lying next to him when the dog raised his head and sniffed the air. Mitch watched the dog push up into a sitting position and continue to listen to something in the woods.

Axel started to growl, bringing Allie to her senses as she awoke and stood up on all fours with her ears tuned to full alert.

She offered a low growl waking Evan. He opened his eyes still half asleep to see the dogs and Mitch watching the woods.

Mitch reached for the bucket of water and tossed it on the fire to extinguish the light. He drew his gun and moved closer to Evan and crouched down.

They could hear rustling in the woods as if someone was running toward them.

"Nooo!" a woman screamed in the distance and then the sound of a thud as something hit the ground.

"No! Please don't! Get off me, let me go!" she screamed.

They heard a man's voice, then struggling and then a loud slap. The woman had stopped screaming, but there was still a sound of rustling in the brush.

Mitch sat back, listening for more signs that the struggle had stopped. "Damn it," he said. "I don't want to do this," he said out loud, wishing that he had not been drawn into this drama.

He moved forward in the direction of the sound of the struggle.

"Mitch!" Evan tried to whisper. "Let me send the dogs."

Mitch gave a nod.

"Axel, Allie, go!" he said as he stretched his arm out and pointed.

The dogs burst forward into the thick brush as Mitch and Evan followed behind them. They listened as the two dogs made their way through the woods.

"Aaaaah!" They heard the man scream as the dogs made contact.

When Mitch and Evan arrived, each of the dogs had an arm and the man was screaming as the dogs tried to pull him in two. The woman was lying on the ground in a twisted position, knocked out cold. It was obvious that the man had raped her.

"Down," Evan commanded the dogs. They released the arms of the man and dropped to the ground, watching him, waiting for him to move.

"Heel," he commanded again and the dogs ran to his side and sat. "Watch him," he said as he walked forward with Mitch.

Mitch raised his pistol to the man's temple. One of the man's arms had been dislocated from the dogs pulling at him. He moaned in pain.

Evan shocked, turned and lost his dinner. His mind couldn't register the scene before him.

Mitch turned to the young woman who looked to be all of twenty five. Her eyes were beginning to flicker open and she began to whimper as she pulled her knees together and tried to turn away from them. "Please don't hurt me!" she screamed trying to stand up, but couldn't.

"Its okay ma'am," Mitch said. "He wont hurt anyone again. Let me help you," he said offering his hand to her.

Reluctantly, she reached for it and he pulled her into a sitting position. The shock of it washed over her as she began to shake, remembering the terror.

"They have my sister," she said. "Please help me."

Mitch glanced over at Evan who looked like he could puke again at any moment. He did not want this hassle. Should have stayed by the fire he thought to himself. He sighed. He was already in it now.

"Where?"

"My house…. A half mile…" she pointed east.

"How many?"

"Four men. They killed my parents and my sister is in there," she said.

"How many guns?"

"They all had a gun."

"Can you shoot?"

"Yes, a little," she snubbed and tried to catch her breath.

"Evan, we can't just leave them," he said. "Are you in?"

"Yes, I guess," he replied.

"I gotta know that you have my back if need be," Mitch said.

Evan looked down at his pistol on his hip and then looked up at the girl. "I got your back," he said.

Chapter 29

Mitch kicked the man. "Get up," he said, shining his penlight at him and pointing his gun.

The man rolled over on his right side as his left arm dangled from its socket. The man turned back over to face Mitch as he pulled his right hand up holding a pistol. Mitch fired and hit the man in the temple. The man would move no more. Mitch heard Evan begin to retch again, wondering if the boy was up to the job at hand.

Mitch walked over to the now dead man, removed the revolver from his hand and checked to see how many bullets were in it. It was loaded and he handed it to the young woman, and held his hand out to help her stand.

She stood on shaky legs and then walked around for a minute before saying, "This way."

They carefully made their way through the woods, listening for any sound that might indicate that the other men had heard the shot and come to rescue the now dead man.

As they slowly crept closer to the house, Evan walked behind Mitch and the young woman. He commanded the dogs to heel and they followed him obediently.

They stopped in the patch of woods thirty feet from the house.

The house was lit by candles in two rooms. It was a one and a half story home with white board siding. It sat on a block foundation about three feet high.

Inside, Mitch could see three men sitting at the dining room table. A pretty young girl that looked to be around eighteen walked in carrying a pitcher. Her face was red and she had been crying. She was clearly afraid to approach the table, but did so and hurriedly put the pitcher down and turned to depart. Before she could, one of the men reached out and pulled her to him roughly and onto his lap. He began to move his body against hers as he held her tightly against his lap. The girl began to struggle, and with her eyes closed tried to pull away from the man.

His arms went around her waist and his body pushed her to a standing position. He kept her body pinned to his as he reached up and turned her head to his, bringing his mouth to hers. Mitch watched the girl bring her right arm up and quickly brought her elbow down and into the man's ribs. The man released her as he tried to catch his breath and she turned around to face him, bringing her knee into his groin. He doubled over and she pushed him away from her and turned to run.

One of the other men stood up from the table just as she was about to dart through the door and slapped her across the face knocking her to the floor.

"Evan, take the front. I'll go in the back," he said. "You watch for anyone outside," he said to the young woman.

"Sharon," she said.

He nodded.

"Heel," Evan commanded the dogs and they fell in line next to him.

In the darkness Mitch quietly made his way towards the back porch with his gun drawn. He wondered where the fourth man was but couldn't wait any longer since the girl was in danger.

Mitch climbed the six steps to the top of the porch and slowly made his way to the door. He tried the knob and it was unlocked. He turned it and carefully pushed it open and stepped into the long hallway that went from the back of the house to the front and joined a large foyer at the front door. Mitch caught sight of Evan leaning against the wall next to the door that led into the dining room, with his gun pointing up to the ceiling and the two dogs behind him.

Evan pointed at the dogs and motioned to Mitch that he wanted to send the dogs first.

Mitch nodded and watched as Evan signaled the dogs to go and they burst forward into the room. They scrambled into the room behind them with their guns drawn. Allie jumped the man nearest the girl and was on top of him as he tried to fight the dog off.

Axel had one of the men pinned in a corner and was daring him to move as his body rocked towards the man barking.

The third man was leaned up against the wall and was fumbling to pull his gun from his pants.

Mitch fired and the bullet ripped into the man's chest. His body slid down the wall leaving a red, sticky, strip of blood.

With his adrenaline flowing, Mitch turned and shot the man standing in the corner, and then shot the man on the floor, scarcely missing Allie who was on top of him.

Mitch heard the gun fire from behind and then felt a burning blow to his back. He stood for a moment and realizing that he had been shot, he fell to the ground.

Evan turned towards the direction of the sound to see the fourth man lying on the ground. Sharon stood frozen in place holding the gun.

The girl on the floor began to crawl away from the activity in the room. When she reached the wall, a puddle began to form beneath her as she lost control of herself.

Sharon caught sight of her sister Maggie on the floor and dropping the gun she ran to her side.

Evan turned his attention to Mitch as he knelt down and felt for a pulse. It was faint, but he was alive. He reached down and pressed his hands on the wound as blood continued to soak his hands.

"Get some towels," he screamed over his shoulder at Sharon.

She stood and ran from the room and a few minutes later, returned with an armful of towels and peroxide. She knelt beside Mitch and poured the peroxide over the wound before pressing down on it with a folded towel.

"Is there a doctor nearby?" Evan asked.

"No. But the veterinarian lives a mile from here," she said.

"How would I get there?"

"Take my road…" she began to give him directons, when Maggie interrupted.

"I'll take him," she said standing.

"Be careful."

Maggie and Evan started towards the door.

"Axel, Allie, stay," he commanded the dogs as he and Maggie went out the door.

Sharon looked over at the dogs who watched their master go into the dark woods from the window.

Mitch began to stir on the floor as she held the towel in place. He moaned as he tried to turn over. She reached for his arm and helped him turn over on his side carefully.

"Take it easy," she said warning him not to move too much.

She reached for another towel and placed it over the exit wound.

"Can you hold this?" she asked him.

"Yes," he said reaching for the towel.

"Evan?" he asked.

"He and Maggie went for help," she said.

Mitch nodded and passed out again as Sharon sat holding pressure on his wound.

An hour had passed and when Mitch awoke again Sharon managed to help him stand and walk to her parent's bedroom where he laid down on the king size bed.

"My God," he said as he drifted out again. Sharon didn't know if his exclamation was because of the luxury of a soft bed or the pain from his wound.

Axel and Allie were still in the dining room and began to growl at the sound of horses hoof beats. Sharon went into the dining room and retrieved one of the handguns that lay on the floor.

She moved to a front window and peeked out the curtain. There were three of them on horseback she thought to herself. Axel thrust his nose into the curtain to peer out the window. He began to wag his tail when he caught sight of Evan.

Sharon placed the gun in the chair and rushed to the door to open it for them. They had found Dr. Ward.

"Come in. He's in here," she said leading the way into the bedroom.

Evan and Sharon stood quietly as Dr. Ward examined Mitch.

"He is a lucky man," Dr. Ward said. "The bullet just grazed his ribs. It passed clean through," he said as he began to sew up the wound.

He reached into his bag and pulled out a bottle of Penicillin and a bottle of Banamine, along with a handful of syringes.

He handed them to Sharon and said, "The directions are on the bottle. I will stop by in a week to check on him," he said. "Come and get me if he develops a fever."

"Thank you Dr. Ward," Sharon said.

The old man nodded and said, "My condolonces on your parents."

"Thank you," she said again.

Maggie had come into the room and waited until Dr. Ward left to speak. "The bodies are starting to stink. What are we going to do with them?" she asked Evan.

"Bury them," he said as he left the room with Mitch sleeping soundly. Maggie followed him out of the house and went into the garage to get two shovels.

At two a. m. Evan and Maggie began to dig a large hole to put the four bodies in. The night air was cool and made the work easier.

Sharon sat with Mitch until the medicine had taken effect before she went outside to help dig the hole for the grave.

"Is your father going to be okay?" Maggie asked Evan breaking the silence as Sharon joined them.

He realized that in the rush of things, they had not been introduced. "My name is Evan and Mitch is not my father," Evan said.

"I'm Maggie," she said continuing to dig.

In the darkness, they dug until the hole was nearly five feet deep and then they went inside to drag the four bodies from the house and onto the back porch.

Evan used his horse to drag one body at a time off the porch and into the hole until finally at the break of dawn, they finished.

"I have to go back to camp and get our gear," he said.

"I'll give you a hand," Maggie said. It was the least the she could do since he had saved her life.

"I'll check on the patient," Sharon said starting for the house.

Evan held the reins of the mare for Maggie to mount and then carefully handed them to her. She had only ridden a few times in her life and she looked unsteady atop the horse. Evan lifted the reins of his horse over its head and turned to place his foot in the stirrup and rested his seat deeply into the saddle, as he urged his mount forward. The horses and humans alike, moved slowly into the woods weary and exhausted.

Chapter 30

Mitch stirred in the bed. Trying to reposition his right leg brought a sharp pain into his back where he had been shot. A sound of agony escaped him as he tried to move back to erase the pain. He grimaced, and remembered the gunfight two nights prior.

The door to the room creaked open slowly as Sharon stepped in. "Hi, you are awake," she said smiling. She walked to his bedside and reached for his arm to help him sit up.

"Move slowly," she said.

"Not a problem," he replied letting her help him into a sitting position.

She pushed two pillows into place for him to lean back on.

"Are you hungry?" she asked.

"I can eat something."

She smiled, happy to finally see him awake. "I will be right back."

Sharon returned a few minutes later and entered the room carrying a tray filled with grits, a biscuit, shelled pecans and coffee.

She placed it in front of him and he smelled the aroma of the coffee before taking a sip. "Thank you," he said. "It has been a long time since I've slept in a bed and had breakfast cooked for me." His thoughts turned to Rachel and their last breakfast together.

"You are welcome," she replied. "I think that you earned it after saving my life the other night."

"How is your sister?" he asked still groggy from the medicine.

"Maggie is doing okay. She's tough."

"Like her sister," he said remembering how Sharon had bounced back quickly after being attacked. He wondered if she was dealing with the trauma or trying to hide from it by staying busy.

Sharon answered him as if reading his mind.

"Mitch, I learned a long time ago that not all people are bad. I just met four of the worst a few days ago. Yes, I would have loved to beat the hell out of the guy. But he's dead now. I am alive. I don't intend to spend another negative thought on it. Life goes on," she said.

He frowned. "How old are you?" he asked.

"Twenty-six. How old are you?" She threw right back at him making a face at him.

He laughed and reached for his side. "I am old enough to be your father young lady," he said.

"You don't look it," she said smiling. "So, is Rachel your wife?"

He looked surprisingly at her, wondering how she knew about Rachel. "She is my fiancé and Evans mother," he said and offered no further information. He didn't want to talk about Rachel to anyone, as if he wanted to keep her all to himself.

"You called out for her while you were sleeping," she explained.

"What did I say?" he asked.

"Just her name," she lied.

"Where is Evan?" he asked changing the subject.

"He and Maggie are out hunting. Our food supply has dwindled down to very little. That was the last of the grits," she said pointing at the bowl.

She reached for the syringes in the drawer next to the bed and pulled the medicine bottles out of her pocket. She lined the bottles up and began to withdraw the contents of the Banamine with the syringe.

"What is that?" he asked.

"Pain medication and antibiotics," she said. "Do you remember Dr. Ward coming by?"

"No."

"Don't worry, I am a nurse."

Mitch watched her as she worked and suddenly they heard a loud roar of a jet fly over the house.

Their eyes met. He had forgotten that they were near Fort Hood, but it was a welcoming sound that meant that his country hadn't been entirely crippled.

"You know that you could see about getting a job at the base," he said.

She nodded thumping the air bubbles out of the syringe.

"Yes, I was planning on traveling to the base just before those thugs attacked us," she said.

"You see," she moved her arm through the air to the hospital equipment that lined the wall. "My father was dying of cancer."

Mitch looked at the pain on her face. "I'm sorry."

"Thank you. At least he's not hurting anymore," she said.

She reached over to his arm and gave him one shot and then the other. "You won't be either in a few minutes," she said. "The Banamine will make you sleepy."

"You are giving me horse medicine?" he asked incredulously.

"It was either that or nothing. We ran out of medicine for my father two weeks ago," she said.

"When Evan returns, tell him that I want to see him," he said feeling the effects of the Banamine starting to work.

"I will. Get some rest," Sharon said lifting the tray and leaving the room.

She carried the tray into the kitchen and put the dishes into the bucket of water to soak and then went out onto the back porch to wait for her sister and Evan to return.

The late October day was overcast and the air was chilly as she sat down in the rocking chair and pulled the thick blanket snugly around her. Her right hand moved to the gun clipped on her side. She rocked in the chair and soon dozed off. She had been asleep for a while when she awoke to the sound of Allie and Axel coming up onto the porch.

Evan and Maggie appeared from the woods and rode into the yard. She didn't see any game tied onto the horses which meant another day of no meat.

"No luck?" she asked worriedly.

Maggie shook her head.

"Not a damn thing," Evan said. "We didn't even see a bird."

He tied his horse and walked up onto the porch and leaned up against the porch rail. He began to pace back and forth. His mind worked better when he was moving. He was considering their options. Their food supply would last three days tops. They could shoot one of the horses, one of the dogs, or he could ride the eighteen miles to Fort Hood. If he rode hard, he could make the trip in two days. But what if he got there and there was no food to be had? Then what? They would be forced to shoot one of the horses.

"Mitch was awake earlier," Sharon said. "He asked to see you."

Evans face brightened for a moment and he turned to go into the house. He walked through the foyer, past the stairs and into the bedroom where Mitch lay sleeping.

Evan walked quietly across the floor and sat down in the chair next to the bed trying not to wake the patient. It was of no use as Mitch spoke quietly, "Hey man."

"Hey. How are you feeling?" Evan asked.

"Rough way to get a nice warm bed," he said smiling weakly.

"Did you see any game?" They knew from their travels that the game was getting scarce.

"No."

Mitch was quiet as he pondered the situation.

"Evan, since Fort Hood has jets coming in and out of there, they must have communications. I think that you should ride to Fort Hood and see if you can get a message to Brian," he said.

Evan nodded his head. "I think you are right," Evan agreed.

He didn't like the thought of leaving him and the two girls alone to fend for themselves. But if he didn't make the trip they would surely starve. The five horses were thin and even if they butchered them, there would scarcely be enough meat to last through the winter. And they would have nothing else.

Mitch drifted off to sleep while Evan sat in the chair. He wondered if his mother had made it to the Rocking B. He knew within him that his twin brother Eli was okay. If something had happened to him he would have felt it. He prayed silently that Dad, Cassie and Simon were okay. He sighed as he stood and left the room.

*   *   *

Mitch sat in the chair on the front porch taking in the view of the pecan orchard that ran along each side of the driveway all the way to the road. The Hollis pecans were the best that he had ever tasted, but after a week of eating them, he could hardly stand the thought of eating another.

His gaze went to Evan and Maggie who were saddling up four of the horses.

He watched Evan lift the saddle up and into place. From the front porch, he saw the mare flinch and stomp her back foot in protest as the saddle came to rest on her back.

Maggie pointed to the cinch and asked him a question that Mitch couldn't hear. Their eyes met and something told Mitch that they had become close since he had become bedridden.

Today was the first day that he had been out of bed, but they had no choice but to leave to find food.

Evan decided that they would all make the trip to Fort Hood and there had been no argument.

Sharon walked out onto the porch carrying a blanket for Mitch and a can of Ensure. She had found two cases in the closet when she was packing her things. She had forgotten that her father wouldn't drink the chocolate flavored liquid and that her mother had put the two cases in the closet.

The temperature was dropping and it looked like the day would be cold for their trip. Evan and Maggie had brought the lawn mower cart out of the garage and worked on it all day to make it suitable for Mitch to travel. Evan had found some tools, a tarp, a few pieces of plywood and some old PVC pipe. With the hammer and a handful of nails, he attached the plywood to the floor of the cart to elongate the bed. He then curved the PVC pipe over the cart and covered it with the tarp. The bright blue cover stood out from the cold winter scenery. He had removed the lawnmower hitch as well and fastened a rope hitch that one of the pack mares would be able to pull comfortably.

Sharon sat with Mitch on the porch as he fought to stay awake. She had waited to give him the shot of pain medication just before they left so that he would sleep for a few hours of the trip.

Evan and Maggie finished hitching the small wagon to the mare who didn't seem to mind it. He nodded to Sharon when it was ready. He and Sharon half carried him the few steps to the wagon and helped him in. When he was comfortable, Sharon went back into the house for one more walk through and returned with a few more blankets for Mitch.

The small wagon train slowly moved down the driveway and to the road. Sharon followed behind the small cart and pulled her horse up to look back at the house that had been her home. She glanced towards the fake graves next to the real ones. They were covered with rocks and had a wooden cross. Evan had suggested the caches and he had even gone so far as to burn her and Maggie's names on the crosses that marked the cache. She hoped that it would prevent thieves from taking their family belongings. She squeezed her horse into a trot as a tear slid down her face.

Chapter 31

Brian hurriedly walked from his tent. He had a meeting with the Commander and he was running late. His assistant Kelly joined him at the corner of his tent and her short legs struggled to keep up with him as he walked quickly to his destination.

The group from the Rocking B had arrived nearly four weeks earlier and already it seemed as if they had been there a year.

Tents had been set up outside the base for the hundreds of refugees that were coming in on a daily basis. They were offered a case of MRE's and a gallon of water per person. Each person was required to sign in and register with the base. If they had their own tent they were sent to join the others that had the same. If they didn't have a tent, they would join the other refugees in the large military tents that had been set up for housing.

Brian looked up to see Eli approaching in full military uniform carrying a backpack and his weapon. Today was the day that he and Chad would be flying out to the front lines. Brian fought the lump in his throat as he watched his grandson move closer to him. Kelly, with her clipboard and pen in hand, stood behind Brian and watched the two men greet each other.

Eli smiled nervously. "I came to say goodbye, Grandpa," he said looking like the soldier that he had become.

Eight weeks of basic training wasn't possible now as the country was at war. He would be getting on the job training, which scared Brian to death. His grandson was leaving the base a young man, but would be something entirely different if he even returned. He reached out to hug him. "You be careful," he said and stepped back from him. He brought his hand to his forehead and saluted his Grandson. Eli snapped to attention and returned the honor.

He pivoted on his heel and walked away.

Brian blinked back the tears and said a quick prayer for him before pulling back the flap of the tent, stepping inside and holding the flap for Kelly to enter.

Commander Williams was leaned over a large map of Texas spread out on the table.

He was talking to another officer and pointing to a location on the map.

"Governor," the commander said.

"Commander," Brian said joining in.

"The Mexican army has taken San Antonio. We are fighting them in Houston, Austin and all the way over to El Paso," Commander Williams pointed with his stick.

He sighed heavily. "The problem is that they have a foothold in every major city in America," he said looking defeated. "This plan has been in the works for years. If we plan to re take the border, it is going to be a major undertaking," he said.

"What's the ETA on additional ground troops?" Brian asked.

"Two days."

"Fighter jets are enroute now. ETA is 0200 hours."

Brian looked at his watch. "That is four hours. Has the drop order been given?" Brian asked.

"Yes," The commander said.

Brian nodded. "I am returning to my ranch. You will be able to reach me by radio. Please keep me informed," he said as he turned to leave the tent with Kelly following behind him.

Brian turned the corner to go to his tent to see Ben standing outside waiting for him.

"Hey Brian," Ben said interrupting his thoughts.

"Hello Ben. Did you see your brother off?" he asked as he continued to walk towards his tent.

"Yes sir," he nodded. "I got my orders to leave for Austin tomorrow."

"What time?"

"0600 hours." he said.

"I will be there to see you off son," Brian said. He couldn't leave and let the boy fly out without someone to see him off.

"That's not necessary sir," Ben said protesting, although grateful for the offer.

Brian reached for his shoulder. "I know. But I want to be there," he said.

"0600," Brian said and turned to go.

Ben stopped walking and watched him leave. He really didn't know what to do now that Chad and Eli had left. He thought sure that they would all three be in the same squad. He walked through the compound and went to the gate that led out to the civilian area.

People were lined up along the fence, as far as the eye could see, waiting to get to the registration table. He walked over to the Information board to read the recent entries of the people that had arrived. He didn't recognize any names. He looked out over the forlorn crowd. His eyes came to rest on a very skinny German shepherd dog in the distance. Too bad he thought. No dogs allowed inside the compound. People that had sacrificed their own food for their pets lives had been forced to give them up once they arrived at the base. He watched as the dog lay down next to a small tarp covered wagon. The dog had a collar on with a tag. Ben decided to walk over to take a look at it, if the dog would allow it. Axel pushed up into a sitting position and began to growl at the stranger approaching his territory. He lifted his nose to the air and began to wag his tail. He recognized Ben.

"Hey fella," Ben said to Axel holding his hand out for the dog to smell him. He reached out and read the name on the tag.

"AXEL. I belong to: Reed K-9 Center."

"What the hell?" Ben exclaimed. He looked into the wagon to see if there was anyone in it but it was empty. There was no one around. "How did you get here boy?" he asked the dog. He sat down on the cart and pulled out a stick of beef jerky and held it out to Axel.

The dog nearly took his hand off as he grabbed the meat hungrily and ate it.

Allie appeared from nowhere and began to bark aggressively at the stranger that had invaded her space. Ben decided that it would be smarter to move away from the wagon and wait for the owners to return. He backed up and then turned to go to the registration gate but instead collided into Evan. Ben pushed away from him and stood back looking at him. He looked like a skeleton with unkept hair and a ragged beard. His clothes were dirty and he smelled to high heaven. And then he recognized him.

"Looking for me?" Evan asked tiredly with little expression, as he held his box of MRE's and balanced a gallon of water on top. He shifted the weight to one arm.

Ben stood shocked to see him. "A different version but yes," he said. He embraced his friend and stepped back.

"Man, am I glad to see you?" Ben said.

"Me too, man."

Evan walked over to the cart. He sat the box of food and jug of water down and leaned against the edge of the plywood. His energy was depleted and could hardly stand.

"You don't mind if I eat do you?" he asked tearing open the box. He pulled out the beef stew, opened the package and began to eat it cold.

"Not at all," Ben said reaching for the jug of water to open for his friend.

"What are you doing here?" Evan asked.

"I came with your Grandfather and brother," he replied. "You haven't seen them?"

"No. We didn't even know that you were here," he said opening another MRE.

"Who is we?" he asked.

"Mitch Carlson, Sharon and Maggie Roberts. Mitch is in the hospital ward, with a gunshot wound. Where is Grandpa now?" Evan asked.

"Come on, I will take you to him."

Evan finished the cold meal and turned up the jug of water and drank a fourth of it to wash down his food.

They stood to leave. "Axel, Allie, stay," he said over his shoulder.

They approached the gate to enter the compound and a soldier stepped in front of them.

"No clearance, no entrance," the soldier stated firmly.

Ben saluted and reached down for his I.D. that hung from his neck. "This is Evan Reed, grandson of Governor Russell. If you would like to explain to the governor why you didn't let him pass, you be my guest."

The soldier considered for a moment the implications and stepped aside. Evan followed Ben throughout the compound until they arrived at the tent of Governor Russell.

Ben knocked on the two by four that stood next to the flap.

"Governor Russell, its Ben. There is someone here to see you," he said.

"Enter."

Ben pulled the flap back for Evan to step inside.

Brian had his back to him and was tucking in his shirt.

"Grandpa," Evan said as his body began to sway. He was exhausted and couldn't believe that he was standing before his grandfather.

Brian frowned. Eli just boarded for Houston.
"Did your flight get delayed?" he asked as he turned to see Evan standing before him. "Oh, my God, get him a chair" he said too late to Ben as Evan toppled to the ground.

Ben radioed for the medics and Brian sat down on the ground holding his grandson, remembering when he was a child. His skin was clammy and pale.

The medics arrived and transported him into the hospital. Brian spoke to one of the doctors and asked if Mitch could be moved next to his grandson and he agreed although miffed at the extra work it would take.

Sharon approached Brian and held her hand out.

"I am Sharon Roberts. Your grandson saved my life. My sister and I rode in with him and Mitch," she said holding her army issued nurses uniform.

"We are waiting for a doctor. And they are about to move Mitch over next to Evan," Brian said. "I cannot believe that they made it all the way from the border, with a war raging."

"Love is a great motivator," Sharon said looking disappointed as the medics brought Mitch to rest next to Evan.

"Thank you for helping take care of our guys," Brian said.

"I think that you have it backwards," she smiled as she went to meet her sister down the aisle. Brian watched as Sharon spoke to her sister and then Maggie shoved her armful of items into her sister. With a terror stricken face she rushed to Evan's bedside.

"What happened? Evan? Can you hear me?" she said pitifully. She reached for his hand and leaned towards his face.

"Hey," he smiled at the girl.

Brian left the two alone and walked over to Mitch.

He had an I.V. hooked up and he was resting but not asleep.

"Rachel?" he asked.

"She is safe at the Rocking B. She is waiting for you, frantically, I might add," Brian said smiling. "I will radio them and tell them that you and Evan are okay. If the doctor releases you, we will leave for the ranch right away," he said reaching for Mitch's hand, shaking it before standing to leave. He could hardly wait to get back to his tent and radio Rachel.

"Kelly, contact the ranch for me, would you?" he asked happily as he returned to his tent.

She looked at him surprised at his light mood. "Yes sir." He listened as she placed the call.

"BLR 227 station two to station one over." There was no answer.

She repeated the call, "BLR 227 station two to station one over."

Still no answer. She looked to Brian for further instructions.

"Keep trying. Send for me when you get through," he said stepping through the tent flap.

What has happened? He had kept radio contact with the ranch the past month that he had been gone. It wasn't likely that the radios had gone out. Unless.... the ranch had been compromised.

He shook the thought from his head. After all, he had to see a man about a dog.

221

Chapter 32

Life on the Rocking B ranch had over the past few weeks become routine. The planning and practice drills had paid off. Everyone knew their job and their schedule which made things easier as they adjusted to a new way of doing things. The three strike rule was in place. Fortunately, no one had tried to buck the system and things ran smoothly from day to day.

There had been a few incidents where people were turned away at the perimeter and they tried to fight their way in, but had been unsuccessful. Word soon got around that the Rocking B was not an easy target and things returned to business as usual.

Aaron and Pedro had joined the community and assumed duties which helped with the replacement of the men that had left for Fort Hood. Pedro was reluctant to befriend anyone and pretty much stayed to himself or with Aaron.

Rachel awoke in stall number four of barn two, that she shared with two other women. She lifted her arm to look at her old wind up watch to see that she had about thirty minutes before she left for

Arkansas. Her first thought each morning was either of Mitch or her family. She sat up on the cot and looked at her things packed and ready to go, by the stall door. She had waited at the Rocking B in hopes that Evan and Mitch would make it safely, but they hadn't yet. There were days when she just couldn't bear the thought that they just might be dead. Today was one of those days. She sat forward and felt sick to her stomach again and struggled to stand to run to the wash stall in case she vomited. She made it just in time as the heaves hit her.

After she finished, she reached for the hose that hung from the ceiling and washed away the mess that she had made. She then sprayed the water into her hand and rinsed her mouth out before she reached for the bottle of bleach and sprayed the area on the floor. She returned to her room and dressed. She wore her camo and her pistol was clipped under her left arm, her hair was in a pony tail. She tied her boots, reached for her coat, and pulled her pack into position on her back before she stepped out of stall four, slid the door shut and fastened the lock.

She made her way down the aisle to see that Charlotte Redden was about to begin school in stall one.

"Good Morning Charlotte," she said waving.

"Good Morning Rachel," she replied. "I hope you feel better. Have a safe trip home." She had watched Rachel run to the wash room and heard her retching again.

"Thank you," she said as she continued towards the exit.

Ten weeks. She had been here ten weeks. She stopped in her tracks and brought her hands to her face, her eyes wide. She looked around her suddenly feeling stupid as she hurried her steps to the house to find Lisa, who was in the kitchen washing dishes. Rachel dropped her pack at the door and hurried in to stand shoulder to shoulder with her. Rachel turned her head and looked at her.

"What's the matter honey?" Lisa asked worriedly looking at the pale face that stared back at her.

"I need a pregnancy test," she said, her eyes welling up.

Lisa reached for the dishrag and dried her hands before reaching out to pull the girl into an embrace. She reached for her hand and led her into the pantry. Lisa walked to the end of the room and pulled the step stool over to the corner and climbed up three steps to the top of the shelf for a Rubbermaid container that held twenty five pregnancy tests.

She climbed back down and handed the box to Rachel who turned and went across the hall and into the bathroom. Lisa walked over to the clipboard, made the correction on the inventory sheet and went out into the hallway to wait. She heard the toilet flush and a few minutes later Rachel opened the door to emerge from the room.

Rachel nodded her head and her lip began to tremble. She was happy but yet terrified. She knew that now was not a good time to be having a baby. She had three C- sections with the births of her other children. She knew the odds of her having the baby naturally were against her. They might both die. Mitch's baby... Her hand instinctively went to her abdomen.

"Everything will be okay. Don't worry, this is God's bright shiny gift in a dark desolate time," Lisa said, suspecting her very thoughts.

Rachel smiled half heartedly and walked out to the patio to sit down. Lisa followed her and sat down as well looking at her worried goddaughter.

"Are you still going to make the trip?" Lisa asked.

"This changes everything," Rachel replied, beginning to wonder if she should risk the trip now. She shook her head. "I don't think so," she said. She inhaled deeply and breathed out a sigh of relief. "Do you think that I can get my old job back?" she asked.

Lisa laughed. "Are you kidding me? Get in there," she ordered her happily.

Rachel walked past Lisa and into the radio room to relieve Tim of his duties. Lisa watched Tim smile, stand and leave the room as Rachel sat down and read the notations that Tim had made on the call log.

She began by adjusting the controls to try and reach her family in Arkansas. She had yet to make contact, which worried her even more, since they did have a radio there.

Marie arrived to take her seat next to her to begin her day as well. For the next few hours the two would turn knobs and make the call signals to try to reach the outside world.

Rachel sat in front of the radio and turned the controls but to no avail. "It's dead." She looked over at Marie who was shaking her head.

"Mine too," she said.

Rachel frowned. It didn't make sense. The radios ran on different batteries and surely they both couldn't have quit at the same time, she thought to herself.

"I'll go find Marcus," Rachel said standing and pushing her chair back. Marcus was the tech guy for the group, as well as one of the gardeners.

She walked through the kitchen and out onto the patio. The bright sun struck her face and she had to adjust her eyes after sitting in front of the radio in the dimly lit room for four hours.

She walked into the office of Barn one to look at the work schedule for the day to see where she might find him. She scanned the paper to see that he was working in Garden two and then she heard it, gunfire in the distance. She stood listening for a few minutes as the sound grew louder. She ran from the barn to the backside of the house where the antenna wires entered the house to connect with the radios. The wires had been cut. She turned and ran towards the barns. "Breach! We've been breached!" she screamed as she ran. People began to scramble to their assigned areas as Rachel ran into Barn two to help Charlotte gather the children. The phrase "We have been breached," echoed throughout the compound as people ran.

Rachel's heart was racing with fear, when she stopped at the stall. She took a breath to compose herself and heard Charlotte inside talking to the young ones.

"Alright children, do you remember the game that we played last week?" she asked forcing a cheerful face.

"Yes!" one of the little boys yelled out.

"Everyone stand, retrieve your packs, get in line and follow me," she said.

Rachel slid the stall door open and met eyes with Charlotte. Their eyes said everything they felt but couldn't say out loud in front of the children. "Good luck. God help us. I'm scared. Can I do this?"

Rachel watched as the fourteen children filed out behind Charlotte holding hands. The youngest child of six was the closest to Charlotte and the oldest at the end of the line was a girl of thirteen.

They began to run slowly towards the house with Rachel following with her pistol drawn covering the small group as they made their way towards the house amidst the organized chaos that was going on around them. The gunfire was getting heavier and was moving closer to them as they made it to the back door and rushed in while

Lisa held it open for them. Marie was standing in the communications room and was holding the door open that had lay hidden behind the bookcase for fifteen years. Charlotte and the line of children filed into the room. Rachel heard Charlotte say, "Good job children! Now the next game is going to be?" she inquired of them, and again the young boy answered. "The quiet game!" he whispered as loudly as possible.

"That's right," Charlotte said quietly before bringing her finger to her mouth, motioning for the game to begin.

Lisa stood at the door scanning the compound for Michelle and three other mothers to arrive with their younger children, and seven of the elderly group. She caught sight of them as they rounded the corner of barn one. The gunfire was rapidly moving closer and Lisa began to wave them forward to hurry. The small group filed through the doorway and joined the waiting children, in the shelter room.

Lisa shut the front door, locked it and walked over to the door to the pantry and entered the room. She stood and reached up to the top shelf for the paint ball gun and hurriedly made her way to the back door of the house. She stepped out to fire the paint ball gun at three of the trees, marking their trunks with the yellow colored paint, leaving a message to the others that the children and elders had made it safely into the shelter.

She didn't see the Mexican gunman step out from behind a tree and fire his gun before it was too late. She felt the stinging bullet hit her midsection and knock her over. When she fell to the ground the last thing that the gunman saw before he died was Rachel, blood spattered and wide eyed, standing ready with her pistol.

"Lisa!" she screamed her name and fell to her knees next her body.

"You are going to be okay," she lied to her surrogate mother. She reached down and slid her arms under hers and began to drag her towards the hidden basement room. Marie rushed out to help lift Lisa up and the two women carried Lisa into the safety of the room.

There were ten adult size backpacks that held three days of food, a headlamp, and survival items.

Rachel heard the Velcro rip free as she snatched the first aid kit from the side of one of the backpacks. She tossed it at Marie with one hand and with the other hand, pressed on the gushing wound that Lisa had sustained.

226

"She's gone honey," Marie said reaching for Rachel. "We must go, now."

Rachel looked down at Lisa to see her eyes fixed and tried to find a pulse. Horrified, she backed away from her, unable to speak.

Marie gently pushed Rachel towards the hole in the floor and watched her descend the ladder into the tunnel.

The door that was hidden behind the bookcase was a metal safe door and had been installed years earlier. In the floor of the hidden room was the metal trap door that led into a three hundred foot tunnel that ended in another safe room with two blast doors as well. From there, they could follow the escape tunnel to reach the outside world.

Marie was in charge of sealing the entrance. She pulled the bookcase door closed and then swung the heavy metal blast door closed and locked it. Then, when Rachel was free of the hole, she dropped the first backpack down to her. She watched and waited for Rachel to move it out of the way. After the last of the backpacks were lowered Marie stepped into the hole, pulled the heavy metal hatch door closed and descended the ladder in the dark. When she reached the last rung of the ladder, she heard a roar above her head and the ground shook. She hurriedly joined the group in the tunnel as they made their way along with the headlamps lighting their way to safety.

Chapter 33

Mitch awoke in the hospital bed. He was glad to be able to sit up in the bed unassisted. It had been three days since he had been brought to Fort Hood. He was able to move about with less pain every day and he was beginning to get anxious to be on his way.

Evan had been released after receiving fluids and was now staying outside with the cart and the animals. He and Maggie had become close and she hardly let him out of her sight unless she was working in the hospital.

Mitch sitting in the bed, watched Sharon down the aisle as she went to each patient and gave them their meds. She was a pretty girl with reddish brown hair and blue eyes. Finally, she approached him smiling.

"Good Morning," she said happily.

"Good Morning."

"I am not going to even ask you how you are feeling. I can see that you are ready to get out of here," she said, handing him his paper cup of pills and a glass of water.

"Yes I am," he said.

"Breakfast trays will be out soon," she said turning to move on to the next patient, even though she wanted to stay and talk to Mitch.

He leaned his legs off the bed to sit on the side and slowly moved to reach below the bed for his clothes. His ribs were taped so his movement was limited but he managed to dress himself without much pain. He looked down at his cowboy boots and was wondering if he was up to leaning over to put his socks on when Sharon reappeared with his breakfast tray, casting him a look.

"What are you doing?" she asked sternly.

"Will you help me get my boots on?" he asked.

"No! I will not. The doctor hasn't released you yet," she said, not ready to see him leave.

"Sharon, this bed is for someone who needs it. I don't. Now either help me get my boots on, or I will walk out of here barefooted," he said stubbornly.

She sighed and then she knelt down in front of him. She lifted his foot and slipped his sock on gently before looking up at him.

His eyes met hers. "Thank you," he said fondly.

"You are welcome," she said, as she finished helping him get his boots on. She leaned up to bring her face close to his and kissed him on the lips and waited for a response but there was none.

Disappointed, she looked into his eyes and said, "I hope she's worth it."

He reached his hand up to touch her cheek. "She is," he said, not wanting to hurt the girl. She reached for his hand and squeezed it before standing up to leave.

"You better eat before you go. Take advantage of a free meal while you can," she said.

He watched her go on to the next patient and cheerfully bring them their trays. He turned back to his and devoured the scrambled eggs, bacon and toast and then drank the orange juice. He reached for the packets of powdered creamer and sugar and slipped them into his shirt pocket, before sipping on his black coffee.

It was not yet daylight as he looked down the aisle to see some of the other patients still sleeping as he swung his legs off the bed to stand to leave the hospital ward. The base would be awakening soon and he guessed that Brian would be up if not already working.

A young soldier was approaching.

"Where would I find Governor Russell?" he asked.

"Straight ahead and turn left," the soldier instructed.

Mitch thanked him and proceeded to see the Governor.

He knocked on the board and he heard him say, "Enter."

He was sitting at his small table having breakfast, with Axel and Allie lying next to him. The dogs rose to greet Mitch with their tails wagging. He reached to pet the dogs before straightening up in pain holding his mid section.

"Good Morning Mitch. Have a seat. Coffee?" he asked.

Mitch carefully sat down and nodded.

"They release you?"

"No. I left."

"I was coming to see you this morning. Look, I am arranging for helicopter transport to the Rocking B as soon as possible. I am trying for first thing in the morning. Rachel will be very happy to see you and Evan," he said smiling.

Mitch nodded, considering his offer.

"Brian, the only possessions that I own now are my five horses and what they carry in their packs. I wish that I could just hop on that chopper and fly on over to the Rocking B, but I have got to stay with my horses," he said, disappointment lingering in his voice.

Brian handed him a cup of coffee and sat down across from him before taking a sip of his own.

"I understand. Will you sell me the horses?"

Mitch looked at him disbelievingly. He knew that Brian didn't have any use for the horses and he was offering to do him a huge favor.

"Brian, I can't in good conscience …."

"Now hear me out," Brian interrupted him.

"Rachel couldn't be my daughter any more than if I had fathered her myself. I love that girl. She loves you. I would do anything to see that you two are reunited. Name your price," he said stubbornly without dropping his eyes.

Mitch smiled. "Brian, you know that the dollar has collapsed. Money is no good now. The horses are as valuable as gold these days," he said.

"Yes. I know that. Will you take twenty ounces?" Brian offered him.

Mitch couldn't believe him. Twenty ounces of gold was about the equivalent of twenty thousand dollars before the war had started. He sat quietly and sipped his coffee as he pondered the issue. If he stayed with the horses, it would take him at least a month to get to the Rocking B. With winter setting in, the horses might not make it at all. If he accepted the offer, he could be holding Rachel in his arms tomorrow. Slowly, he began to nod his head in agreement.

"Sold," he said before reaching his hand across the table to shake hands with Brian.

"Good deal," Brian said reaching for a pen and paper. He quickly scribbled an IOU to Mitch in the amount of twenty ounces of gold, signed it and handed it to him.

"I will give you the gold when we arrive at the Rocking B. I don't exactly carry that much on me."

"That will be fine." Mitch knew that he was good for it.

"Thank you. I assume that Evan is flying back with us?" Mitch asked.

"Yes. So are Maggie and Sharon. Evan didn't want to leave Maggie and she refused to leave her sister. Since Sharon is a nurse, she will be an asset to the ranch," he said.

"I'm glad to hear it. They are good kids."

Brian sipped his coffee and wondered if he should tell Mitch that his sister and brother were dead.

"Mitch, there is something else. Aaron arrived at the ranch just before I left. He had been shot and was stable when I left," he said.

"Were Celia and William with him?" he asked worriedly.

"No. Just his cousin Pedro."

"I see. Thank you for telling me."

Brian was glad that he didn't ask him directly about his family. Aaron or Rachel should be there to tell him, he thought to himself.

Mitch swallowed the last of his coffee and stood to leave.

"I will see you later. I have a lot to do before we take off."

"Mitch, I am glad that you agreed to sell me the horses."

"It was a hard bargain. Thanks Brian," he said smiling as he pulled the flap back and stepped out of the tent. It was hard to believe that he might actually see Rachel by tomorrow. After all of this time, it seemed like an impossible dream. Allie whined and darted through the flap to fall into line at his side. As he walked, the bitch stayed with him. There were makeshift tents set up and people camping as far as the eye could see. He looked into the distance, until finally he saw the garden cart covered with the blue tarp and the five horses hobbled nearby.

Evan and Maggie were sitting outside next to a fire cooking something when he approached.

Evan had shaved, cut his hair and was dressed in army camouflage. He looked thin, but a whole lot better than the previous week with some color doting his cheeks.

He stood when he caught sight of Mitch and ran to embrace him.

"Did you hear? We are going home," Evan smiled.

"Yes, I did," he replied. "Hello Maggie. How are you?"

"Better," she said smiling and then cast her eyes toward Evan.

"Good," Mitch replied. The girl didn't spare any words, he thought to himself.

He walked past them to the horses. They looked better too and Evan had done a good job taking care of them the past couple of weeks. He reached for the halter of his horse and pulled her head to him. She nickered a greeting and pulled away to drop her head to resume grazing on the dry, frozen grass stubs.

He ran his hand over her back and rump. She was thin but looked to be regaining some weight. He reached for her rear hoof and checked to see that it was clean and then stood and patted her before turning back to Evan, who had walked over to the horses with him.

"Thanks son, for taking care of them for me."

"Sure. What will happen to them, when we leave?" he asked, instinctively reaching out to touch the horse. "Your grandfather has bought them. I don't know what he plans to do with them."

Mitch turned to the cart and reached in to pull his backpack out. He opened it up to see that it had been left untouched and everything was there. He removed his .38 special, checked to see that it was loaded, returned it to the others in his pack and zipped it back up. His long guns were still wrapped in a blanket and his sleeping bag placed in a corner of the cart.

"If you don't mind, I thought I'd bunk here tonight," he said pointing to the area next to the cart.

"Are you kidding? You will sleep in the cart. Mom will beat me if she finds out that I let you sleep on the ground with you being injured," he said grinning.

"We just wont tell her then, now will we?" smiling, he waved and turned to go, with Allie falling in line.

*   *   *

Brian peered through the binoculars scanning the distance towards the Rocking B, trying to determine if the plume of smoke was near the ranch or the ranch itself. He didn't mention to the others that they had lost radio contact with the ranch but now seeing smoke, he was worried.

Two hours earlier he had met with the pilot and co pilot and discussed procedures and orders. They were merely civilian passengers hitching a ride and were to stay clear of any enemy fire and allow the soldiers to do their jobs. They had looked at the diagrams of the maps and decided that it would be best to bypass the ranch and hike back should it be determined that the area had been compromised.

The roar of the two Blackhawk helicopters made it difficult to carry on a conversation, so the small group remained quiet while Brian would occasionally converse with the pilot through the headset that he was wearing.

Mitch sat, with Allie and Axel at his feet, next to Sharon looking out the window. Evan and Maggie sat behind them, with their gear surrounding them.

As the helicopters approached the ranch and slowed, Brian saw that the smoke was indeed coming from the Rocking B. He raised the binoculars again to see that it was barn number three that was on fire. Bodies littered the compound and he didn't see anyone from his ranch moving about. He scanned from barn number three to the others and then to the house and smiled with relief, when he saw the yellow paint dotting the trees. Yes, they had made it into the shelter. He glanced at the pilot, who didn't return the look but instead spoke into his mouthpiece attached to his headset, to headquarters.

"Roger that. Location has been compromised. Proceeding to alternate destination," the pilot said.

234

Brian knew that the alternate location was a mile north of the ranch. The first helicopter carrying the passengers would land and unload. The troops from the second helicopter would unload and move in on the Ranch to secure it before Brian and the others would be allowed to return. Two soldiers would remain with the civilians until the all clear was given.

Mitch sat quietly with the others in the back and surveyed the bodies littering the ground as the helicopter continued past. He tried to scan each body to determine that Rachel wasn't among them, but they were moving too fast and he couldn't see clearly enough. He felt the helicopter touch down and make contact with the ground. He and the others quickly scrambled to gather their gear and exit the chopper. They ran with their gear, slowly toward the tree line of safety. Allie and Axel began to bark in the excitement, ready to work. Their small group watched as the two helicopters lifted off and turned south towards the ranch.

Brian turned to the others.

"I believe that some of the members made it into the shelter," he said looking at Evan and Mitch. Evan smiled nervously before answering.

"I saw the yellow paint." He didn't mention the dead man lying next to the painted signal.

"Let's go," Brian said as he turned to go home.

"Sir, our orders are to remain here until the primary location is secure," the young soldier said, stepping in front of Brian.

"Son, by the time we get there, it will be. Now step aside or kill me, because I'm going home." Brian waited for the young man to decide before he brushed past him with the others following.

"Brian," Mitch called out before hastening his steps and catching up to him.

He fell into line with him before asking. "Where are we going?"

"To the underground shelter near the main house," he replied.

The two soldiers moved into position, with one at the front of the line, the other at the end of the line as they escorted the small group through the woods.

Chapter 34

Rachel and Marie were at the back of the line as they finally made it to the safety of the dimly lit room. The musty underground shelter was barely big enough to contain the thirty one women, children and elders. Some of the children were crying and asking for their mothers as Charlotte and Michelle tried to comfort them.

Two of the walls were lined with shelves of food, water and medical supplies. The small toilet was located in the tunnel, which offered some privacy. The other two walls held six beds that folded up to make more room as needed. In the corner of the room was a doorway to the ladder that led to the exit shaft.

Rachel approached Michelle and put her arm around her shoulders. She had not taken the news of her mother's death well and began to cry again when she felt Rachel near.

Rachel knew that she had to keep it together, as she fought the urge to fall apart. She would cry later, if she lived.

"Quiet," Rachel said loudly to the group, getting their attention.

She took a deep breath, turned back to Michelle and wiped a tear from her face affectionately. The young woman had refused to take part in the preparations over the years, unable to believe that her world would ever be altered.

"I am going back to the ranch," she said.

"No Rachel. Please don't go," Michelle begged her, terrified, as she clutched her arm.

"Michelle, I will be very careful, I promise," she said softly. "Now you take care of the little ones while I'm gone okay?" she said trying to help her focus on something else. She walked to the first aid box on the far shelf and reached into it, to retrieve an envelope.

"If I don't return within two hours, open this," she said waving the envelope and handing it to Marie.

She hurriedly reached for her rifle strap and lifted the gun up over her head and into place on her back. She opened her backpack flap, withdrew a box of shells and slipped them into her pocket, and then reached for a small set of binoculars that easily fit into her other pants pocket. She made her way to the ladder and climbed the twelve rungs until she reached the top. The cold metal handle of the hatch door turned stiffly and then clicked loose. She closed her eyes and said a quick prayer before drawing her pistol in readiness as she pushed the heavy hatch door open to the daylight on the other side. She blinked her eyes to adjust them to the brightness and looked around her before climbing out and then she quietly pulled the door to her and down, to close and lock it back securely.

With her heart pounding, she lifted the gun up and back over her head to rest in the crook of her arm as she walked into the woods that led in the direction of the ranch. The winter cold hung in the air as the afternoon sun shined brightly and with no clouds in sight. On another day in time she could have seen herself hiking with the children and the dogs, but not today as she was in another world now.

As she approached the outskirts of the ranch, she heard sporadic gunfire, but nothing like before. She made it to the edge of the woods and pulled her binoculars out. She lay down on her stomach and looked through them into the distance. She scanned the compound before coming to a small group of Mexican men that held guns pointed at some of the ranch members, among them were Marcus, John, and Dustin. She could hear the blood pounding in her ears as she watched for a moment before scanning to the left to come to rest on Pedro

Sanchez whose rifle was strapped on his back. He walked among the invaders saying something to them, before turning back to the captured men and raising his pistol and shooting Marcus. She gasped as she watched Marcus body fall to the ground, unable to process what had happened. Pedro pointed his pistol at Dustin, waving it to motion for two of the invaders to take him away.

Then, in the distance behind her, she heard the approaching sound of helicopters. She watched the armed men scatter when one of the helicopters locked on its target and dropped down as the gunner on the helicopter opened fire.

John bravely turned on his unknown captor and struggled with the man amid the attack from above. Rachel watched him skillfully overtake the man and snap his neck before successfully winning the dead mans weapon and running towards barn one.

Suddenly, she heard the sound of a twig snap behind her and, before she could turn a man came down on top of her with his hand over her mouth. She struggled, before hearing a whispered "It's Aaron. Shhhh."

She closed her eyes tightly, as the thoughts began to race through her head. Is Aaron in on this? Did he help take over the ranch? Why? How did he know that I was here?

He rolled off her and pointed behind them as they slid their bodies along the earth and out of sight of the gunmen. They crawled a safe distance, stood and began to carefully sneak away from the ranch.

"Are you alright?" Aaron asked.

She nodded her head warily watching him, wondering if she should run or face him. He reached out for her arm and she jerked it away, as she swiftly turned and pulled her pistol to bring it within inches of his face.

"What is going on?" she asked him angrily, feeling betrayed.

"Rachel, if anything happens to me, you must know something. Celia and William are alive. They are being held captive on the Circle C. Pedro and his men took the ranch and he forced me to get him in here. He plans to kill Brian and take over his ranch. Then, he will have Texas all for himself," he finished quickly.

She listened to him horrified, still holding the gun locked on his face.

"But Brian isn't here. I don't understand…" she began.

"One of the helicopters just flew by and dropped him north of the ranch," he explained. "Pedro's contact told him that Brian was returning today. My guess is that he is on his way here, now on foot. We cannot let him get to the ranch until it is safe. Rachel, we are on the same team here," he said nervously holding his breath.

She looked at him weighing what he had told her, wondering if she should believe him. Most likely, if Brian had seen that the ranch was under siege he would have flown past it and landed. That much made sense. And with the radio knocked out, he couldn't communicate that he was returning home today. She wanted to believe him, after all, Mitch did. But things were different now. She decided to convince Aaron that she believed his story, at least until she had reason not to.

"Okay," she said. "Let's go see if we can find him," she said lowering the gun and returning it to its holster.

"First, let me change my pants," he said sarcastically, as he held his arm up to point the way, deliberately avoiding touching her.

Rachel led the way through the woods and towards the area that she thought the helicopters may have landed before taking off, again. Brian would have avoided the shelters exit shaft, so he must have asked the pilot to land north of it, since the woods were thick around it.

As she quietly scanned the brush in front of her, she heard movement and crunching of brush in the distance.

She stopped and held her hand up, motioning for Aaron to stop as she dropped to one knee. She brought her weapon up and waited for the sound in the woods to make its presence known.

Allie burst through the brush with Axel following behind her. The two dogs stopped when they saw her. At first, Allie began to growl before she recognized her and then her tail began to wag. She and Axel began to bark excitedly and dance around her, happy to see their long lost master.

Disbelievingly, she looked at the dogs. She lowered her gun and fell back on her heels as she waited, wondering where they had come from. She was afraid to hope that it meant what she thought it meant... that possibly... Before she could finish the thought the lead soldier stepped into view with his gun drawn.

"Face down on the ground!" he yelled.

Startled, she dropped her weapon, raised her hands and lunged towards the ground, as Aaron followed suit. She could hear movement in the brush, and then Brian burst into view.

"Stand down soldier!" He commanded as he ran forward to help lift Rachel up off the ground. He held her for a moment before asking, "Are you alright?"

She nodded her head as the tears began to flow, relieved to see him but yet not wanting to tell him about Lisa.

"Brian… Brian….I'm sorry…. I couldn't save her. I tried to…" the words gushed out as she cried.

"Lisa? Lisa?" he shook her for the answer and she nodded. "Oh my god nooo…" he said, holding onto Rachel tightly as the grief washed over him. She held the only real father that she had ever known as his world crumbled at the loss of the love of his life.

"The others?" he managed to whisper before pulling her to arms length.

She stepped back to look at him sadly. "Michelle and the children are in the shelter. Dustin is at the ranch. I saw him just before the helicopters descended," she said.

She felt a hand on her waist and turned around to see Mitch standing before her. Her mouth dropped open just in time for him to cover it with his as he kissed her.

She knew that kiss. She brought her hands to his face and leaned back, unable to believe that she was looking at him for real. She leaned forward and kissed him again, hungrily, as if to make up for the lost days. Then, slowly she pulled away and smiled. Out of the corner of her eye, she caught sight of Evan standing with two women, watching the glorious reunion. She held her arm out unable to take her eyes off Mitch, and Evan came into their embrace.

She smiled at her son, relieved to see him. She couldn't believe that at last the wait was over.

"Thank you for bringing my son home," she said lovingly to Mitch, reaching up to touch his face as if to prove that he was real and standing before her. Suddenly, remembering that they were not alone, she released her grasp.

She turned to see that Brian was standing with Aaron who had his hand on his shoulder. It looked as if he had told Brian about Pedro. Rachel holding tight to Mitch's hand, pulled him over to Brian and Aaron as the others gathered around.

"This reunion is going to have to wait. We must get to the ranch," Brian said.

"Brian, let us handle this. Please go to the shelter and we will come and get you when it is safe," Aaron pleaded. "You are one of a few of the government officials that are left alive. We need to keep you that way," he said.

"Not a chance in hell," he said angrily before turning to Rachel.

"Take Sharon and Maggie to the shelter. Stay there with them until the ranch is secure," he said.

"Brian…" she began to protest, but he quickly shut her down.

"Do it," he said, suddenly looking like a stranger, as she watched the anger on his face.

She nodded. "Be safe," was all that she could manage to say. She turned to Mitch and kissed him, then reached for Evan and hugged him to her with a pleading, fearful look as the men made their walk towards the ranch to take back what was theirs. She stood with the two women watching the men, slowly one after the other, disappear into the woods.

When they were out of sight, Rachel turned to face Sharon and Maggie. They were both beautiful young women she observed.

"I'm Rachel," she introduced herself and smiled tiredly.

"I'm Sharon, and this is my sister Maggie," she replied looking at the woman that Mitch was so crazy about. Her first impression of her was that she was independent and strong but now she seemed hopelessly lost, struggling to hold on to hope. Sharon wanted to dislike her but instead found that she felt sorry for the woman who had just been reunited with the man she loved and her son, only to see them leave, possibly never to return.

"This way," Rachel said, reaching for her weapon and heading towards the shelter hatch that lay hidden in the distance.

When they reached it, Rachel using the butt of her gun, knocked on the hatch door three times, waited and knocked on it again. They heard a click and slowly the hatch began to open as Marie faced them fearfully. The relief covered her face when she caught sight of Rachel.

"We are coming in," Rachel said and waited for Marie to make her way back down the ladder before turning to Sharon and Maggie.

"Are there any guns in your packs?" she asked.

"No," Sharon and Maggie answered in unison, nervously.

"Toss you packs in first," she said over her shoulder before leaning into the shaft and announcing, "Clear the hatch."

"After you…" she said as she watched first Maggie drop her pack into the hole, sit down on the hatch opening, turn and slowly descend the ladder, and then Sharon.

When it was clear, she went into the little hole and carefully closed the hatch before joining them in the shelter.

When she got to the bottom she turned to face the small group who were waiting anxiously for any news from above.

"Everyone, meet Sharon and Maggie," she introduced. "Please make them feel welcome. They returned with Brian, Mitch, Evan and an army squad just in time to help defend the ranch," she said as the small group happily reacted to the news.

She held her hand up to quiet them and continued.

"We were instructed to return here and wait until it was clear," she said, leaning her gun against the shelter wall and turning to Sharon and Maggie. The groups faces fell as they realized that the fight was not yet over and returned to their seats.

"So, tell me how you came to be here?" Rachel prompted as she sat down next to Sharon who began the short version of the story, editing it for the children's sake.

Rachel listened intently upon hearing how Mitch had been shot when he and Evan fought the men to save Maggie, and how they had arrived at Fort Hood and then proceeded on to the Rocking B. The unspoken words were evident that Sharon had developed feelings for Mitch. Just looking at Maggie, Rachel knew that she and Evan were something more than just friends and concluded that these women were here to stay.

Chapter 35

The two young soldiers moved to the front of the line to lead the small group of men quietly through the woods. As they got closer to the compound, they could hear screaming from some of the women that had been caught unaware when the attack began.

Brian walked to a small rock and then turned and walked ten paces. He knelt down and began to dig in the soft dirt with another flat rock that he found nearby. After he had dug a small hole, he hit his intended target of a white PVC pipe that he had buried long ago.

He finished digging out the long cache, and reaching in he pulled the rope that was attached, to free his prize.

He quickly unscrewed the six inch white pipe capped at both ends and poured out the contents that held an M1, ammunition, clothes sealed in a plastic bag along with a first aid kit and three days worth of food. He examined the gun to make sure that it was in good working order before he loaded it, stood and proceeded to make his way to the perimeter of his ranch.

Aaron quietly filled Mitch in on what had happened after he left the Circle C, as they walked along at the back of the line.

"Not five minutes after you left, eight Hummers drove down the driveway, carrying Pedro and his men. They moved the vehicles around behind the barns and waited for Celia, William and their families to get there. Pedro told me that he was part of a task force with the U. S. and that they needed to requisition the ranch for a base to hold the border." He shook his head. "I'm sorry boss, but I believed him. After Celia and William arrived, Pedro and his men took us all hostage. From what I could gather, Pedro was one of the men that planned the attack. I didn't know for sure until a helicopter landed and he forced me to go with him. He told me that if I did what he instructed, then Celia and William would be released. Just before we got to the Rocking B, he shot me in the leg. He said that it had to look real." Aaron looked up to see that they had arrived at the perimeter of the ranch.

Brian moved to the front and then went down on all fours as he made his way to a safe position behind a pine tree. He lay down on his stomach and brought his binoculars to his face to scan the back of the house where the yellow painted signal was located. His binoculars stopped at the body of the dead Mexican and then he moved on. There was no activity around the house. He scanned from the house to barn one and stopped, watching for any movement. Nothing, but then he saw the barrel of a gun pointing from around a pine tree near the barn. It was shaking. He moved the binoculars a little further to the right to come to rest on a young Mexican man who held the gun. He scanned away from the man to see if he could see any other threats, and he did. There was another man hidden across the compound in a thicket of privet. Brian continued to scan the compound and when he finished he counted three men posted in strategic locations. He motioned to Aaron to come up next to him, which he did. He handed him the binoculars and asked him if these were Pedro's men. He nodded his head yes. One of the young soldiers had crawled up to his other side and was observing as well. Brian turned to him and brought his two fingers to his eyes, then signaled three, to motion that he had seen three men. He then picked up his gun and gave a nod. The young man found the three targets and motioned to Brian that he would take out the one located to the left of the compound. Brian nodded and turned back to Aaron motioning for him to take out the third target. The three men readied to aim their guns on the targets and pulled the trigger in unison.

Brian caught the young man right between the eyes, as the young soldier hit his target in the chest. Aaron hit his target but merely wounded him. As the wounded man scrambled to get away, Brian quickly turned his gun toward the third target and managed to finish him off with another well aimed shot.

The young soldier motioned for him to stay put as he and the other solider stood and made their way to the back of the house with the one covering the other. They made it to the back door that still stood open and disappeared inside. A few minutes later, one of the soldiers reappeared in the doorway and gave the all clear for them to make their way in, as he moved to the corner of the house to cover them. Brian could see the other soldier speaking into his radio mic. He finished the call just as he, Mitch, Aaron, and Evan along with the two dogs made it inside.

Brian looked around the house to see a gaping hole in the room that once was the kitchen. He reckoned that the trail of blood that led through from the back door to the hidden room was Lisa's. He quickly turned away to move closer to the front window to see if he could see any movement around the barns, hoping to see Dustin.

He brought his binoculars to his face to see beyond the barns as two soldiers that had captured three men were moving them at gunpoint towards the house. One of the men was Pedro.

"Sir, orders are for you to stay here until we have finished securing the compound," the young soldier said, hoping that there wouldn't be an argument. Brian didn't respond but kept watching the three men as they were ordered to sit down.

Brian dropped the binoculars. "I think that it is over," he said, as the radio confirmed it and the two young soldiers left the house to join their squad, with the others following behind.

"Sergeant, can I have a word with you?" Brian inquired.

"Governor," he greeted stonily.

"This man has important information on the MR," Brian motioned towards Aaron. He listened as Aaron described what had happened at the Circle C and how Pedro was involved. Brian, uninterested, turned to leave as he heard the Sergeant tell the two soldiers to take Pedro into custody and secure him.

Brian felt as if he were in a daze. He walked slowly past barn one and continued walking on scanning the people that were making their way back towards the main house. Finally, he caught sight of his son Dustin whose leg held a tourniquet around his thigh. John and a man, that Brian didn't recognize, were assisting Dustin as they made their way back to the safety of the compound. Brian thought about other fathers who had faced the daunting task that lay ahead of him. How do you tell a son that his mother is dead? He stood looking at his son and when their eyes met, Dustin instinctively knew that something was terribly wrong, just by the look upon his fathers face. Brian watched as he asked the two men to help his son sit down, and Dustin waited for him to come to him with the bad news.

"Who is it?" he asked simply.

"Your mother," he replied, as he sat down next to his son and clung to him for dear life, knowing that their lives had been forever altered.

Dustin lost control as the news hit him that his mother was dead. He should be celebrating a victorious win, but instead it didn't matter now. Nothing mattered now, but that his mother was gone.

"Michelle?"

"She's safe in the shelter," he said standing and reaching for his sons hand to pull him into a standing position with Johns help.

"Go get that leg looked at son. I will meet you at the hospital ward in a little while," he said turning to go towards the main house. She loved this house, he thought to himself as he looked at it knowing that it would never be his safe haven again.

He entered, and walked towards the hidden room. When he reached the bookshelf he retrieved the key, unlocked the door and, stepped inside.

Brian walked over to the woman that he loved and fell down next to her body. He pulled her to him and tried to hold her but her body was already stiff. He sat next to her as their shared lives flashed through his head like he was watching a movie. And then he remembered the conversation that they had shared right after they began to make preparations.

She had made him promise that if something happened to her, that he would allow his heart to be touched again by another. She had persisted until he had promised her. And he had done so, because he didn't want to talk about it any more, unable to bear the thought. He had hoped that he would go first and then his lie would never have to be remembered. But he hadn't and his grief overwhelmed him as he lay down next to her for the last time.

He laid next to her for what seemed like an eternity, before he heard the knock from the hatch in the floor. He knew that he could not hide or hold back the world. He swallowed hard and turned towards the hatch to lift it open to see Marie standing on the ladder sadly looking up at him. He reached for her hand and helped her up into the little room.

"I am so sorry Brian," she said. He nodded his head unable to speak. She held a blanket. "Do you want us to take the children back through the woods?" she asked, not wanting to intrude on his last moments with his wife.

He shook his head, before finding his voice. "No. Let me," he said reaching for the blanket and turning around to lay it over the still body of his wife. He tucked it around her securely so that the children would not see and said, "Okay." He went to the door and opened it to see Mitch and Evan, along with some of the other members of their group waiting to be reunited with their families that were in the shelter.

"Mitch, Evan, give Marie a hand," he said as he brushed past them. Trying to hold it together, they watched him, make his way through the group of people that had gathered in the house as they offered him their love and support. Finally, he reached his bedroom and shut the door.

Chapter 36

It had been two days since the attack on the ranch. Later that evening, Brian finally emerged from his room and began to lead once again. He called a meeting and the appointed leaders that were still among the living came and they all discussed the tasks that lay before them. When the decisions had been made, Marie typed up the notice and posted it on the boards in the two barns that still stood.

They had decided to dig a mass grave for the groups' sixteen people that had been killed in the attack and they would erect a monument to hold their names.

The twelve bodies of the attackers would be hung around the outside perimeter of the compound to serve notice for all to see.

Commander Williams had ordered the two army squads to stay put until further notice as he strategized his next move, and finally the word had come in this morning.

The Circle C had been retaken from the Mexican resistance. Celia, William and their families were alive! Mitch had learned that Commander Williams had, at the request of Celia and William, established a base on the Circle C in order to reclaim the border and he was happy to hear it since, that would offer them some protection.

After posting the notice that an open invitation to travel to Fort Hood had been announced, none had signed up. Aaron had been granted passage to return to the Circle C but decided to stay on at the Rocking B. Brian who was returning to Fort Hood, would be riding with Pedro and the two captured men, whose fate was still yet to be decided. He was determined to see them brought to justice.

It was dark and the moon was full as the small band of people sat quietly around the campfire on the patio, enjoying each others company, glad to be alive. Evan had gone into the pantry and found a few cases of beer and two bottles of wine.

Mitch held Rachel as they sat together on the rocker/glider watching Evan and Maggie hand out the drinks, for those who wanted to celebrate. The win was bittersweet however as the Rocking B was still in mourning and the war was far from over.

Rachel glanced across the yard to see Aaron talking to Sharon. She leaned closer to Mitch, happy to be with him, sad that Lisa was gone, angry that they had been forced into this new way of life, and she missed her children. Her emotions were running high and she knew that the increased hormone levels had a lot to do with it. She still hadn't told Mitch that she was pregnant and after thinking about it, decided that she couldn't wait any longer.

"Come to the house with me?" she asked.

"Baby, you should know by now that I will follow you anywhere," he said looking into her eyes.

"My god, I love you so much," she said and reached up to touch his face. She felt like the luckiest woman in the world.

 He smiled at her and stroked her arm, thinking that this was where he belonged, with her.

They stood and clutching each other like teenagers, made their way into the empty darkness of the house and sat down on the sofa. Mitch pulled her close and began to kiss her neck and she smiled, feeling the tingling sensation travel through her body.

"Okay, wait," she said reluctantly but letting him continue.

"You do know that there could be consequences to our actions," she said, breathlessly. His mouth made its way to hers and he kissed her hungrily, before answering her.

"Don't worry, I'll be careful," he said.

"It's a little late for that," she said as he moved back to her neck. He stopped kissing her and leaned back to look at her. In the moonlight, shining through the picture window, she could see his face.

"What did you say?" he said.

She smiled.

"I am pregnant," she announced, unable to keep it to herself any longer. She watched his face and waited for it to change from shock to overwhelming joy, but it didn't.

"Say something," she said, beginning to worry, as Mitch contemplated the very idea.

"How? Are you sure?" he asked. "Isn't it dangerous, at your age, to be pregnant?" he asked worriedly.

"Mr. Carlson, are you saying that I am old?" she said teasingly, trying to lighten the conversation.

"Don't joke about this Rachel," he said, fearfully. "I just got you back, I can't lose you again," he said, his voice breaking. He knew the risk, since she had had the three C-sections. He stood and began to pace, feeling trapped in a situation that held no answer. "Oh dear God. What are we going to do?" he said more to himself than to her. If she had the baby, she could die. If she decided to abort it, she could die. It was a losing proposition. He returned to her and dropped to his knees in front of her. "Rachel, Rachel..." he muttered. "I'm sorry baby, I should have been more careful."

"Stop it," she said gently, taking his face in her hands and leaning forward to kiss him. "I will not look at this as anything other than a blessing," she said. "God has been with us through this whole, horrible mess, and I refuse to see this any other way." She leaned forward and kissed him.

"You are an amazing woman," he said. "How do you do it? How can you believe so strongly in a God that could have prevented all of this?" he asked.

"Because you are here, with me," she said. "I prayed every day that God would bring you and Evan back to me, and he did. But he didn't stop there. He blessed us with a new life. He blessed you with another chance at a family to love. Britta used to say that after the suffering, the blessings come." She reached for his hand and brought it to her abdomen that would soon expand with the growing life inside of her. He returned to his place next to her on the couch and pulled her to him.

"You always know just what to say to calm me down," he said contentedly, as they sat holding each other and he considered being a father again.

They sat together for a long while and as they listened to the small group outside the window, Brian emerged from his room and turned on the hall light, startling them both.

"I was just about to come and find you two," he said with empty eyes and sitting down at the table in the now repaired kitchen. They stood and joined him at the table.

"Rachel, before I returned home, I spoke with Commander Williams about their K-9 unit. They need to get some more dogs and I suggested you might be able to help with that. What do you think?"

"I don't know Brian. I haven't been home in months. I don't even know if the dogs are still there at this point, or my family," she said sadly. "I can't make a promise without knowing that or the shape that they might be in. I wish that I could, but until I know more, I just can't say."

He nodded his head. "I understand. You do have Axel and Allie. You can take Victor and Hammer. They might need a little reminding, but they will get the job done," he said. "Now, let's just say for the sake of argument that the kennel is still in place and the dogs are fine. Would you be interested?" he asked.

She cast her eyes down before turning to Mitch. He nodded.

She turned back to face Brian. "Yes."

"What?" Mitch blurted out, surprised at her. He had thought that she was going to tell him no because she was pregnant, and now he was really trying to figure her out. She squeezed his hand, as if to reassure him.

"Will I be able to take a maternity leave?" she asked smartly.

"What?" Brian shot back at her. It was his turn to be surprised.

"Rachel! Rachel!" was all that he could say. Tears came to his eyes as he leaned across the table and kissed her on her forehead. "Congratulations."

He looked at them both. "I wish Lisa could have heard that."

"She was the first one that I told," Rachel said smiling at him and swallowing the lump in her throat.

"Seriously Brian, I am going to need a surgeon when the time comes," she said, her tone pleading.

"We will plan on flying you in to Fort Hood, a few weeks ahead of time," he said.

"Woman, you about stopped my heart," Mitch interrupted, breathing a sigh of relief. She leaned over to kiss him sheepishly.

"Alright then," Brian said. "There will be a helicopter here next week to pick you up and take you home to assess the condition of the dogs," Brian said.

"What?" Now it was her turn to be surprised. She was shocked, since the thought hadn't even crossed her mind until now, that she was going home.

www.ingramcontent.com/pod-product-compliance
Lightning Source LLC
Chambersburg PA
CBHW072215170626
46813CB00003B/956